"Leigh continues to do what she does best . . . really hot love scenes, dangerous enemies, and deadly revenge."
—*RT Book Reviews* on *Ultimate Sins*

"*Midnight Sins* has everything a good book should have: suspense, murder, betrayal, mystery, and lots of sensuality . . . Lora Leigh is a talented author with the ability to create magnificent characters and captivating plots."
—*Romance Junkies*

"[An] erotically charged tale woven tightly around a chilling suspense about love and betrayal. *Midnight Sins* features some outstanding characterization and a plot that unfolds to reveal a horrific tangle of events that lead to the unthinkable. You won't want to put this book down until you have read the very last page."
—*Fresh Fiction*

Elite Ops

"Leigh delivers . . . erotic passion. This is a hot one for the bookshelf!"
—*RT Book Reviews* on *Renegade*

"Overflowing with escalating danger, while pent-up sexual cravings practically burst into flames."
—*Sensual Reads* on *Black Jack*

LORA LEIGH

dirty little lies

St. Martin's Paperbacks

This is a work of fiction. All of the characters, organizations, and events portrayed in this novel are either products of the author's imagination or are used fictitiously.

DIRTY LITTLE LIES

Copyright © 2016 by Lora Leigh.

For information address St. Martin's Press, 175 Fifth Avenue, New York, NY 10010.

ISBN: 978-0-312-38912-3

Our books may be purchased in bulk for promotional, educational, or business use. Please contact your local bookseller or the Macmillan Corporate and Premium Sales Department at 1-800-221-7945, ext. 5442, or by e-mail at MacmillanSpecialMarkets@macmillan.com.

Printed in the United States of America

St. Martin's Paperbacks edition / September 2016

St. Martin's Paperbacks are published by St. Martin's Press, 175 Fifth Avenue, New York, NY 10010.

10 9 8 7 6 5 4 3 2 1

For my gracious, wonderful,
most patient editor Monique
who hasn't threatened to kill me once.

That I know of . . .

This one's for you.

prologue

Why was she still here?

The beauty of the place she had always thought of as home, the peace of the tree-shrouded mountains that surrounded it, and the murky depths of the river bordering it weren't so peaceful now as they had once been. Pristine green grounds surrounded her uncle's two-story white-and-red farmhouse. Horses grazed in their fenced-in pastures, and a hint of fall lent a bite to the late-evening air.

This was home.

She'd been raised here, feeling secure and loved despite her mother's often abrasive, less-than-affectionate personality. In all the years she'd understood that her mother bore her no love, Grace had nonetheless felt as though she belonged.

Until now.

Now she just felt spooked, as though she were being watched. Like a deer sensing itself in a hunter's sights.

Dammit, she didn't need this.

Staring out at the Tennessee River as it drifted lazily past the Maddox farm, Grace admitted to herself that she wasn't exactly certain why she was still here. She'd been packed and ready to leave on the day of her mother's funeral. After all, what right did she have to be in her uncle's home when it was her mother who had destroyed that uncle's life? Lucia had had her own sister, Uncle Vince's wife, Sienna, murdered. She'd tried to murder his daughter. She'd lied, murdered others, and for so long had worked to destroy not just the family, but everyone they protected.

Grace hadn't been certain where she was going at the time and leaving wasn't what she wanted. She'd wanted to make things better for her family, for the friends who had suffered. A family that pleaded with her to change her mind. To stay. To remain despite her mother's crimes.

Her uncle Vince and his three forceful sons, Cord, Deacon, and Sawyer, weren't exactly easy to fight against. Like the mountains themselves, they were immovable, shadowed, and often treacherous when encountering the enemy.

She wasn't the enemy, though.

Was she?

Rubbing at her arms against the chill wind blowing off the water, Grace tried to tell herself that her mother's crimes weren't her own. No one knew what Lucia Maddox had done except the family. Lucia's crimes had been dealt with quietly to preserve the secrecy of the government-backed militia her uncle headed. The one Lucia had tried to destroy.

Her mother.

She was the daughter of a traitor.

Yeah, that one was going to look really good on her résumé, wasn't it?

It sure as hell hadn't helped matters when it came to the man she'd been certain would finally decide to become more than just a friend. But Zack Richards had pretty much been MIA whenever she was around after Lucia's crimes were revealed.

Big surprise.

Quiet, intense. An accountant. As different from her military family as one could be.

"Miss Grace?"

Grace whirled around from her view of the river to stare up at one of the farmhands her uncle Vince employed. A stable hand standing six feet with a rangy build and brown puppy-dog eyes. Longish brown hair fell over one eye, giving him a boyish look.

"Hey, Richard." She smiled up at him before heading back to the farmhouse.

Rich was nice, unassuming, but something had her spooked regardless. So spooked that suddenly she just wanted to be in the house, surrounded by her uncle and cousins.

"I'm sorry about your momma," he said softly as they moved into the backyard.

From the corner of her eye, she watched the large Rottweiler Zack had given her the year before lurking in the leafy bushes to Rich's right. For once, the dog wasn't jumping around, chasing moths, or trying to get the stable hand to play.

The unusual behavior from her normally rambunctious pet made Grace's nerves tingle. She hated feeling so frightened. The last eight weeks had been hell, and she wasn't in the mood for the nerves that jumbled inside her at the oddest times.

"Thank you, Rich." She nodded, reminding herself that she knew this man, she'd been raised around him. Hell, he'd helped her cousins teach her to drive when she was just sixteen.

"Miss Grace." His hand settled on her arm heavily, drawing her to a stop as her heart began to beat fearfully.

"I'm sorry, Rich." She shook her head apologetically. "Cord's waiting on me—"

"No, Miss Grace." His hand tightened around her arm, restraining her, his face filling with regret. "Mr. Cord's in the stables with his brothers. No one's waiting for you."

A glint of metal, the blade of a knife, gleamed from his other hand as Grace felt panic set in. "Rich?"

At the whisper of his name, the look on Richard's face shifted from regret to grief. "I'm so sorry, Miss Grace," he said softly. "I'm so sorry. Just tell me where the files are, and I'll let you go. I promise."

Files?

This was a nightmare. He wanted files? Even if she knew what the hell he was talking about, he wouldn't let her go. He'd gone too far for that.

"What files?" Play along. She could play along with this just for a minute, just until she could find a way to escape him.

"Miss Grace, helping your momma was a really bad idea." He sighed again, muscles bunching in his arm above the knife hand. "The files have been gone this long . . . nothing's hurt if they stay hid, I guess."

He was going to kill her.

Sweet Jesus, he was actually going to use that knife on her.

"Have you lost your ever-lovin' mind, Richard James?" she burst out, sheer incredulity snapping through her. "I never helped Luce so much as change a lightbulb. Get your head out of your ass and let me go." She jerked her arm and for a second, just a second, she thought he'd actually let her go.

His hold relaxed, pain contorting his features just before resolve filled his eyes.

Yep, he was going to kill her.

Grace twisted in his grip, obviously surprising the farmhand as her foot swept out and connected with his knee while an ear-piercing scream left her lips. At the same time, her Rottweiler, Magnus, gave a vicious snarl a streak of fiery pain lacerated her thigh.

She was damned if she'd make it easy for him!

chapter one

Annapolis, Maryland
Brigham Estate

Damn, he didn't want to be here.

Pulling into the circular drive of the Brigham Estate, home of the Brigham Security Agency, Zack Richards fought back the coil of rage and betrayal that tensed in his gut every time he was ordered to show up.

The Brighams liked to call themselves his family; he liked to call them a pain in the ass. He would gladly have kept well away from them if only that were possible. Unfortunately, his uncle, the head of the Brigham family, had found a way to get Zack back to D.C. periodically.

Alexander Brigham hadn't found a way to make him like it, though, and Zack made certain his uncle knew how very much he despised each visit. A bit childish, perhaps, but it kept Zack from hitting a man whose health was said to be suffering.

Zack hopped out of the mud-spattered pickup he'd driven in from Tennessee and strode across the drive to the imposing two-story brick colonial and up to the wide, wooden front doors, wishing he'd get a chance to pound on the wood and expend a little of his irritation. Instead, as usual, just as he set foot on the porch, the panels were opened smoothly by one of the young agents Brigham employed.

"Mr. Zack, Mr. Brigham's assistant will show you to the office." The younger man nodded to the aging assistant, Peters, who waited at the end of the huge foyer.

Nodding, Zack strode past the agent and over to his uncle's assistant, scowling at the other man. "He ordered this little visit . . . and now he's not available?" Zack sneered as the assistant turned and led the way down a wide hall. "Why am I not surprised?"

Not that the assistant deigned to comment. Or to speak at all until they reached the office. "Mr. Alex will be right in, Mr. Zackary," Peters stated, his precise lack of inflection raking Zack's nerves more than normal.

John Peters still stood tall and stiff, his shoulders militarily straight, his expression—well, he was rather devoid of any particular emotional look. For as long as Zack had known the man, he'd never seen a single emotion, opinion, flash of sympathy, compassion, like, or dislike on his long, now aging face. His gray hair was still marine short, though now it was silver gray rather than the nondescript brown of his youth.

Zack went straight to the bar, lifted the decanter of Alexander Brigham's finest aged Irish whiskey, and poured a short glass half full before tossing half of it back with a grimace of pleasure. Refilling the glass, he tried to convince himself that this meeting wasn't going to piss him the hell off within five minutes of Mr. Alex's entering the room.

He knew better, though. Getting ticked off was just a given.

He turned back to Peters with a slow, mocking tilt of his brow. "Sure, Peters," he drawled. "Tell him to take his time. I'm in no hurry."

The assistant inclined his head with a measured move before turning on his heel to retreat from the office, closing the door silently behind him.

Zack gave his head a little shake. The man never failed to amaze him—and maybe even intimidate him just the slightest bit.

While moving around the office, Zack stared up at the mahogany shelves filled with books from floor to ceiling. He noted the cherry hardwood floors, a heavy mahogany desk the size of a bed, the comfortable leather chair behind it. A Victorian settee and matching chairs were placed in front of the fireplace on a centuries-old tapestry rug, while the walls on the opposite side of the room held portraits of four generations of Brigham patriarchs.

Bastards.

Taking another sip of Ireland's finest, Zack continued to pace around the room. He shifted priceless figurines from their various places, turning them, sliding them forward or back.

Childish, he admitted again with a sneer, but it did so irritate Old Man Brigham. His uncle's irritation would increase with each object he had to reset and place just so.

Zack walked behind the enormous desk. Once he took a seat in the heavy, far-too-comfortable leather chair, he shifted picture frames and, not for the first time, removed the silver frame of a laughing red-haired young woman, her gray eyes filled with life and love. He slid open a bottom drawer of the desk and placed the picture there, facedown.

It wouldn't take Brigham long to find the portrait, but his uncle would get the message loud and clear. Closing the drawer, Zack turned his attention to the files stacked on the desk, intent on pulling pages from inside the folders and distributing them haphazardly throughout the pile.

One file label caught his attention, causing his jaw to clench and suspicion to tear through him. He opened the folder and scanned the pages carefully, white hot fury rearing inside him.

A weekend meeting in D.C.? It was no more than a ruse. He just hadn't imagined the depths of the deception involved.

Zack quickly closed the folder and shoved it under his jacket, holding it in place beneath his bicep. As he stalked to the door, it pushed open and Old Man Brigham himself stepped inside the office.

"Zackary?" A frown flitted across his heavily lined face, disapproval glinting in his gray eyes. "You needn't come looking for me—"

Zack grunted at the admonishment. "I was just on my way out."

"The hell you say!" The protest was rife with arrogance.

"The hell I did say." Zack stepped around him, barely glancing at his uncle as he entered the hallway.

When he neared the wood-encased steel entry doors, the agent stationed there opened the panels with a smooth flourish, his expression as bland as Peters's when Zack strode past him.

Come to think of it, the entire household, family and help alike, showed little if any emotion. Ice water ran in their veins; he was certain of it. Pure, coldhearted logic and a touch of the psychotic.

Stepping into his pickup, Zack tossed the file to the seat beside him before starting the motor and putting his foot heavily to the gas. He probably left a few skid marks on the old bastard's brick driveway.

At least, he hoped he had.

Any other time, he'd have felt a measure of pride over that. If he wasn't already so damned pissed. If he didn't want to leave the skid marks on that son of a bitch's head instead.

Driving through the iron gates with inches to spare as the electronic release eased them open, Zack headed back to Loudon, praying he was in time. Whatever had made him believe that the Brigham family would keep their damned noses out of the mess that had arisen in the mountains of Tennessee at the beginning of summer?

He should have known better. They'd sent a traitor home in a casket with no judge, no jury to order the execution. Why imagine they'd give the Maddox family so much as a warning before executing a possible threat, and without a shred of evidence other than the traitor's word for it?

Forget "innocent before guilty." The Brighams believed it was innocence that had to be proved, rather than guilt.

Glancing at the file that lay on the seat beside him, Zack could feel that core of rage, normally carefully hidden, rising inside him once again. And not for the first time, he thanked God he was never part of the family his mother had fought so hard to be free of.

And he never would be part of it, no matter their seeming desperation or their threats or their games. He wouldn't have a moment's hesitation over foiling their plans—and this time, he might even be looking forward to it.

The strident pulse of his cell phone in the pocket of his jacket drew his attention. Hitting the Bluetooth control on the steering wheel, he answered with a terse "Hello?"

"You alone?" asked Jazz, his foster brother.

"As can be," he answered, clenching his hands on the steering wheel, filled with a heavy foreboding at the other man's far-too-serious tone. "We have a problem?"

Jazz's fiancée, Kenni, was the long-lost Maddox princess. For eight years, she'd been the target of a traitor determined to kill her. The Maddox family suspected that the traitor wasn't working alone.

"Kenni, Slade, and Jesse are fine," Jazz assured him. "But we have a big problem. Grace Maddox was attacked yesterday evening, at the Maddox farm. Her assailant escaped. Her uncle Vinny's not letting anyone in or out—even Kenni. That Rottweiler you gave her last year managed to catch him off guard, but one of the farmhands sent a message to me that the dog was hurt pretty bad. I haven't been able to find out more."

Vince wouldn't dare refuse to allow Zack to see Grace. It would be the one time Zack would use the power the Brigham name gave him. And Alex Brigham would back him up, no matter the problems he and Zack had. No matter the plans the bastard might have to take Grace in for interrogation. He'd still back Zack.

All Jazz could tell him about Grace now though was that she was alive. Son of a bitch.

Tiny, delicate, as sweet-natured as anyone he knew, that was Grace. Fighting off an assassin would be impossible for her.

"Put our men on alert," Zack told him, the rasp of rage in his tone clear now. "I'm just leaving the estate—"

"Slade has a plane waiting at a private airfield about twenty minutes out of D.C. You remember Chaz McDougal?" his brother asked. "His plane is hangered there."

Tall, red-haired, Scottish to the core, and detested by the Brigham family, that was Chaz McDougal.

"I'll be there in five," Zack assured him. "I'll have the pilot notify you once we're airborne."

"No need, Chaz is flying you in himself and knows to contact us at lift-off," Jazz informed him. "Get here fast, Zack. They're not letting any of us in, Kenni's sick with worry, and we have a report that Mad Max and Beau-Remi are heading in from NOLA. Things could be getting ready to get bad."

Kenni Maddox and her cousin Grace had worked together for two years to try to uncover the traitor threatening Kenni's life. Neither woman had suspected how close that threat had been, though.

Maxwell Maddox and Beauregard Remington, Grace's half brothers, were a whole other set of problems.

Big problems. The kind neither Zack nor the Maddox family needed right now.

"As quick as Chaz can get me there," he promised. "I'll call as soon as we land."

Disconnecting, Zack hoped—for Alex Brigham's sake—that the Brigham family hadn't ordered that attempt. If they had, the war brewing in the Tennessee mountains would end up boiling over, and that was something none of them wanted.

Except, perhaps, whoever had been working with the traitor who nearly murdered Kenni Maddox more than once. They still hadn't identified the accomplice, but he knew it couldn't possibly be Grace Maddox.

The file was gone, just as Alexander had suspected it would be. Staring down at the disarranged papers on his desk, he blew out a relieved sigh and shook his head.

Behind him, Peters was carefully resetting the figurines to their proper positions. Books were out of order; the framed picture of Zack's mother was missing once again. No doubt stored in the bottom desk drawer Alexander kept unlocked for Zack to hide it in.

The boy delighted in upsetting the office, but even more, he seemed to enjoy hiding the picture of Alex's baby sister—Zack's mother, Nicole—to show his disregard for the family. There was no changing his mind, and Zack refused to hear why his mother had run away to the mountains of Tennessee or what had been the cause of her and her husband's murders.

The boy was nosy as hell, too, hence the reason Alex had left the file for him. Making a move against anyone in Zack's hometown—Maddox, the Kin, or otherwise—would ensure his nephew's complete hatred, especially where that girl Grace was concerned. At least this way, he could say he'd given Zack a chance to save her. If she was innocent, then his sister's son would delight in thinking he was rubbing it in Alexander's face.

The sound of Peters's cell phone ringing and the assistant's quick response drew Alexander's attention. The other man listened attentively for long seconds, the corners of his eyes tightening in concern at whatever the other party was saying before disconnecting the call.

"Sir, there's a development in the Loudon situation." Peters stepped closer, his brown eyes showing a glimmer of concern. "It would seem Grace Maddox was attacked at her uncle's home last night. She's been wounded, and the pet Mr. Zack gave her last year is reported to be seriously injured. News of the attack has also reached her half brothers in NOLA. Should we send a team in?"

NOLA? Mad Max and Beau-Remi? Have mercy!

God help them all if those two became involved.

"Her condition?" Alex rasped, the fingers of one hand curling into a fist as frustration began to rise inside him.

Dammit, this wasn't supposed to happen. Word of her mother's confessions shouldn't have leaked, not yet.

"Her family has all access to her limited to her uncle and his three sons," Peters reported. "There's no report on her condition or the extent of her injuries."

The other man worked on the electronic pad he held, his fingers quick as he began searching for information.

"Send Victoria in alone," Alex ordered, knowing his daughter would gain access to the family before anyone else from the house or the agency could. "She and Grace are friends, and the family seems to like her. They shouldn't refuse to allow her to see the girl. Have a team on standby, just in case the situation deteriorates. Whoever our enemy is, they're moving to start a war between the Kin and the agency. We can't allow that to happen."

He'd seen it coming for years. It was the reason his sister, her husband, and Grace's father, Benjamin Maddox, had been targeted to die over two decades before.

He waited as Peters typed, his assistant's fingers moving quickly over the tablet despite his age.

"The team will be ready to head out by nightfall, but Miss Alexandra demands to speak with you first. I've already sent orders to our pilot to expect her."

Alexander nodded at his assistant's quick response.

"And it would appear Mr. Zackary has stopped at the McDougal property. Our contact within his estate reports Mr. Chaz is flying him to Loudon himself."

Alexander grimaced at that piece of information. "Figures," he grunted. "Damned Scots bastard. I should have known Zack was friends with him. Loyalty to the family isn't exactly in his vocabulary, is it?"

There were days he wished his father were still alive just so he could prove how wrong the old man had been all those years ago.

"I believe Mr. Zack merely likes to poke at you however possible," Peters defended the boy yet again.

"Mr. Chaz isn't a bad sort, though, as you've stated yourself. He's not exactly his father."

"Yet," Alex snorted before giving a heavy sigh and gazing around the office once again.

He tried to remind himself that his nephew, the son of his beloved baby sister, just didn't understand the past. He feared Zack, like his parents, would never allow himself to hear the truth either. Not that any of them were blameless, but neither were any of them monsters.

It was a lesson young Grace Maddox would be learning soon as well.

chapter two

A woman should have a warning before a man like Zack Richards stepped into her bedroom. Time at least to comb her hair, maybe look a little more presentable after being attacked by some maniac and nearly losing the pet Zack had given her as a present the year before.

Magnus was just a pup when he'd been delivered to Grace with a big, half-chewed blue bow around his neck. The accompanying card had warned her that the rambunctious puppy was a brat. Someone to get into trouble with. She'd laughed at that, and loved the pet at first sight. And now she'd let Magnus get hurt. She didn't think she'd ever forgive herself for that. Facing the man who had given her the gift wasn't easy.

The fact that she was obsessed with him didn't help.

Grace glared at her cousin Cord as he stepped in behind the tall, auburn-haired, gray-eyed object of her greatest irritation and arched his brow at her with mocking knowledge.

Cord knew how she felt. He knew how hard seeing Zack would be for Grace, especially after the weeks she'd spent being ignored and turned away from, feeling reviled by him.

This sucked.

"Grace." Without so much as a *hello, how are you,* or *get ready,* Zack flipped the blanket back from her, pushed the hem of her gown as far as possible on her thigh, and glared at the bandage high on her leg.

"For God's sake!" she burst out, completely shocked, amazed he'd do something so forward, especially while Cord looked on.

She slapped at his hand as it neared her flesh, jerked the blankets back to her waist, and held on tight. "Who the hell are you, and where did the real Zack go?"

Quiet, intense, *staid* Zack Richards would never just jerk her blankets off her, no matter the reason. He was polite. He wasn't alpha material. Never raised his voice or acted so dominant.

There wasn't so much as a glimmer of apology in his gaze now. As a matter of fact, it was as flat and hard as her uncle's and cousins' had been after her attack.

"Have you found the bastard?" Zack turned his gaze back to Cord.

Cord shook his blond head, his deep, intense green eyes darkening with fury as the muscles in his body seem to flex dangerously.

He felt responsible, as did his brothers and her uncle. But the attack hadn't been their fault; it would have happened sooner or later.

"We have a team searching for him—he won't get far." Cord bit out between clenched teeth. "Magnus took a chunk out of his arm before he managed to use that knife to get away from the dog. We have our best trackers after him."

Grace felt pain tighten her chest. She was used to Magnus lying at the bottom of her bed, his large body comforting when the nights were too quiet and too lonely. Zack would never have gotten so close to her without permission if her pet were here.

"What's Magnus's condition?" Brooding, dark with fury, Zack's voice sent a chill racing up Grace's spine.

When had he learned to mimic that kind of authority, that lack of mercy?

"Serious," Cord breathed out in a rough sigh. "He'll make it, but it's going to take a while. He'll be with the vet for a week or better."

She'd had enough. The two of them were talking over her scantily clad body as though she weren't even there. "My bedroom is not a freaking office or meeting area!" Grace snapped, fed up with the discussion as mortification burned through her. "Go have your little pow-wow somewhere else, if you don't mind."

Her pulse was racing, her skin felt overly warm, and even the ache in her leg where Rich's blade had sliced across it paled in comparison to the ache that bloomed under her skin whenever Zack was around.

She didn't need this.

Not right now, not while she felt about as unattractive as possible or while facing a side of Zack she'd never imagined.

"I do mind." The belligerence caused her eyes to narrow on the normally polite, sometimes teasing man she'd set her heart on in the past several years.

She might consider changing her mind on that one if he kept this behavior up. "Well, isn't that just too bad." She sliced her narrowed gaze toward her cousin. "*My* bedroom. Both of you can leave."

Cord's arms went across his chest as a frown lowered his dark blond brows. Her attention was quickly pulled from him when Zack just sat beside her on the bed.

Her bed.

As though it belonged to him.

"Get out of my bedroom—"

"Let me see your leg first." The attitude of command and the pure arrogance in his expression nearly had her jaw dropping.

"Not happening." She held on to the blankets with a death grip now, the sheer irony of the situation nearly laughable. "Guess you should have shown a little interest before now, right? What the hell are you doing here, anyway?"

Not once since she'd found herself bleeding, cradling the whimpering form of her dog, and screaming for her family as rain began pouring down on them in the backyard did Grace imagine Zack would even give a damn. Let alone show up or pretend to care.

Not that he was pretending to care. He acted as though it were his right, as though her leg belonged to him. Asshole attitude, and she didn't like being taken unaware by it.

Surprise flickered in his gray eyes. "I'm here because you were hurt, dammit—"

"So?" she enunciated with precise disdain. "It's not like you showed up when that horse threw me last year, or when I broke my ankle the year before that. So why now?"

She could actually have dealt with this side of him then. She might even have played up the injuries just a tad to evoke a little compassion and maybe even that first kiss from him that she dreamed of. That was before the past eight weeks. Before he'd looked at her like she was a traitor's daughter and refused to speak to her at the funeral of the woman who gave birth to her.

He'd ignored her, turned his back on her, and he was here now for what reason, exactly?

"Tell her I checked up on her every time, Cord—" he began ordering her cousin.

"Doesn't count if I don't see you," Grace assured him with false sweetness. "Now, leave. I'm tired."

And any chance she'd had of even a one-night stand with Zack, let alone a future romance, was gone. Her mother had made certain of it. And now, Richard James had guaranteed it.

"Told you she wasn't in the mood for company," Cord seemed to remind him when Zack flicked him a hard glance. "Especially from you. She's been put out with you of late."

Cord had told him? Exactly what else had her cousin been blabbing about?

"Why don't you play I-told-you-so with Zack downstairs, Cord?" she gritted out between clenched teeth. "Away from me."

Cord lifted his gaze to the ceiling as though praying for patience.

"Because he knows better than to try," Zack snorted at the question. "He's just here to make sure I don't get frisky with the pretty little invalid."

Get frisky?

Her stomach clenched at the very thought even as anger slapped at her pride. That kind of teasing was just wrong. She'd waited years for him to try to "get frisky," as he called it. She'd given up weeks before, and wasn't about to put herself there again. No thank you. Wasn't happening.

Now, if she could convince her girl parts of that, then she might get through this little meeting without humiliating herself in the worst possible way.

"I'm sure getting frisky is the last thing on your mind," she stated with mocking sweetness. "God forbid quiet, staid Zack Richards should lust after a traitor's daughter." She flicked her cousin a hard look. "My virtue is perfectly safe."

For a second, Cord's expression went perfectly blank before incredulity gleamed in his eyes and he gave a slow, disbelieving shake of his head.

"Cord. Leave." Zack's brook-no-refusal tone of voice actually had her thighs tightening.

"I don't know, Zack." Rubbing at the back of his neck, Cord looked between them before a grin tugged at his lips. "She might shoot you with that gun she has hid under her pillow. And she does know how to use it. Maybe you two need a referee."

They needed more than a referee right now.

"Both of you go—"

"Now, Cord." Zack's tone deepened; it actually rumbled with the demand.

Giving a mocking snort, Cord shrugged in his it's-on-your-head way before giving her a knowing little smile and turning on his heel.

The door closed behind him seconds later, leaving

her in her bedroom with no panties or bra beneath the short little gown she wore, alone with Zack.

And she hadn't even brushed her hair.

If his cock got any harder, it was going to bust through the front of his jeans.

Zack stared down at the delicate, far-too-helpless form of the young woman he'd forced himself to stay away from, and felt the knowledge of what was coming cement in his soul.

God knew he'd never wanted to hurt her, never wanted her to see the man he was, but hiding it from her now would be impossible.

What quirk of impishness had made fate decree that the one woman he couldn't seem to stop lusting after was exactly the type of woman he could never keep? He needed a woman who was less delicate, harder, better able to handle whatever danger might erupt in their lives and help him protect whatever family they might have together. A woman as helpless, sweet-natured, and defenseless as Grace wasn't a woman who could do that.

Though, he had to admit, she was showing a little more gumption now than he'd suspected she possessed.

"Can I see your leg now?" he asked, injecting what he hoped was gentleness in his tone.

"You can kiss my ass and get the hell out of my bedroom." She lifted her head from her pillows just enough to emphasize the feminine fury brightening her emerald green eyes. "Right now."

Zack blinked down at her and almost grinned.

That thought of baring that pretty, curvy little butt was a hell of a temptation.

Dark blond hair curled becomingly around her face and bare shoulders from where she sat propped against her lacy pillows, dressed in that virginal little white nightgown, in her girly little bedroom while fire filled those green eyes.

She looked almost put out.

"Now, Grace, settle down." Once more, he had to control a grin. "Let me see how bad you were hurt, then we'll talk."

The color of her eyes deepened, going from emeralds to jade in the space of a heartbeat as her little jaw clenched and her pouty lips thinned in displeasure.

Damn, she'd been cute as hell before—now, hell, he might be mesmerized. For a minute, anyway.

"We are not talking, Zackary Richards—"

He was tired of being nice about it. Catching her off guard, he jerked the blanket back, pushed her gown up again, then froze.

The breath rushed from his lungs, his balls went tight, and Zack could have sworn every drop of blood in his body went straight to his dick.

Sweet, sweet heaven.

Silk-soft flesh touched his fingers, bare, so bare there and warm that it took every ounce of strength he possessed not to push her back against those pillows and spread her pretty thighs farther.

Grace was just as still, and as he stared at the soft flesh he'd revealed, a hint of feminine dampness began to gleam against the bare folds.

"How pretty," he whispered instead of pulling back, aware of her stillness and the sense of anticipation growing between them. "I always knew you'd be so sweet and pretty there."

And so small. Her mound was just as small and delicate as she was.

She was hurt! another part of his mind was screaming at him. The bandage covering the knife wound was just inches below his fingers, a swath of blinding white against satiny, sun-darkened flesh. She'd just been attacked, nearly killed, and all he could do was imagine pressing his lips right there, where that gleam of dampness was gathering on the slowly swelling folds.

What would it be like to take her? he wondered. To watch that sweet flesh stretch around him, taking him inside her—

To keep from mounting her in a haze of lust, he jerked his gaze from the temptation to meet her eyes and nearly groaned at the arousal he saw there.

She wanted him, but he'd always known that, hadn't he? At any time in the past few years, he could have had her in his bed, could have lived out every fantasy he had of touching her, taking her.

"This wasn't what I intended, Grace," he breathed out, knowing he was lying to her.

He'd known the second he saw that file on Alex's desk what he was going to do. There was only one way to protect her while proving her innocence, and that was by taking her to his bed. Alex Brigham knew the hell he'd pay if he dared to strike against her then.

"Of course it isn't," she murmured, realization flashing in the jade green of her eyes. "Sucks knowing a traitor's daughter is aroused by you, doesn't it? Must just sicken you inside."

She slapped his hand away and jerked the blankets up again as he fought to process the accusation.

"Is that how you think I see you?" He moved closer, the hunger hardening him further as she glared at him, resentment and anger darkening her eyes. "Do you think I blame you for Lucia's actions? That anyone does?"

"Well, someone does," she snapped back. "Otherwise, I wouldn't have been attacked, and Magnus wouldn't be so hurt that he's not here to bite your damned ass for pissing me off."

The large Rottweiler had been no more than an overgrown lapdog until the farmhand attacked her. Zack was more than a little surprised when he'd heard how savage the animal became and how well he defended Grace without having had any specific training.

"The fact remains, Magnus is not here," Zack pointed out, the flaring shades of green in her eyes almost mesmerizing. "And I am." He leaned closer, causing her to press herself farther into the pillows. "And trust me, sweetheart, that lust goes both ways."

She exhaled a delicate little snort. "In your dreams."

The breathless response assured him it wasn't just in his dreams, Zack knew.

The pout on her lips fascinated him, drawing his gaze from the brilliant green of her eyes to the sweet, tempting curves. In that second, a single thought came to him: In all the years he'd been teasing her, lusting for her, there was one thing he'd never done.

"I've never kissed you, have I, sweetheart?"

He had never kissed her. He'd never touched her. All the fantasies she'd ever had of them being together had never been realized. And now . . . now she couldn't have any of them.

"If I know Cord, he's waiting right outside my door," she warned him, dismay nearly strangling her. "Don't make me call for him."

Something dark and far too hungry lit his gaze for just a moment, just long enough for her to glimpse it, for her heart to shatter with the knowledge that it could never belong to her.

Her? Not just a traitor's daughter but also someone accused by that very traitor, her own mother, of being part of the conspiracy. She didn't have a chance with a man like Zack Richards. If he'd stayed away for eight weeks because of Lucia's crimes, how much worse would it be when he found out Lucia had accused her of having the very information everyone was seeking— and of waiting for the right time to sell it? No, she didn't have a chance.

"Grace, sweetheart, are you threatening me with your cousin?" Amusement flickered in his gray eyes now. "I had to have heard you wrong. You wouldn't do that, now, would you?"

Since when had nice, polite Zack Richards turned into a smart-ass, anyway? And hell yes, she would. . . .

Maybe.

God, she was so weak. She was hurt, and so cold inside, she didn't know how to combat it. And she'd wanted Zack for so long, so much so that no other man had compared to him.

"I want you to leave, Zack." She had to force the words past her lips. "Go home, go wherever you've been for the past eight weeks, and stop playing games with me, because I can't afford how very bad you'll hurt me."

He didn't move. With one arm braced over her legs, his gaze locked on hers once again, he just stared back at her, intent.

Calculating?

"Scared of me, Grace?" he asked her, his voice gentle—too gentle. The sound of it caused her breathing to tighten in trepidation.

Not in fear, but in feminine caution and a whole lot of suspicion.

"I'm not scared of you, Zack," she assured him, wondering if that was true. "But neither am I interested in what you're offering."

She could feel the yawning fires of hell licking at her heels for that particular lie.

She was interested in whatever he might have in mind at the moment, or any other moment; she just couldn't allow herself to accept it. There was too much danger involved. Zack wasn't a gutter fighter like Cord, or even like his foster brothers, Jazz and Slade. He was an accountant, completely nonviolent but entirely too sexy.

"You are a liar, darlin'." A grin tugged at his lips, just at the corner, while his gray eyes gleamed with amusement. "And we both know it."

Because he'd seen her response to him.

Grace leaned forward carefully. "Just because you can make me respond physically doesn't mean I want you involved in whatever the hell is going on right now. And we both know you don't really want to be involved."

His gaze seemed to darken then, to chill until his eyes were like cold, hard slate.

"Afraid for me, are you?" A hint of mockery filled his tone. "Think I can't protect you, little girl?"

At any other time, he might have been amused, Zack told himself.

"You're an accountant, not a soldier. And I don't want anyone else hurt." Pain darkened her eyes. "Especially you."

Especially him.

"Because I don't play war games with your cousins and bloody my knuckles every chance I get to prove I'm strong enough to suit you?" He had to laugh at that one, despite the insult.

"Because it's not your fight." Fists clenched, her expression tight with anger and fear, it made him wonder at the decision to hide who he was, what he was from her all these years.

She didn't think he could protect her. That thought ran through his mind on repeat, infuriating him with each pass.

It was a dare.

A challenge.

He'd never imagined Grace would have the nerve to step that close to the danger zone where he was concerned. Few people did, male or female.

Lust, anger, fear for her. They all collided then, wrapped around him, and broke the restraints he kept on the inner demons trapped inside. That darkness, that hunger he'd denied himself, and the aura of nonthreatening courtesy he was always careful to maintain.

In that second, they were gone, and a part of him wondered if he'd ever recover from it.

"Then I'll make it my fucking fight, how's that one?"

He moved before she could anticipate it, one hand sliding into the back of her hair, the other gripping her hip while he loomed over her, pressing her back to her pillow.

Before she could utter a cry or so much as whimper, his lips covered hers, and in that second, he realized why he'd stayed away from Grace Maddox.

Zack didn't ask for the kiss; he didn't warn her first. He owned the kiss.

His lips mastered hers. His tongue slipped past, parting hers in surprise. Then his lips slanted over hers, and it was nothing like what Grace had imagined this first kiss would be.

It was better.

It was hotter.

It completely consumed her senses and shot to hell any preconceived notions she might have had about Zack as a lover and the pleasure he could give her.

He mastered her senses with his kiss, stole reason and resistance before he pushed his hand beneath the blanket to the sweet flesh hidden there. His fingers slid into rich, heavy dew and swollen folds of flesh as the heel of his palm pressed into the engorged bud of her clit.

And right there, between one heartbeat and the next, she cried out into his kiss, her body bowing, moisture rushing over his fingers as sweet, quiet little Grace came in his hand with a strength and desperate hunger like nothing he'd known in his life.

In that moment, Zack knew that this woman was the greatest weakness a man could possess. Especially a man who didn't dare allow weakness into his life.

chapter three

Now what?

Stepping into Vince Maddox's office nearly thirty minutes later, Zack felt that punch of the inevitable still ricocheting through his senses. The second Grace exploded like dynamite in his hands, he'd known he was in more trouble than he ever imagined he could be. And he'd imagined quite a bit of trouble where she was concerned.

And she was madder than hell at him.

The thought of her flushed face, anger gleaming amid the pleasure sparking her eyes, had left him wanting nothing more than to feel her coming for him again.

Damn, she made him hot. It had taken everything he had to pull back—to keep from crawling over her, tearing his jeans from his hips, and pushing inside the sleek, wet depths of her. As she'd climaxed, her nails had dug into his shoulders, her body bowing, pushing closer to him, unconsciously seeking more, searching for every second of pleasure to be found.

"'Bout time you showed up," Cord growled from where he sat in a heavy leather chair next to his father's desk. His brothers, twins Deacon and Sawyer, sat on the other side, sprawled in matching chairs as they glared back at him.

"Call Jazz and Slade off," Vinny demanded as soon as the door closed behind Zack. "Those two are like a coupla junkyard dogs."

With an arch of his brow, Zack took a seat in the leather sofa facing the desk. "What are they doing?" he drawled, knowing damned good and well what they were doing.

Vinny leaned forward, propping his elbows on his desk, his dark green eyes shadowed with grief and the knowledge that his wife had been murdered by her own sister, his own daughter nearly killed more than once by the same woman.

The past two months hadn't been easy on Vinny or his boys. The truths now being uncovered had the power to chip away at the faith they had in the work they did. And Zack couldn't blame them, but he was damned if he'd let that lack of faith destroy Grace.

"They're parked at the gates, refusing to move. Kenni actually threw a tomato at the guards stationed there, and now she's threatening to neuter them!" he snapped furiously.

Something resembling a smothered chuckle came from one of the twins at his right, but when Zack glanced at them, both men were staring at the rounded tops of their boots with intense concentration. Turning back to Vinny, he caught the other man glaring at his sons.

"That sounds like Kenni," Zack agreed somberly. "They're lucky she hasn't used the Taser Jazz bought her."

Vinny's eyes rounded in something akin to horror. "He gave her a Taser gun? Did he lose his mind?"

Zack's initial reaction had been similar.

"He didn't want to lose another of his antique cork-screws, I guess." He shrugged. "I thought it was a smart move."

Kenni was nearly murdered by a henchman of her aunt's. She'd killed him by plunging one of Jazz's an-tique corkscrews straight into his heart.

Zack was still impressed with the move.

Vinny shot him a killing look rather than agreeing with him.

"As for her current threats," Zack continued. "I sug-gest you let Kenni check on her cousin, let Jazz and Slade in on the situation, we share info, and we all get along." He let his look harden. "Or I take Grace out of here, hide her myself, and Jazz, Slade, and I handle all this on our own."

Four sets of varying shades of green gazed back at him with suddenly icy expressions.

"Do you want to die, Zack?" Cord asked softly then, his beach cowboy look doing little to soften the cold em-erald gaze.

"Not today, Cord," Zack assured him facetiously. "Check back with me tomorrow. I have a feeling deal-ing with your cousin will be more detrimental to my careful control than I ever imagined she could be."

"Just kill him now, Dad," Cord grunted, not in the least amused.

"You could do that." Zack gave a short nod of his head. "Of course, if you do, I won't be able to tell you about my little visit to the Brigham Estate yesterday." He met each man's gaze once again. "I'm sure you want to hear about that." Zack relaxed back in the sofa, propped his ankle on the opposite knee, and watched the three men silently as they exchanged looks.

Finally, Vinny gave a hard shake of his head, his expression becoming heavy and filled with grief once more. "You'll break her heart," he said, his tone saddened. "You've already wounded it with your disregard for her over the past eight weeks."

"Better her heart broken than her life taken." A broken heart would keep her breathing, at least. "Alex Brigham had a file detailing Lucia's interrogation. She claimed Grace was helping her and that she was holding a flash drive containing evidence pointing to Lucia's partner. The leader of the silent coup you've been battling since Grace's father died. The only way we'll save her is if Brigham is convinced she's my lover. He won't strike out at her if she belongs to me. Not for any reason."

"And what makes you so fucking special?" Cord burst out just as his father lifted his hand for silence.

"Dad, you can't believe that—" Deacon leaned forward in anger only to receive a silencing look from Vinny.

Sawyer sat still, simply watching. He was the only one who would have worried Zack, if he'd had anything to worry about.

"You're going to play that card, Zack? After all these

years?" Vinny asked softly. "For a girl you've steered clear of since she first showed any interest in you? You wouldn't play it for yourself, but you're playing it for her?"

The implication that he was letting this get personal wasn't lost on Zack.

"Whoever targeted Grace is the same bastard who killed my parents as well as your brother and your wife." Zack dropped any pretense of casual amusement. Leaning forward, he stared back at Vinny, fighting to control his anger. "Sierra Maddox is the reason I was sent to Toby Rigor." Vinny's first wife had seen things even Vinny hadn't wanted to see. "Losing Kenni all those years nearly destroyed Jazz. I want that bastard, Vinny. I want him bad. And if this is what it takes to smoke him out, then fuck him, it's time he learns who he's dealing with."

Something flashed in Vinny's eyes, there and gone before Zack could identify the emotion.

"Very well." Vinny sat back in his chair, that casual attitude Zack had displayed moments before now infusing the Maddox patriarch. "Introduce yourself, then. Let Cord, Deacon, and Sawyer know who they're dealing with. Let them know why you, Jazz, and Slade hold the potential to divide the Kin."

His teeth clenched. He should have known Vinny would take this particular tack.

Finally, his lips curled mockingly with the knowledge that Vinny thought he'd back down. "Zackary Richards," he stated clearly. "Son of Zackary Richards Sr. and Nicole Brigham—Alexander Brigham's youngest sister."

Silence filled the room for long moments.

"Son of a bitch." Cord sat forward in his chair, his gaze sharp, suspicious. "Toby Rigor knew who you were, didn't he?"

Zack inclined his head. "And he took steps to ensure I'd always be safe. Steps that are still in place."

His foster father had been one of Vinny Maddox's most respected team leaders, as were his friends. And now those friends, and the sons of those friends, were sworn to carry on that protection.

Several times over the years, those Kin leaders had backed Slade, Jazz, and Zack equally whenever they'd butted heads with the Maddox family, whenever needed and with such covert precision that Vince Maddox never identified any of the men and women behind it. And they'd tried.

"And you're willing to extend that same protection to Grace?" Vinny asked then. "As well as holding back the Brigham family, no matter the cost to yourself?"

"To find the bastard who killed my parents and her father," he agreed, "you're damned right I am. I want this traitor, Vinny. I want it stopped. Now."

Secrets.

They were a part of the Tennessee mountains, part of their heritage as well as the very existence of the Maddox family and the government-backed militia they called the Kin.

"And you're willing to use Grace to catch him," Vinny sighed, "because you believe she's guilty."

"Because I know she's *not* guilty." Zack denied the charge, ignoring the narrow-eyed suspicion suddenly creasing Vinny's expression. "Grace wouldn't betray her father's memory, or the cousin she knew was alive for two years before Kenni ever admitted to Jazz who she was. If Grace were helping Lucia, then Kenni would have been dead before Jazz ever realized she was in trouble."

Kenni and Grace had already admitted that to the family. Grace's love for Kenni, for the family, wasn't in question.

"Then Luce lied," Vinny stated. "Grace can't be in possession of that information."

The disappointment in the other man's tone was enough to send irritation flashing through Zack. He wondered if Vinny wouldn't have preferred Grace be guilty just so he could get his hands on that information.

"If Grace even thought she had something the family needed, she'd turn it over in a heartbeat," Zack agreed. "And she was too young when Benjamin died for him to have entrusted anything in her care."

"Then how do you intend to learn who Luce's partner was?" Cord asked.

"I won't have to learn who it is," he assured them, tapping the fingers of one hand on the arm of the sofa. "Luce swore Grace has it. Whoever's been heading this attempted coup will be desperate to get it, or to kill her so she can't reveal it. They have no idea who within the Kin backs me, or how many back me any more than you do. Whoever it is will get desperate now. They're going to convince themselves they're smart enough, strong enough to take her from me. I'm going to prove them wrong. And uncover who they are at the same time, however I have to."

Sawyer spoke up then, an edge of disgust in his tone.

"By using Grace. When it's over, you'll leave her broken, Zack."

He repeated his earlier statement. "She'll be alive."

Grace would be alive, and that should be all that concerned her family. At the heart of it, he was afraid that part played too large a role in his own plans as well.

He'd begun thinking of her as his in some ways, long before now. He didn't like it, but he also tried not to hide from himself. And Grace was a part of him he couldn't define or make sense of.

"What do you need?" Vinny asked rather than protesting further. "How do you intend to play this little game of yours?"

It wasn't a game, but so long as the Maddox family believed it was just that, then the safer Grace would be. The Brigham family would know better, unfortunately. Just as Zack knew it. There were secrets they shared, secrets that would end up not just hurting Grace but destroying him as well.

"Grace is too weak to protect herself. You raised her to be the replacement princess when you thought Kenni was dead." He ignored the shocked anger in their faces. "She's delicate, with no fighting skills and a trusting nature." He shot the four men a scowl. "It's like letting a puppy loose in a den of wolves. You set her up as bait from the moment you took her into your home."

Grace hadn't even been born with the fiery, stubborn nature of the Maddox Clan. She smiled sweetly at everyone when she asked for something, and for the most part, they indulged her. The princess could do no harm, until the true princess returned. Now she was a target.

"That's how you see Grace?" Vinny asked heavily. "Weak and defenseless?"

"She's a country club debutante," Zack reminded him, though without scorn. "Through no fault of her own. She can't survive in this world you've carved out for her. The very fact that she is so defenseless has made her a target."

The four men stared at each other as though assessing what Zack had said, perhaps not believing it, but they had to see the truth of the matter.

"You didn't train her, even to the extent that Kenni had been trained," he continued. "At least Kenni knew how to hunt, to shoot, and to fight. Grace has none of those skills. The only chance she has is to align herself with someone who has the strength to protect her, and will spend his life doing just that rather than his job within the Kinship. You set her up to die."

And it pissed him the hell off. Over the years, it had driven him to distraction to know that Grace had no idea how to fight if the situation warranted it. And with the Kin, the situation would eventually warrant it.

"You didn't answer my question, son. How do you intend to protect her?" Vinny asked with that dangerously soft voice that seemed to affect anyone who heard it.

Anyone but me, Zack thought. He wasn't scared of Vinny any more than he was frightened of his uncle, Alex Brigham.

"First of all, the information regarding my parentage goes no further," Zack insisted. "Secondly, I'll be taking care of Grace from here on out." And here was where he expected the blowout: "As her lover."

Surprisingly, Vinny's brow lifted in subtle, amused

mockery, his green eyes lighting with it before he glanced at her cousins. Each of the other three men was too quiet.

The patriarch finally shrugged. "Grace can choose her own lovers. Any plan you come up with, she'll be made aware of, though. So it isn't our agreement you have to procure, but hers."

Zack stared back at them suspiciously. Well, now, wasn't he expecting more of an objection?

"Grace is a grown woman," Vince continued, obviously reading at least part of the wariness Zack could feel tightening through his body. "I'm not stupid, and I don't expect my boys, Kenni or Grace to live by some antiquated code of moral conduct. If she wants a lover, that's her business. I may question her taste in men"—his look assured Zack he was the questionable male—"but that's her business, not mine."

Her cousins appeared on the verge of outright amusement, though, especially Sawyer. He kept rubbing his hand over his cheek as though trying to hide the twitch of his lips.

"So let me in on the fucking joke," Zack growled.

"No joke." Sawyer finally chuckled, shaking his head. "No joke at all, man. I'm still stuck on the 'puppy in a wolf's den' image. I have to remember that one."

He wasn't the cousin known for his tact; that was for damned sure.

"Yeah, a sweet little golden retriever, that's our Grace," his twin, Deacon, agreed a little too solemnly. "All bounce and fluff and no teeth. We like her like that. She's a calm, comforting influence on all of us."

"It could get her killed," Zack informed him.

"We see the error of our ways now," Cord injected, anger slipping into his tone as Zack turned to him.

It was time one of them realized what a mess they'd created.

"As Dad said," Cord ground out, "who she takes as a lover is her business. Whether or not she agrees to actually let you into her bed for the sake of her safety is up to her as well. But she will know what's going on and what your plans are."

"You'll allow me to inform her of them," Zack demanded, the tension in the room causing the hairs at the back of his neck to lift in warning. "I'll be damned if I need you turning her against me before I even tell her what's going on."

"Agreed," Vince voiced before his sons could object. "You have twenty-four hours. Get your gear—you can have the suite next to hers."

He frowned at that. "My home is more secure—"

Vince leaned forward, his weight bracing on his arms as he propped them on his desk. "The suite next to hers, Zack," he reiterated with dark warning. "Grace will remain here until you can prove she'll be safer at your home. She has a job to do here, and no one else can do it. Live with it or leave. Your choice."

The phone on Vinny's desk buzzed at that moment, bringing a grimace to his lips as he jerked it to his ear with a brusque "What?" His lips flattened and he disconnected the call without a response. "It would seem Kenni is now stalking up the drive along with Jazz and Slade." He pushed his fingers through his hair in frustration. "Dammit, I wanted her out of this."

A father's lament, Zack thought with regret. A father who had already lost his daughter once.

"Grace helped her, Vinny. She won't stay out of it. Even for you." As much as Zack regretted it, as much as he hated it, there was no keeping his brother or his brother's fiancée out of the coming mess.

Vinny glared at him. "You're going to become a problem, Zack."

His lips quirked at the accusation. "I've always been a problem, Vinny. I just didn't let you see it. Until now. But I'll be damned if I watch another defenseless young woman die for this family. Not again."

Not Grace.

Cord snorted as he rose to his feet, mocking amusement filling the sound. "I almost pity you," he stated, his green eyes filled with ire as he glared down at Zack. "Almost."

With that, he turned and stalked from the office, leaving only a tension-filled silence Zack had no intention of disrupting.

Let them think what they wanted. No one hated the thought of hurting Grace more than he did. Just as no one could possibly hate the fact that she was involved in this more than he did. That was the hand being dealt to them, though, and none of them had a choice but to play the cards they were given.

Especially him.

chapter four

"I'm so sorry, Miss Grace," he said softly. "I'm so sorry. Just tell me where the files are, and I'll let you go. I promise. . . .

"Miss Grace, helpin' your momma was a really bad idea. . . ."

That night, Grace was still trying to make sense of the attack, to make sense of what was going on.

Rich had been so certain she had whatever files he wanted, just as he'd been certain she was helping her mother, Lucia Maddox, betray the Maddox Clan.

What files?

Despite the sting of the stitched wound on the outside of her thigh, Grace paced her bedroom, going over each second of her recollection, desperate for answers and all too aware that Zack was in the connecting room.

Her television droned on in the background, the late-evening news reporting its doom and gloom. Normally, she'd pay more attention to it; tonight, her attention was far too fractured.

She couldn't even keep her mind on the fact that someone wanted her dead for something she didn't even possess. Oh, hell no, let's not concentrate on the fact that her dog was nearly dead and a friend had tried to kill her, not when Zack Richards was in the other room. Not when he'd made her body respond to him despite her best efforts to keep that from happening.

Let's just jump on the orgasm free-for-all and torment herself with memories of it as she did in the hours before she'd forced herself to go over the attack again.

Her body was all for it. It was begging for a second helping. It was greedy. Her inner trollop was still cheering for Team Richards, no matter her attempts to shut it down.

Still far too sensitive, memories of that afternoon plaguing her, Grace tried to tell herself she wasn't going to allow it to happen again—but she knew better.

Damn, he was good. So damned good. The feel of his kiss, the stroke of his fingers—

Nope, not going there.

She shook her head, grimacing at the effort it took to pull her mind back from reliving that pleasure and make herself concentrate on preserving her life instead.

What in the hell made Rich think she had any sort of files or that she'd been helping a traitor? It made no sense.

Everyone knew what little use Lucia had for her only child. Her mother had reviled not just the stepsons who came with her marriage to Benjamin Maddox but also the daughter who adored her father. Her father had been her hero. If anyone had been Daddy's little girl, then it was Grace. She'd been devastated by his death.

So why would she be accused of helping Lucia?

Frowning into the dimly lit interior of her bedroom, she paced the length of the room again. Or rather, limped her way across it.

The slice on her upper leg was deep enough to require stitches and, no doubt, if Magnus hadn't been there to protect her, would have been far worse. Her pet's injuries had nearly been fatal.

Dammit, she'd grown up with Rich. She'd known him for most of her life. Why attack her? Why not just ask for whatever he thought Lucia had given her?

Nibbling at her thumbnail, she went over the attack again, played it back, forward, tried to remember each nuance of his voice, every word the farmhand had said. When nothing there made any more sense than it had before, she tried to remember each meeting with her mother before the day Lucia had been taken from the house by the Brigham agents.

In the weeks before that, Lucia had been even more caustic, more insulting toward Grace than ever. Grace had stayed out of her way as much as possible. Of course, she tended to do that regardless, simply because Lucia's gibes always had the power to hurt, to make Grace feel as though she were the flawed one because her mother couldn't love her.

Grace had had her own concerns, though. Trying to stay one step ahead of Cord and any threat against Kenni, she'd been consumed with ensuring her cousin stayed hidden and safe. There was little time for anything else.

And now, she had to deal with Zack.

Just when she thought life could calm down a little . . .

At least she'd been able to shower, with some help from Kenni. Her hair was washed and neatly brushed rather than tangled around her face. She'd felt like a bedraggled orphan earlier in the day.

"I can think of better ways to spend the night than pacing the floors."

Swinging around, Grace barely managed to contain a surprised cry, both at the pain caused by the movement as well as by the sight of Zack leaning in the doorway connecting the two bedrooms.

Freshly showered, he hadn't yet combed his dark auburn hair; it framed his face with roguish messiness that looked far too sexy. His chest and feet were bare. Hard, tight abs flexed as he scratched at the light sprinkle of hair on his chest. The only reason he was on the right side of decent was the snug jeans, zipped but not buttoned, hanging low on his hips.

She wanted to lick him.

Bite him.

All night long.

What in the hell had possessed her uncle to allow him to spend the night?

"Uncle Vinny catches you in here, and he'll skin you alive," she hissed, hobbling back to her bed, grateful she'd changed from her gown to the silky black pajamas Kenni helped her into after her shower.

"He'd have to catch me first." The arrogance in his tone was too natural to be faked. Which meant he'd kept that side of himself hidden over the years. At least from her.

Before she could pull herself back to the mattress, she felt Zack quickly lift her and then gently settle her against the pillows.

"I could have done it myself!" she snapped, at odds with herself and the liquid pleasure now coursing through her. "I'm not a damned invalid."

"That knife wound to your thigh says different," he grunted, easing back before once again sitting at the side of her bed as though he had every right to do so.

"I was doing fine," she reminded him irritably. "Magnus is much worse. Besides—" She breathed out heavily. "—I have to head to D.C. to the Brigham Estate next week. I need to work out some of the soreness."

The monthly meeting with the Brigham Agency couldn't be put off. Besides, she was friends with Victoria Brigham and had promised to attend her birthday party. She'd actually been looking forward to it.

"Like hell." The scowl on Zack's face caused her to tilt her head and stare back at him in surprise while arranging the blankets to her waist.

"What's like hell?" she asked absently, trying not to focus on his lips. Especially the lower one with that slight fullness to it that she just wanted to nibble at.

Lick.

Maybe even bite.

She didn't think all night long would be enough time.

"What the hell are you doing, making a trip to the Brigham Estate?" The irritation in his tone had her refocusing on listening to him rather than biting him. "You have no business there."

Grace stilled. "Really? According to my uncle and Alex Brigham, I have a monthly meeting there, just as

I've had since I took over the position as Uncle Vinny's assistant. One weekend a month. They insist." She waved her hand negligently. "I tend to go along with such requests, though." She smiled sweetly. "Considering it is my job."

So much for that friendly, quiet accountant demeanor he'd been lying to her with over the years. He was just as hard-edged and arrogant as her cousins. Well, they'd learned better than to try to run over her through the years. If Zack insisted on sticking around the Maddox household, he'd learn as well.

Probably the same way her cousins had: the hard way.

"Not anymore, it's not," he assured her, staring at her as though he couldn't imagine her doing such a thing.

It was the Brigham Estate, not a brothel, for pity's sake.

"Has Uncle Vinny canceled the meeting?" she asked with deliberate confusion. She tended to play with morons. It was a game of sorts.

"He will be." The reply was one of complete confidence.

"When he informs me that I don't have to do my job, then I won't do it." She smiled once again. "Until then, plans are on. I'll be heading out at the end of next week."

And Uncle Vinny would not be telling her she couldn't go. The private meetings with Alex Brigham and his son Madden were more necessary now than they had ever been. Besides, she was really looking forward to that party. Her dress was waiting at the estate, the price alone ensuring she attended. It had taken a hefty chunk from her account.

"Did you somehow miss the fact that your life is in danger?" Zack rose furiously from the bed, shot her glare, then turned away to stalk to the other side of the room. Turning back to her, he tried to tell himself to stop lusting after her and attempt to talk some sense into her. She did not have to obey her uncle no matter the danger to herself.

"I'm certain Uncle Vinny is taking every precaution, he always does." She shrugged, remembering the warning Cord had given her earlier not to let Zack know about her self-defense training or just how stubborn she could be.

Evidently, whoever had targeted her was taken in by the appearance she and her family had deliberately kept up over the years: that she was meek and helpless. After all, Vinny would never allow someone who was weak to know the details of the Kinship. Hell, even Luce had believed the ruse. She'd often reminded Grace how little her uncle trusted her simply because she was so weak-minded.

It was laughable at times.

Hard-edged, military-trained Kin leaders were known to hang their heads or eye her nervously whenever they pissed her off, but her own mother hadn't seen who she really was. Obviously, neither had Zack.

Blame her stubbornness on him, Vinny had always suggested, and she did just that.

Always appear wary of Vinny's temper, Cord, Deacon, and Sawyer had advised her.

They'd preached that to her for years simply to ensure she was never targeted because of her job. Vinny never respected anything but strength. If she didn't appear to embody that innate strength, then no one would suspect she held his secrets. Now it wasn't her job endangering her, but the mother who should have fought to protect her instead.

She'd be amused, but she'd grown out of caring about her mother's motivations in her teens.

"Vinny took every precaution yesterday as well, didn't he?" Zack sneered. "That bastard nearly killed you and your dog. What would you have done if not for Magnus, Grace?"

Put that knife in his throat! she thought furiously. She wished she had done that instead of trying to pull back and play helpless, hoping to keep him alive for questioning. He hadn't expected her to fight; she hadn't expected Magnus to attack so viciously.

She'd misjudged the situation, and it pissed her off.

"Zack, you will have to take this up with Uncle Vinny," she told him again, keeping her voice calm. "Both my half brothers, Baer and Banyon, will be accompanying me, and I understand you'll be there as well. I'll be perfectly safe," she pointed out.

Asshole. Cord had already discussed Zack's meeting with the men in her family with her earlier.

"You weren't safe in your own home—"

"We had no idea I was in danger," she pointed out with such innocent logic, he ground his teeth together in frustration.

Zack could feel the irritation beginning to work up his spine even as lust tightened his balls. She was staring at him as though she had complete faith in her family to protect her when they'd failed her once already. The second time could mean her death.

She was sitting there in her girly bed as though nothing and no one had touched or could touch her. So certain she was safe. So certain no one would ever hurt her again.

God, it was killing him.

A golden retriever puppy in a wolf's den. Sawyer's words haunted him.

With her soft, golden blonde hair framing her face in lush waves and falling to her shoulders, she looked too soft, too tempting. Those big green eyes were innocent, so filled with faith. And she was so damned tiny that he wondered if he'd break her when he actually managed to get her beneath him.

Going slow and easy would be hell, but he'd do it. There was no way to fake being lovers. The act had to be legit. It was the only way to draw out the traitor intent on killing her. Once rumors that he was the missing Brigham nephew began to circulate, then her enemies would know there was no way in hell the Brigham family would move against her so long as she was in his bed. It would also ensure no orders went out against her from the Brighams. That avenue would be effectively closed to whoever was targeting her.

This way, the enemy would have to do his own dirty work and contact Zack. And everyone in the Kin knew exactly how Zack felt about the Maddox Clan, other than Grace, as well as the Brigham family. He'd made no secret of it.

"Grace," he tried again as he crossed his arms over his chest and glared back at her. "This isn't a game. It's your life. Do you want to die?"

She lowered her head, the fall of hair obscuring her

expression as she seemed to staring at her fingers where they lay on the quilt covering her.

Delicate fingers with pretty oval nails. Nails that had clenched into his shoulders earlier as her hips arched, pressing the slick flesh of her sex into his palm as she came for him.

"You should leave, Zack," she finally said softly, still refusing to look at him. "I understand we all have an important meeting in the morning, and I need to rest."

Important meeting, her ass. According to Cord, Zack was going to inform them how he intended to protect her. He thought she was just as weak and defenseless, just as malleable as Luce had believed.

He was in for a surprise.

Just because she couldn't reveal her training didn't mean she couldn't reveal her temper, and he was testing it sorely at the moment.

"Not until we have this resolved." He stalked back to the side of the bed, watching her carefully when she glanced back up at him. The way the slight tilt of her eyes seemed more pronounced, the dark emerald color gleaming with a hint of anger, her flushed cheeks, the stubborn set of her chin.

Why had he never noticed that determined little curve before?

"It is resolved. Unless Uncle Vinny tells me otherwise, then I'm heading to D.C. at the end of next week. You can go with me, stay here, go home, go back to work, I don't care." She stared straight up at him then, pure green fire making her eyes brighter.

A grin tugged at Zack's lips. "Do you think you're going to get stubborn on me, Grace?" he asked her, scooting next to her hip on the bed and watching as her petite nostrils flared in irritation. "After this afternoon, do you really think it's going to work?"

She stared back at him resolutely. "It was good, Zack," she surprised him a second later. "It was real damned good, and I'm sure it can get better." And not once did she bat an eyelash. "And I'm sure I'd promise you anything you want once you started touching me, just to have it again. But don't doubt, I'll lie straight to your face and once I'm out of this bed, I'm going to do exactly what I want to do, and exactly what my job entails I do. Consider that before you try to use sex to control me. That control lasts only while we're in the bed."

He'd be damned. She believed every word spilling past those pretty little lips, didn't she? She was so convinced that what he could do to her, what he could make her feel would be so easily overlooked once her bouncy little ass came off the sheets?

He shook his head in amused regret. "Ahh, baby, one of these days, you won't be under Vinny's roof. You'll be in my home, in my bed, where I can show you different. Then we'll see how brave you are."

She gave a little shrug. "The chances of that happening before we go to D.C. are slim. I'll take my chances."

She would take her chances, would she?

Zack braced his arm across her hips, leaned forward until his lips were less than an inch from her, and warned her softly, "I'm not one of those little boys who pant after your cute ass. I'm a man, Grace, and one you don't want to dare."

Her lips parted, her breathing heavy. Zack watched

as a flush suffused her face and pure want filled her eyes. "I didn't barge into your bedroom, making demands," she whispered, breathless, her tongue poking out to dampen her lips. "We both know you can make me want you—it's a game you've been playing since I was eighteen." The hurt that flashed in her eyes then surprised him. "You are indeed a man, Zack, but I'm not a stupid girl anymore. Don't make that mistake. Now, stop teasing me and let me go to sleep. It's been a helluva two days."

He leaned forward just that little bit, then captured her lips at that moment when she thought she could turn away from him, thought she could escape the hunger raging through his system. He deserved one more taste of her before morning came. Before she learned what a bastard he intended to be.

He deserved the pure, unvarnished need he tasted in her kiss, the way she flowed into him, melted against his chest, and let him in. Her arms snaked around his shoulders, those delicate nails pressing into bare skin, pricking at his flesh with heated need.

Oh, he was going to have her. Not tonight, not until she knew what she was facing, knew what they were doing. He didn't want fairy tales in her eyes when she stared at him. Fairy tales didn't exist, but this did.

Her lips parted for him again, her tongue tasting his as he possessed her with his kiss and pulled those hot whimpering little moans from her throat. This was what he wanted to see in her eyes. The need for this, the aching hunger, and a woman's knowledge that she would come to him, no matter what, just for this pleasure alone.

That she was his—

At that thought, he jerked back, staring down at her, shocked at his own musings, at the depth of need beginning to burn in his veins. Pure, raging lust mixed with a hunger he'd never allowed himself before and wouldn't tolerate now.

Rising quickly from the bed, he glared down at her, jaw clenched, his body demanding he take her, lust tearing through him with a force he'd never experienced before.

What the hell had she done to him?

She accused him of teasing her since she was eighteen? Hell no, it wasn't her he'd teased; he'd been teasing himself, killing himself with the need for her. And he was damned if he could figure out why.

"Get your rest, Grace," he growled, the discipline it took to force himself away shaky at best. "Rest well, because after tonight, you may be far busier than you ever imagined."

chapter five

Tension lay thick in Vince Maddox's office the next morning when Zack stepped into the room, the files he'd put together gripped loosely in one hand. The space reminded him far too much of Alex Brigham's office. Perhaps not so stately or so expensively decorated, but the appearance was more or less the same. Dark wood, walls, and floor offset with large windows positioned to allow maximum light. Tall bookcases filled with suitably impressive titles, among them historic and military tomes.

He hadn't glimpsed a single modern paperback on the dust-free wood. It was enough to send a chill up a man's back.

Vinny sat at the other end of the room behind the heavy executive desk with his sons positioned on the two sides just as before while Grace stood with her back to the room, arms crossed, staring pensively out one of the large windows.

The pale blue sleeveless dress she wore emphasized her delicate figure, but rather than the high heels he was used to seeing her in, she had a pair of white flat sandals on her feet. The change in footwear made sense, considering her wound.

Bruises marred her upper arm; he knew others marked her side. His jaw tightened before he reached Vinny's desk and took the chair the other man waved him to.

"Sleep well?" The edge of snide anger in Cord's tone had Zack lifting a brow mockingly.

"Very well," he assured the other man. "You?"

Cord gave an irritated grunt, his brooding gaze flickering with ire.

Vinny spoke to his niece, his voice gentle as he looked across the room to Grace's back. "Grace, could you join us, sweetheart?"

"I can hear just fine from here, Uncle Vinny," she assured him, and though her tone was well modulated and lacking any anger, Zack swore he could still feel heat in it.

"I'm sure you can, but I'd prefer you come over here and sit with us. Let's at least try to be civil about this until we find out what's going on exactly."

Tossing a file in the seat beside his own, Zack leaned forward and placed all but one folder on Vinny's desk without addressing the fact that Grace had yet to take her seat. "This is the information I've put together since returning yesterday morning, along with a copy of the file I stole from Alex Brigham's desk," he announced. "I think you should go through it before we begin talking."

Grace took her seat silently as Vinny passed a file to each of his sons before flipping through the one he kept for himself, a frown darkening his brow as he scanned each page. Beside him, he could hear Grace breathing quickly, and he caught the look of horror as it came over her face.

"You couldn't tell me this yesterday?" Vinny finally snapped, glaring across his desk at Zack.

"I didn't have all the information yesterday. All I had was the few pages at the front of the file that I took while at the estate. The rest I put together from favors owed and various contacts I've made within the Brigham Agency," he assured Grace's uncle. "They're going to come for her, Vinny, as will Luce's partner. You might be able to protect her from Kin traitors, but you can't protect her from the agency, and you know it."

He didn't have to look at his own file. The orders Alex Brigham had been putting together to have Grace brought in for questioning were bad enough. The report on Luce's interrogation—her accusations that Grace had been helping her and still held vital information missing for over twenty years regarding a deep-level traitor within the Kin—was the same as a death sentence for Grace. A sentence Zack refused to accept.

"This isn't true!" Horror and a realization of the depth of her mother's betrayal filled Grace's strangled whisper. "Uncle Vinny, it isn't true."

Tears filled her voice, and the sound of them tightened Zack's chest. She knew as well as the rest of them did what was coming if they didn't find a way to prove her innocence or reveal the information Luce had sworn she possessed.

"Dammit, Grace, I know that," Vinny swore, his expression darkening with fury as Zack sat back in his chair and waited.

"This is bullshit," Cord muttered, suddenly tossing the file he held and its contents across the floor, the pages fluttering for a moment before settling silently. "They can't do this. I'll be damned if we'll let them do this."

"If we defy them, it will destroy everything the Maddox family has built over the generations and it will throw the protection of not just this area in danger, but it will affect the other families in the network as well," Zack pointed out. "The Maddox Clan is the strongest, but even that strength won't be enough to save her, Cord. You know that."

The Brigham Agency wasn't bound by normal laws, just as the Kin weren't. There were checks, balances, and there were traitors. Far more, it appeared, than they had ever imagined.

"I'll leave . . ." Grace whispered.

"And go where?" he asked, turning to her, finding it harder to rein in his own fury than it had ever been. "Where will you go, Grace, that the agency or the Kin can't find you? There were only a few of those low-level bastard traitors searching for Kenni, and she lost her uncle fighting to stay alive. How will you survive against the agency or the Kin they convince to go after you?"

She was so fucking pale, it made him want to slam his fist into a Brigham face.

Emerald eyes sparkled with tears as soft pink lips tightened to control their trembling and a sense of hopelessness flashed across her face. "But I didn't do this."

The file shook in her hands as she lifted it for just a moment before letting it settle back to her lap.

He hadn't seen that look on her face since she was five years old and standing beside her father's grave. The vulnerability and uncertainty mixed with overwhelming grief and pain. It was bad enough knowing her mother had betrayed the family in general and was the reason for her father's murder. But to realize the woman who should have nurtured her was instead so evil, she'd sacrifice her daughter as well was tearing her up inside. And there wasn't a damned thing he could do to make the pain go away for her.

"I'm going to assume you have a solution?" Vinny snarled. "That's why you're here, right?"

"How can he have a solution?" The tears in her voice didn't detract from the anger, the pain, or the confusion. "How can he help when it's obvious you or the Kin can't?" She turned to him then, shaking her head. "And how did you get this information? You hate the Kin and the Brighams, yet you were able to steal files from the estate?" Disbelief flickered in her gaze. "Really, Zack? Did you turn into a cat burglar overnight?"

The question came quicker than he'd anticipated. Grace was smart, though; he should have expected it.

"Did you verify this information, Uncle Vinny?" Desperation filled the question, the search for something, anything to change the situation apparent in her tone.

Turning back to Vinny, Zack let his gaze lock with the other man's.

Vinny's expression was heavy with knowledge of the

sacrifice Zack was making. And it was a sacrifice. A lifetime of secrets, the attempts to deny who he was and where he came from were over.

"Uncle Vinny?" Grace whispered, the silence in the room becoming as heavy as the tension.

"I don't have to verify it," Vinny said quietly. "I know Zack was at the estate when you were attacked. He's there every month, just as you are."

Cord wiped his hand over his face before leaning forward in his chair, elbows on his knees, his hands hanging between them as he stared at the floor.

He'd always known the time for secrets was going to be over soon. It had been a damned good fight, and he'd managed to stay one step ahead of the Brigham family all his life.

He'd known the truth would eventually come out though.

"Why?" Grace whispered. "Why would the Brighams care about someone who so obviously hates them as much as Zack hates them? What does he have on them?"

Zack shook his head. "I don't have anything on them, Grace. It's what they know about me."

He rubbed at the side of his jaw; the bombshell he was about to drop would be devastating for her. The rumors of the reasons behind her father's and his parents' deaths had circulated through the Kin for decades. Truth didn't matter. The truth had never been told, the rumor always allowed to stand simply because it was less dangerous to the family and to the Kin.

"What they know about you?" she questioned him, anger rising in her tone. "How can you help me if they have something they're holding over you? What kind of game are you playing?"

"They're not holding anything over me," he gritted out, forcing his fingers not to curl into fists.

"Then explain it, Richards!" Deacon snapped as he and his twin glared at him murderously. "Do you think we're just going to let you waltz out of here with Grace, without giving her a damned good expectation of your ability to protect her?"

"Enough, Deacon." Cord shook his head as Vinny grimaced at the question, his gaze still locked on Zack.

"Enough? Let him fucking explain himself to her." Sawyer came out of his chair to stand next to Grace. "He's full of shit."

Zack's lips quirked. He had to give it to the twins—they were just as explosive as Cord was dangerously quiet.

"Ever known me to lie to you, Sawyer?" Zack asked him, turning in his chair just enough to watch Grace's face as he spoke. "Have I ever lied to you, Grace?" he asked her softly.

She licked her lips, the lower curve trembling again before she managed to restrain it. "It doesn't make sense, Zack." She swallowed tightly. "There's nothing you can do. . . ."

"I'm the only one who can keep you alive," he assured her. "I promise you that."

"It takes more than a promise, Zack," Deacon snarled.

"Alex Brigham will never let an agent or a Kin under this family's control touch you once he believes you belong to me," he stated, hardening his tone, hardening the compassion and anger inside him. "He'd die and go to hell before he'd touch you, because he knows if he does, and I ever learn he's behind it, then I'll snap my mother's inheritance up so fast, it will make his head spin. And if anything happens to me, then he loses control of it to the heirs I've named in my stead. There's no way he'll win, and he knows it."

"And what makes you so fucking important to the Brigham family?" she snapped. "Why would you or your mother matter?"

"I'm Nicole Brigham Richards's son," he stated. "I'm Alex Brigham's lost nephew, Grace. And I could rip that agency and that family apart if it's what I wanted. And I will if they ever endanger me or what I consider mine, and that's something Alex Brigham won't chance."

She seemed to stop breathing for a moment. "No," she whispered. "You're lying."

"I stayed away from you all these years because I knew how betrayed you'd feel if you learned the truth," he sighed wearily, knowing the time for hiding was at an end. "Just as I knew I wouldn't let you go once I decided you were mine." He reached out and touched her cheek gently before pulling back when she flinched. "This way, you can hate me until hell freezes over for a reason. For something I've done rather than something someone else did."

The rumor that her father had died protecting the missing Brigham heir haunted her, he knew. Vinny had warned him more than once that if Grace ever learned he was that missing heir, she'd never forgive him for the death of the father she'd so loved.

"I'd rather face an interrogation." Jumping from her

chair, dumping the file to the floor, she moved away from him quickly.

Rising as well, Zack let his lips quirk satirically. "Well, that's too bad, sweetheart," he informed her, hating himself, hating the Brighams, and letting her hate him all she needed to. "Because I'm not nearly so willing to let the bastard who killed my parents and your father escape, now that I know how close he is. Luce was in on it every step of the way, working directly with the bastard who arranged it. It stops here." It would stop before it endangered her further; he'd make damned sure of it. "Because I'm damned tired of living under the shadow of it. Resign yourself to it. You might not be willing to be a lover, but by God, you better be a good-enough actress to convince everyone we know that you are, because that's all that will save any of us now. Including the family willing to put their lives and the lives of the men who follow them on the line. Because that's all that's going to call that fucking family off and make it stick until we find the evidence to clear you or until we find the evidence period." He turned and stalked to the door of the office. "And I'll be a son of a bitch if I'll feel guilty for a second of it." He slammed the door closed behind him.

After stomping through the foyer to the front door, he let it slam behind him as well. His truck was waiting in the front drive now, having been driven back by one of Chaz McDougal's men and left at the farm. Within seconds, Zack was out of the driveway and heading farther up the mountain.

Making a call to his foster brothers to meet him at the office, he resigned himself to their coming anger as well. He'd played the role of quiet, unassuming Zack with a zeal that should have won him an Oscar.

Quiet, yeah, he liked quiet.

Unassuming? That one had never been easy. Just as the summers his foster father had convinced him to spend with the Brighams had never been easy. When Toby told the other two foster sons he had taken under his wing that he'd arranged for Zack to work with the Brighams in the summer after Zack turned eighteen, he hadn't been lying. Zack worked his ass off training to become the killer they'd wanted him to be. As though he'd turn into one of the jackasses he'd despised since first learning of them.

The price of their silence at the time had been high. His mother's father, Alexander Sr., had been a bastard with a capital *B*. Zack had realized within days of first meeting him exactly why his mother had turned her back on her family and run away with her lover.

How they managed to hide within the Kin, Zack had never figured out. Vinny's and Benjamin's help aside, it should still have been impossible to hide from the agents the Brigham family would have sent out after them.

It was a question he'd never been able to get an answer for, though. Not from Vinny and not from Alex Brigham, the man who had once claimed to cherish his baby sister.

Turning into the parking lot of the offices of the construction company he owned with his foster brothers, Zack blew out a harsh breath. Telling Jazz and Slade who he was wouldn't be easy. It was a truth he'd never confronted them with, one he'd fought to hide for as long as he'd known them.

Both men were already there, just as he'd known they'd be. Jazz wouldn't head out to the work sites until after ten, and Slade didn't schedule meetings until ten thirty unless all three of them needed to be present.

When he pulled in beside Jazz's pickup, the RIGOR CONSTRUCTION advertisement on the side of the door brought a quirk to Zack's lips. The other man had flatly refused to have the company information painted on the truck until he'd become engaged to Vinny's daughter, Kenni. Now his brother was settling down, finding the happiness that had eluded him for so long, and working on a future with the woman he loved.

Slade had settled down as well. His time with the FBI was behind him, and reclaiming the woman he'd fallen in love with years ago had settled a core of rage in the man that Zack had once feared would never disappear.

He envied them their lives, envied them the women who loved them. It was a life Zack had never allowed himself to imagine, because he'd known his past and his identity would endanger any family he tried to claim as his own.

He stepped from the truck, strode to the door, and entered the offices, steeling his determination.

Jazz and Slade were at the conference table in the back corner, coffee steaming in the mugs sitting in front of them as their conversation halted, their gazes settling on him.

"Well, aren't you running a little late?" Jazz said, his black brows arching with the comment as mockery gleamed in his brilliant blue eyes.

He wasn't in the best of moods.

"And no bruises or broken bones." Slade grinned. "I

thought Cord and his heathen brothers would have tromped his ass after he insisted on staying the night with little Grace."

Flicking both men an irate glance, Zack moved to the coffeepot, poured a cup of the aromatic brew, then took a seat at the end of the table facing them. "We need to talk," he stated, running the fingers of one hand through his hair.

Damn, he wasn't looking forward to this.

"Think this is where he finally tells us his momma was a Brigham and he's been visiting good old Uncle Alex when he disappears every month?" Jazz asked, his tone a little too calm, a little too conversational.

Zack simply stared back at the two men.

"We've known that one for a while, Zack," Slade informed him. "Ever since I found out it was Brigham agents who helped save my ass in D.C. I'm not the kind of man not to ask questions in those situations."

Hell.

He shook his head, resigned. "Why didn't you say anything?"

"It was your secret." Slade shrugged. "I figured you'd tell us when the time was right for you." He glanced at Jazz. "Asshole over there knew before I did, though, and didn't say a damned thing about it until I told him what I learned after the D.C. operation."

They hadn't even hinted that they knew the truth of who he was, of where he came from.

"Toby told me who you were right before he died," Jazz admitted before sipping at his coffee. "I thought it best to wait for you to come to us." His lips quirked. "Just never thought it would take so long."

They had known and never made accusations, never came to him when they needed to. Of course, Zack had helped where he could, and Alexander Brigham never denied him the resources or information he'd needed.

"I always had your backs—"

"We knew that, always have." Jazz nodded. As the eldest of them, Jazz had always been the one to look out for his younger foster brothers while they were growing up. He'd always seemed to know them better than they'd known themselves.

"Come on, Zack, we knew the power we were gaining within the Kin wasn't because of our good looks." Slade rubbed his jaw and flashed an amused grin. "Though I'm sure that didn't hurt."

Jazz snorted at the comment before his gaze sharpened on Zack once again. "You're our brother, Zack—where your blood came from never mattered. I remember your momma, she was a fine woman and your dad was a damned good man. You're our brother, though, nothing else ever mattered to us."

"I did appreciate the team of agents that watched my back in D.C., though," Slade assured him.

"Yeah," Jazz drawled. "And I know that team that took Luce in for interrogation was already waiting in the wings in case we needed outside help. I appreciated that."

Zack stared down at the coffee in his cup, his chest tightening at the knowledge that they'd kept the information to themselves.

Jazz had to have been about to bust for years.

"You should have said something," he said quietly, his chest heavy, guilt flaying his conscience.

"It didn't matter, Zack," Slade assured him. "You're our brother first, your bloodline doesn't matter. And now, I'm going to assume what's going on with Grace is somehow tied to the reason her father and your parents were killed? Whatever they were doing has finally come back to haunt the Maddox family?"

After pulling out the file he'd folded and stuck in his back pocket, Zack opened it and laid it on the table between Jazz and Slade. "This is everything I have concerning Grace," he said on a sigh. "The information Toby got together for me as well as what I've managed to get from Alexander Brigham over the years is on this flash drive." He pulled the small drive from the pocket of his shirt and placed it on the table with the hard copy files. "My parents weren't killed because of any rumored information that Benjamin Maddox knew where the Brigham daughter and her son were hiding. They were killed for the investigation they were involved in to uncover a possible traitor in the Maddox family. And that's information even Vinny Maddox doesn't have. As far as he knows, the traitor was high-level Kin. The information Alexander had from Benjamin at the time pointed to possible Maddox family involvement. Close relatives, possibly one of the cousins who oversees top-level security."

Brooding, dangerous. The expressions on the faces of his brothers changed with that information.

"No names were mentioned?" Jazz asked, fingering the flash drive.

Zack shook his head. "Benjamin was keeping the information to himself. He told Alexander he wanted to confirm it. Supposedly that was what he was doing the night he and my parents were murdered." Zack sat back in his chair, one finger tapping at the wooden arm of the seat as he narrowed his eyes on the files for a moment. "Vinny has known my identity for years. Vinny knew, and he trusted Cord with the information. The twins and Grace are aware of it now as well. We'll see if it goes any further—though, honestly, I can't see Deacon, Sawyer, or Grace being in league with a traitor. It just doesn't fit. We know Luce was involved in the murders, but according to her interrogation, she didn't give the orders. Though she also swore she didn't know who gave them and that one I just don't believe."

He couldn't make Luce's accusations that Grace was involved fit, and he'd tried. Grace had barely been five when her father died, but she'd idolized him; she would never have betrayed his memory in such a way. Deacon and Sawyer could be wild cards, but like Cord, they'd had many chances to betray the family and hadn't done so.

"If Grace were a traitor, she would have given Kenni up as soon as she realized who she was, two years ago," Jazz murmured. "Killing Kenni before the family realized who she was would have been imperative. Besides, Grace sees Vinny and those boys as her only family. You're right, she wouldn't turn on them."

"So how do you intend to draw a traitor out, Zack?" Slade asked somberly.

Zack nodded to the files. "During her interrogation, Luce swore Grace had the files her father hid and she was just waiting for the right time to sell the sensitive Kin information that was hidden on it, as well as the identity of the traitor. I can keep the Brighams from coming after her by claiming her as my lover—the traitor and missing information, we'll have to figure out for ourselves."

And that was going to be the hard part. Hell, "hard" part? It could become impossible if he didn't play his cards right. Somehow he was going to convince an unknown traitor that Grace was giving him the information. That she was becoming so enamored of him that she was willing to believe in his claims of hating the Kin and the agency enough to betray them.

"You're going to need help," Jazz pointed out. "It won't work if you try to gung-ho this and go it alone. You're gonna need your back covered."

"Hell, he's gonna need all four sides covered," Slade snorted. "Very covertly while still giving the appearance that he and Grace are working alone. Then we sit back and listen to the rumors that start making their way to us."

Zack nodded, then rubbed at the back of his neck. "They still haven't found Grace's assailant. The team sent out after him reported in last night, and there's no sign of him. No way he managed to get out of the county without being seen."

There wasn't so much as a deer path that wasn't being watched by Kin after the attack. The search for Richard James was one of the most intense manhunts Alex had seen in the area.

"I have a feeling, once I have Grace in my house and our traitor is convinced she's mine, he'll make a move. Everyone believes I have no love for Kin and pure hatred for the Brigham family. They'll believe I can be had and so can any information Grace has. I just have to play the game right and make sure Grace plays her part."

"Without breaking her heart," Jazz ordered, his voice stern. "That girl's been half in love with you for years, Zack. Remember that. I don't think you want to hurt her any more than she's already been hurt."

chapter six

She wasn't a child anymore, Grace told herself the next morning as she watched one of her uncle's men carry her luggage from her bedroom to the front door. She didn't get to scream, to cry that it wasn't fair. She didn't get to pout anymore, and she hadn't thrown things since before her father died.

Instead, she stood in the foyer, glaring at her uncle and her cousin Cord along with the object of her anger, Zack, as they stood whispering at the far end of the long entryway. As though she had no business hearing what was being said. It was her life, after all, so she should be privy to whatever the hell their secrets were at the moment.

Her eyes kept straying to Zack more than to her family, though.

As much as she hated what he was doing to her life at the moment, she couldn't ignore the fact that he still drew her. He made her want when she knew she shouldn't want him. He made her want the warmth, the pleasure he'd already given her, a pleasure unlike anything else she'd ever known. Not that she hadn't dated, and often, but those kisses in the past didn't even compare to Zack's kisses, to his touch, to what he made her feel even when she didn't want to feel it.

How she'd ever been fooled into believing he was no more than a quiet accountant, she didn't understand. Had she been blind, or had she just not wanted to see that the man who so fascinated her was even more arrogant than the cousins who drove her crazy? That determined dominance and pure self-assurance never failed to make her want to knock their heads together. Especially when they gave her that you're-just-a-girl look. As though being female were somehow inferior to all their male testosterone.

People saw what they wanted to see, her uncle had always told her. If they want to see weakness, then it would take little to convince them they saw weakness. She hadn't wanted to acknowledge the fact that Zack was just as strong, arrogant, and forceful as her cousins, and he'd never displayed those traits overtly. So she hadn't let herself recognize what she didn't want to see.

He was quiet yet always watchful, always on guard. That fact was in the set of his shoulders, the way he seemed focused on what Cord and Vinny were saying right now though she knew he was aware of every move she was making. How had she managed to miss that steely core of authority she could so clearly see now? Her instincts were better than that; she should have known who and what he was years ago.

How many other mistakes had she made over the years?

She could forgive herself for underestimating Rich—she rarely saw him and had interacted with him even less, so she couldn't have been expected to see the dangerous part of him. He hadn't been part of her life on a regular basis since they were teens.

She normally had an excellent instinct for people; it was how she'd identified Kenni so quickly when the other woman returned to Loudon under an assumed identity. She had known Kenni like a sister when they were younger, recalling mannerisms like a certain tilt of the head, a certain look when irritated. And Kenni had always done "irritated" very well.

Yet she'd missed so many facets of Zack that it was unbelievable.

How many others had she let slip by her?

Had she missed it because of emotion? Because she hadn't wanted to see it? Seeing it would have meant choosing to turn away from the fascination she felt for him whenever he was around.

And admittedly, it was more than obvious he'd intended to hide that part of himself. Especially from her.

Too bad Zack didn't consider it a good idea to *continue* hiding that part; he would have been far easier to get along with if he had.

She crossed her arms beneath her breasts and considered him with narrow eyes.

He'd never spent a lot of time around her. As a matter of fact, whenever she showed up and he was present, he rarely stayed long. A hello, a few quiet smiles, and he was gone.

He hadn't let her see him, hadn't allowed her to know him. No wonder Kenni gave her such odd looks whenever she stated how Zack was so unlike her family. Because Kenni knew better. Because Zack showed her cousin all the things he'd hidden from her.

From the corner of her eye, she caught the wary look Cord gave her. He'd been doing that a lot since the day before. Watching her with that faint expression he used whenever they were arguing. She was completely infatuated with a man who thought that because she was smaller and weaker physically, she was somehow weak-minded as well.

Her lips tightened at the thought.

She was not weak-minded, though it appeared where Zack was concerned, she'd definitely been using blinders.

And she was tired of being ignored.

"Did the three of you forget I'm standing here?" she asked in what she considered a perfectly reasonable tone. "If we're not leaving the foyer, then I'm going back to my room to rest my leg for a while because I'm tired of watching you whisper around like three gossiping little girls."

It wasn't really hurting, just aching a little, and her leg wasn't the reason she was feeling put out by the three of them.

Zack turned to her slowly, his expression borderline incredulous. "Like what?"

Vinny was a little smarter where she was concerned, though. "Sorry, Gracie," her uncle called over to her, an apologetic smile on his face as Cord moved toward her. "We're finished."

"Were we?" Zack murmured, eyeing the stubborn stance Grace had taken by the front door. "I'm still considering the 'gossiping girls' comment."

She didn't look particularly uncomfortable—more defensive, perhaps—but that was Grace whenever he was around. Yet she had Vinny and Cord ready to jump through hoops.

Those green eyes of hers gleamed between heavy lashes a few shades darker than the multihued blond hair she'd pulled back from her face while the sides and back tumbled in rich waves to just past her shoulders. Loose beige pants and a soft white shirt completed her outfit, and once again she was wearing flat sandals rather than heels. A reminder of the attack that had that responding surge of fury threatening to break free.

"Shut the hell up, Zack," Cord muttered. "Let's not piss her off any more than she already is."

Ire flashed in her gaze and tightened her lips, almost causing him to smile. She hadn't liked being pushed out of the conversation he, Vinny, and Cord were having. She'd waited longer than he expected her to before protesting, though.

"Go easy on her, Zack," Vinny ordered. "Give her a chance to acclimate."

Rather than commenting, Zack joined Cord in lifting her suitcases and carrying them out into the late-summer sunlight to the back of his pickup.

There was no way in hell she'd make it if he went easy on her. Vinny and Cord seemed hesitant to allow her any part in her own protection or to make her an integral part of the investigation. Hell, they'd argued to keep as much information from her as possible.

She was stronger than they seemed to be giving her credit for. He'd always known that. Perhaps not strong enough for his way of life, but stronger than she appeared.

That Maddox strength was more than apparent despite the impression she gave of always bowing to Vinny's temper.

She wasn't bowing today; she was glaring at all of them as she made her way from the house to the truck, surrounded by several of the Kin, who shadowed her the second she left the house.

And she knew why they were there. To protect her with their own lives if necessary. And she hated it. Zack could see the fear and anger when her gaze met his, that knowledge that the four men walking beside her would lay down their lives for her. Just as her pet had nearly done.

She slid into the front seat of the truck without argument, her body stiff, filled with angry tension as Zack moved behind the wheel.

"Keep her safe, Zack," Cord demanded, his voice low before Zack could close the door. "You let her get hurt, and you'll answer to all of us."

Zack slammed the door closed, ignoring the other man's warning.

If Grace ended up hurt, then Cord wouldn't have to retaliate—Zack wouldn't be able to live with the thought that he'd failed to that extent. For years, he'd cooperated with Vinny and Cord to place an invisible web of protection around Grace, and still, she'd ended up in danger.

As she'd grown older, he hadn't agreed with the ways in which they'd protected her, but he'd lost the right to object. He'd stayed out of her life, ignored the fact that she was just as fascinated by him as he was hungry for her. A man didn't have a right to intervene when he had no intention of keeping the prize being protected. His

life was far too dangerous for a princess to exist within
it for long.

"Do you intend on telling me what the hell is going
on now?" It was more a demand than a question. There
was nothing pouty or spoiled in her determination for
explanations; the tone of voice was more that of a woman
used to knowing the facts and learning she'd been lied to.

"Yes, I do, Grace," he answered, wondering how she
would handle that truth. "I want to get you to the house,
get you settled in, and get a few things taken care of
first, then we'll talk."

He was surprised she wasn't terrified. He'd glimpsed
some fear, but it wasn't ever-present. She was too quiet,
too thoughtful to suit him. The expressions he glimpsed
on her face at rare times, as though she were figuring
out a puzzle of some sort, sent a tingle of warning flaring in his gut.

Zack kept having to remind himself that she was a
Maddox. She'd been raised by Vinny and Cord for the
most part, and they were as calculating as any man Zack
had ever known. Until now, he hadn't considered the fact
that Grace could have learned some of that careful cun-
ning and the ability to see multiple layers of individuals and events and tie them together. It may be time to
revise what he knew of her, to figure out what lurked
behind the quiet warmth she'd always displayed.

"And I'm just supposed to wait," she sighed after a
moment, frustration edging her voice. "Why doesn't that
surprise me?"

Yeah, sweet Grace was used to being in the know, a
part of that inner circle Vinny shared the secrets of his
world with. Was she so close to the Brighams? he won-

dered. She was friends with Victoria, the reigning princess of the family, so anything was possible. She hadn't been close enough to the family to learn his secrets, though.

"Because you know our world doesn't deal well with suppositions and guesses," he reminded her. "I'm still waiting on a few contacts and some of the answers you're going to need. Give me time to get that information together, then I'll tell you everything I know."

"Everything?" Suspicion lay heavy in her voice.

"Everything, Grace." And God help both of them if she wasn't strong enough to handle it.

Glancing at her again, he clenched his teeth rather than say anything more. She was used to getting even the guesses and suppositions as they came in. Hell, she probably gathered those together for Vince herself.

It was definitely time to unravel the puzzle that Grace evidently was, and quickly.

If Grace had ever had occasion to visit Zack's home, then she would have known the second she stepped inside that he wasn't the man he showed to the world.

It was impossible to see the house from the main road, hidden as it was behind Leyland cypress and other heavily branched pines. Summer or winter, the house was completely hidden until the driver passed the natural boundary and entered the large clearing. On the outside, the multilevel brick home looked unassuming enough at the far end of the wide grassy clearing. The two levels were built against the natural incline of the hill rising behind it, but other than that, it had appeared very traditional.

Bland, a bit plain with no landscaping or areas of color, but still, it had the appearance of solidity and seemed sturdy enough to withstand generations of use.

The inside of his home gave away his secrets, though. The outside might have been traditional and bland, but the inside was another story. Rather than encountering hardwood floors and complementing wood-paneled walls along with bulky masculine furniture, as she was used to, Grace entered a foyer with warmed stone floors brightly lit by strategically placed skylights above. The foyer led into an open-plan lower floor. The large, carpeted living area flowed into more stone floors for the dining room and kitchen.

From the outside, the house seemed to be built right into the hill behind it, when actually there was a large horseshoe-shaped yard with the two sides abutting the house itself.

The furniture, though made for the comfort of a man of Zack's build, still gave the rooms a light, airy feel. A lack of true boundaries lent the room a sense of freedom and of deceptive softness. There was actually nothing soft about any of it.

Stone floors, marble counters, stainless steel appliances in the kitchen, and a marble-topped dining table supported by what appeared to be stone columns.

The total absence of wood was a design choice she was going to have to ask him about soon. It was more than obvious he'd deliberately avoided any heavy wooden furniture.

The large sectional couch and recliner faced a big-screen television enclosed in a glass entertainment center. The sectional was a creamy beige material, the matching recliners in darker hues.

The stairs leading to the second level built above the garage were covered in the same light carpeting as the living room. The bedroom Zack deposited her luggage into was spacious, with glass night stands placed next to a king platform bed. Here was the only allowance for wood, in the dresser and chest of drawers positioned on the wall leading into a bathroom.

Windows looked out over the far side of the property, over the treeline and onto the river that drifted lazily past. She would never have expected such a view, just as she hadn't expected him to have the nerve to take her directly to the master bedroom.

"You think I'm going to just hop right into bed with you?" Turning on him as he placed the last of her luggage in the room, Grace frowned in irritation. "And this is your bedroom." She waved her hand to encompass the room. "Giving your bed up for me? No other guest rooms in the house?" She knew better. There was another bedroom. She'd seen the open door as they moved upstairs.

"You're looking for a fight," he stated, the lack of confrontation or even defensiveness in his voice angering her.

"I'm looking for the man I thought you were," she threw back at him. "The Zack I knew wouldn't take such a thing for granted."

"We're both aware you never knew me, Grace," he pointed out as he walked to a set of wide double doors.

"Here's the closet—one side is empty, make use of it. You also have the right side of both the dresser and chest." He nodded to the two pieces of furniture.

The inside of the closet was huge. She doubted she'd use a quarter of the space he'd allotted her, but that wasn't the point.

"Take me to the guest room, Zack," she demanded. "I'm not sleeping with you. As you've just acknowledged, I don't know you. I don't sleep with men I don't know."

"You do when your very survival requires the impression that we're lovers." The dark, brooding tone that entered his voice sent a chill racing up her spine. And it wasn't one of fear. "Whether or not we have sex is your call. Sleeping together is mine."

That was his call?

"I can pretend to be your lover without sleeping with you," she assured him, fighting to keep her teeth from clenching in frustration.

There wasn't a chance in hell she could sleep with him and not beg him to touch her. It wasn't possible. She didn't have kind of willpower. No woman had that kind of willpower.

"Argue over a decision that's changeable, sweetheart," he warned her. "Now, unpack—I have some calls to make. My office is next to the guest bedroom, by the way, so don't even attempt to move in there. You won't like the consequences." With that, he turned and walked out the door without giving her a chance to argue.

Arrogant ass. He did not have the right to make that call, and he damned sure didn't have the right to be so autocratic about it.

Sleeping with him could not be an option.

"I won't like the consequences? Like hell—" She rushed to follow him, and Zack caught her just outside the door, and before Grace knew it, he had her back against the wall, her breasts against his chest, all without putting the slightest pressure on her leg.

Suddenly, the memory of him in her bedroom, his lips on hers, his fingers between her thighs, bringing a rush of pure pleasure, overwhelmed her. Her breath caught, lips parting, her anger suddenly overcome by so much need that she couldn't make sense of it as his lips lowered to her ear.

She felt surrounded by him. The warmth of his body, harder, stronger, dominant, rushed through her, sapping her determination to remain aloof, to keep her heart protected.

"This is how it is," he whispered against her ear, one hand gripping her hip, the other cupping the opposite side of her neck. "I didn't make that decision lightly. A cleaning lady comes in here daily, and no doubt, she's bribable if anyone wants to find out if we're sleeping together. Now, feel what you do to me?"

The hard length of his erection pressed into her lower stomach, stealing her breath as heat raced through her.

"I remember the other night real clear, sweetheart. Clear enough that I want nothing more than to sink inside that slick, wet heat I found between your thighs. And that's something you don't want right now, not before you know exactly how your life's getting ready to be played with." He nipped her ear, a sensual little bite that had her gasping. "But I can accommodate you if you don't want to wait. I'd happily do so—and if you keep pushing me, I damned sure will. But when the truth hits you, you can't say you weren't warned."

Graced stared over his shoulder, blinking at the wall on the other side of the hall, and tried to tell herself it didn't hurt. "Let me go." The strangled words were torn from her, the demand far weaker than she liked. "Get away from me."

Pushing against his shoulders, she was surprised at how quickly he moved back. Not bothering to so much as glance at him, she turned and hurried back to the bedroom, slamming the door behind her. She leaned her back against it, stared at the bed, at the wide windows that looked out on the river, then at those that looked out on the front of the house.

She couldn't do this.

Oh God, she couldn't do this.

Pressing her hands to her stomach to breathe through the pain burrowing through her, she tried to tell herself she was strong enough, determined enough to make it work. After all, this wasn't about her or Zack; it was about finding a killer, a traitor who would destroy all their lives if possible.

But her pep talk didn't help. It may be about finding a traitor, but it was her life being torn apart, her heart that was going to be ripped from her chest, and she knew it.

She could feel it coming.

Her uncle and her cousins had taught her how to be strong, how to stare down even them and how to hold her own against determined, forceful men. But those men weren't Zack. She didn't get weak for them, she didn't lose her breath at their touch, and she didn't lie awake at night wondering what it would be like to touch them, to have them touch her.

It wasn't her uncle, her cousins, or her half brothers who were going to walk away from this with a shattered heart and broken dreams.

Dreams she should never have allowed herself to begin with.

Shaking her head, she stared at her luggage mutinously. She might have to sleep in that damned bed with him, but that didn't mean she would do it without a fight. And it sure as hell didn't mean she had to unpack the first bag or make it easy for Zack. She didn't have to make any of this easy for him, and it was more than clear he had no intentions of making it easy for her.

Damn, his self-control was supposed to be stronger than this.

And what the hell was he doing, waiting on her outside that bedroom, setting her up to follow him, to give him a chance to touch her again? That was a teenager's trick, not a grown man's.

The reason he'd given her for sleeping in the same bed was the truth. His maid was friendly and far too nosy. She'd be easy to question if anyone asked her whether they were sleeping together or if they slept in separate rooms. And Alexander Brigham would find a way to question the woman. Learning Zack hadn't taken her as his lover would once again make Grace fair game as far as the interrogation Alexander had in mind.

The problem was, he doubted Grace would survive the interrogation. He'd seen too many suspected traitors go through the intense questioning combined with hallucinogenic truth-inducing drugs. It was during one of those sessions that Luce had given Grace's name and swore her daughter had the digital files Benjamin had hidden and that Grace had revealed her cousin Kenni's identity.

Grace had known Kenni was hiding under the Annie Mayes identity for two years. She could have somehow given Luce reason to suspect, but no way in hell did Grace give her cousin up.

The drugs used didn't guarantee the truth. They uncovered whatever the one being questioned believed. Luce could easily have sworn Grace had "revealed" Kenni's identity when the truth was, Luce had made a hell of a guess based on something she'd learned from Grace. How she'd lied about the digital files was what Zack had to find out. That one, he couldn't explain away. And with Luce's death, there was no way to re-question her.

And he'd be damned if he allowed Grace to be subjected to the pain-filled, horrifying episodes she'd suffer with the drugged interrogations. The thought of it turned his guts to ice. She would survive it, she'd probably vindicate herself during one of them, but she wouldn't come out of it without being changed. Whatever trust, whatever faith she had in her world would be shattered forever.

Stalking into the office, Zack stepped around the large glass-and-metal desk before dropping into the heavy ergonomic chair behind it and glaring at the door.

He hadn't expected this. He hadn't expected her to fight him at all. After the attack and the news that the agency was beginning the process to pull her in for interrogation as a suspected traitor, he'd been certain she'd cooperate with whatever measures were needed to ensure her safety.

The fact that she was fighting him this early in the game left him a little off balance. That wasn't the Grace he knew. Or had he ever really known her?

The vibration of his cell phone drew his attention. Grimacing, he answered just before voice mail would have picked it up.

"What do you want?" he answered curtly.

"Now, that's a fine way to greet a cousin," Madden Brigham drawled with a hint of dark amusement. "I thought I'd call and see how you were doing, considering you have the old man frothing at the mouth and the two men he sent after the delectable little Grace cooling their heels in Memphis, awaiting his go-ahead to bring her in. I thought I should check and make certain you hadn't really lost your senses. What kind of game are you playing, cousin?"

"One that will get you killed if you don't keep your damned nose out of it." Not that Madden would follow the advice. He was too damned stubborn to do anything so sensible.

Madden chuckled at the suggestion. "You know me better than that, Zack. Besides I'm probably the only one with enough common sense to realize you're not using your head where this girl is considered. Your dick is a piss-poor guide, take my advice on that one."

"*Your* dick is a piss-poor guide," Zack reminded him ruthlessly. "Mine doesn't have near the poor judgment yours does, so keep your advice to yourself."

A slight, mocking grunt could be heard over the line. "Well, I should warn you, the old man is heading to the airport and flying into Memphis to meet with the team he has there. He's coming for her. And he's convinced that the two of you aren't lovers, that you're just doing this to piss him the hell off because you're so pissed that Luce managed to get a weapon and off herself while she was here."

Alexander was never going to stop, Zack thought, and so he was going to have to shoot his uncle.

"And don't make plans to kill my father, cousin," Madden warned him. "We'd become enemies, and that would be a shame."

"And we're what now?" Zack growled. "I was unaware we were anything less."

Madden laughed at that. "We're cousins," he drawled. "We'll fight and hate and do our best to poke at each other whenever we want. Unless someone else decides they can do the same." His voice hardened. "Then we cover each other's back."

"And you're covering my back how?" Zack sneered.

"I'm letting you know the old man will be there by morning with every intention to take that woman from you," Madden revealed. "I know she's meant something to you for a long time, so I'm covering your back by telling you it's all a game. You stand in his face, and he won't take her—but that won't keep her safe. Find the information she's supposed to have, or run with her. And when you do, find a hole and bury yourselves deep because he won't rest until he has her."

"Then he'll die, Madden," Zack warned him quietly.

"I guess it's time you and Tory choose sides: his insanity, or what's right. Because any attempt to take Grace will ensure the pact between Maddox and Brigham is irreparably broken. They'll turn against you, and so will I, and you don't want that."

"You'd go that far?" Madden asked, his tone mildly curious.

"What do you think, *cousin*?" he questioned the other man, wondering if Madden had ever gotten a clue that he wasn't the only Brigham willing to sacrifice his link to the family for his ideas of right versus wrong.

A heavy sigh came over the connection. "I think I can't complain of being bored at the moment. Take care, Zack. Call me if you need me," Madden suggested before he disconnected the call.

No, Zack agreed, there was definitely no room for boredom.

"Well?" Alexander asked impatiently when his son stepped back into the library, his brows drawn into a frown.

Madden was a good-looking boy, though disillusion had taken the joy from his dark brown eyes years before. The cobalt black of his hair grew a bit longer than Alexander liked, but Madden had been ignoring him where his hair was concerned since his late teens.

At least he gave some consideration to his clothing this time. He actually looked rather nice today. The white dress shirt, even with the sleeves rolled back to his elbows, was pressed and fit his tall, leanly muscled frame excellently. The tail was tucked neatly into dark slacks, his feet shod in expensive black leather shoes while an understated black belt cinched his pants.

"Well." A sardonic smile tugged at Madden's lips. "I wouldn't advise sending in that team—he'll decimate them." He sat down in the heavy leather chair across from the desk. "Then he'll probably come after you. And the Kin will follow him, Father, trust me on that." Ice filled his voice and his dark eyes.

No, this wasn't the same son he remembered from before Madden had joined the military. He was still strong, though, still loyal—of that, Alexander had no doubt.

At least, to a point. That loyalty was growing thinner by the day, especially now in the face of Grace Maddox's suspected treachery.

"You believe her innocent?" Alexander questioned him mildly.

Madden's brow arched with mocking surprise. "I don't think it matters what I believe, Father," he stated, his tone icily polite as he rose from his chair. "You'll do what you do, regardless. You've already proved that one time too many. I made the call for you, though. I assessed his tone and determination based on what I know of him." He paused, his gaze darkening. "Taking her will destroy the Brigham–Maddox loyalties. I'd think about that long and hard before I attempted it."

chapter seven

Maybe it was all a nightmare.

What had she eaten for dinner? No doubt something known to cause strange and frightening dreams, Grace thought the next morning as a feeling of warmth enveloped her. She'd learned a long time ago not to eat mustard on her favorite midnight snack of hot pretzels because of just that reason.

In this dream, Zack had slipped into her room and plastered his naked body against her back. And he was definitely naked. She could feel every bare inch through the black chiffon gown she wore.

Nope, the past few days hadn't been a dream.

"Good mornin', darlin'," Zack rumbled behind her, causing her heart to race as he flattened his hand against her stomach, holding her to him. "You feel good first thing in the morning."

"Is that what you tell all your women?" she asked

suspiciously. The thought of those women had always infuriated Grace. Not that any of them had lasted long, but the fact was, they had had him, while she hadn't had a chance.

"I can't remember a single time I told another woman that." He moved behind her, his head brushing against the top of hers. "And no other woman's ever slept in this bed with me either. They'll be terribly jealous of you."

She snorted at the mocking comment. "It doesn't even matter," she sighed, tamping back her anger. "The only reason I'm here is to prove to the world you're sleeping with me. Otherwise, you'd have slapped me in the guest room so fast, both our heads would be spinning."

Zack cleared his throat, but it sounded more like he was smothering a chuckle. "Your opinion of my self-control is far higher than the truth actually is," he stated with no small amount of amusement. "Wouldn't matter the circumstances, you'd still be in my bed, and that's a fact."

Yeah, that was why he'd ignored her since she was eighteen.

"That's what you say now." She swallowed tight—the feel of his erection against the crease of her buttocks was making her hunger for him.

Heat flamed through her, melting any resistance she might have been able to dredge up had they both been dressed. Damn him, he made her want, made her ache, and she couldn't make it stop, no matter how hard she tried. Zack was a weakness she'd never been able to excuse or rationalize. As far as she was concerned, no other man compared to him, no other had the ability to make her burn like Zack did.

"I need to get up," she squeaked.

Hell, she *squeaked*. That had sounded bad, like a teenage boy whose voice was changing or something.

The low murmur of a chuckle at her ear as his lips brushed against it had her fighting to breathe. The effect he had on her was disconcerting and always made her feel as though the air around her were simply too thin.

"Are you sure about that, baby?" His hand smoothed down her arm, the feel of his rough flesh against her softer skin sending a rush of sensation up her spine. "Are you absolutely certain you want to leave this bed?" He nudged her hair aside with his chin, and the rasp of his overnight beard against her earlobe felt far too good. "Because I'd love for you to stay a minute," he whispered wickedly before catching her lobe between his teeth in a gentle nip.

His leg slid between hers.

She was in so much trouble.

Grace could feel the wild intensity building between them like a thunderhead. She'd spent so many years holding so much back that she had no idea how to let the wildness within her free.

The very thought of doing so was terrifying.

"Made up your mind yet, Grace?" he asked softly, an obvious dare in his tone.

Questions, questions.

Unfortunately, she knew the answer to this one.

She was about to step willingly into a heartache that

there would be no turning back from—she could feel it all the way to her bones.

And there was always the chance Zack was just teasing her, tormenting her. After all, he'd done no more than flirt for years, keeping her hanging, keeping her hoping. He had never called her himself, never invited her out, never seemed interested in more than the friendly flirting they engaged in.

"Do you remember the first time you called me?" Zack asked curiously, a hint of a smile in his voice as he pulled the strap of her gown down the curve of her shoulder. "You were, what? Seventeen?"

She did remember the first time; it was burned into her mind. She'd attended a concert at the park with friends that night, and while walking to her car, she collapsed from a ruptured appendix. Zack had been there. He, Slade, and Jazz rushed her to the hospital, called her family, and Zack had stayed until she was out of surgery and in recovery.

"You gave me your number while I was in the hospital," she reminded him nervously. "You told me to call anytime."

She was sure he hadn't thought she'd take his words as literally as she did.

"You called me at three in the morning," he remembered, his lips lowering to her shoulder. "You instantly informed me that I should be there with you, because whatever drugs they'd given you were keeping you awake and you were bored."

She'd done just that. "And you came to the hospital and talked to me until I went to sleep." And she never had the nerve to ask him why he'd done it.

"I thought for sure the staff would tell Cord, and he'd rip my head off." He brushed a kiss against her bare shoulder. "I knew then you were trouble when I walked in and that little smile curled your lips and you told me you were certain it was going to be nice knowing I'd come when you called."

"You said you'd always come when I called," she remembered, her breath catching as he nipped at her shoulder. The feel of his teeth against her flesh was a shock and a pleasure she wouldn't have expected.

"You should have called the minute Vince learned you could be in danger, brat," his voice rumbled with displeasure just before he licked over the spot where he'd nipped her. "I'll spank you for that at some point."

The muscles of her rear tightened at the threat, at the involuntary curiosity that surged inside her. "Zack . . ." she breathed in roughly. "It's not like that. I didn't have a chance to call. We'd just learned the night before—"

"Grace, you really shouldn't lie to me, baby. It just makes me want to smack that pretty ass of yours that much more."

Oh, wow. What was she supposed to say to that?

Yes, please?

She had a feeling this was a bit more than she was ready for right now. No, asking for the punishment wasn't a good idea, no matter how interesting it might sound. And it sounded very interesting. Zack could make the experience a life changer for her. She was having enough life-changing moments right now—she didn't know if she could handle more. Especially such a sensual one.

"You're awful shy, now that you're in my bed, Grace,"

he growled, a warning in his voice. "Tell me, which one is you? The tactful, graceful little paragon of Maddox virtue, or the wicked little temptress who's teased the hell out of me for years?"

She couldn't breathe. Lips parted, Grace struggled to remember how to draw air into her lungs. "Zack . . ." she tried to protest, though what she was protesting she wasn't certain.

"So demure now," he crooned, his lips moving to her neck. "Let me see the woman who came in my arms the other night. The one who ached for me as much as I ached for her."

She frowned at the rumble of demand in his tone as well as the subtle implication.

"There's a difference between tact and demureness, or weakness, Zack," she assured him, certain he was seeing that weakness he felt she possessed and she was a bit offended that he'd never recognized that she wasn't weak—or else she would never have survived working for Vinny.

"In your case, it's hard to tell, baby. Tact would be using a polite tone when you were telling me you weren't ready to be touched. Weakness is just plain lying about it like you are now."

"It isn't weakness, Zack," she assured him, knowing she'd pay for stepping out of the shadow of patience and tact and freeing the woman she'd always kept restrained inside her. "It was the knowledge that not my uncle, my cousins, or the man who refused to get a clue would know what the hell to do with me if I gave myself to them exactly as I am." She jerked the blankets from her, turned, and stared up at the faint mockery in his expression. "And you knew you couldn't handle me," she informed him disdainfully. "Or you would have done more than shoot me a few hot looks and give a suggestive compliment here and there over the past few years. I might have been hiding, but at least I wasn't a coward. I was simply all too aware that you were having too much fun running—"

Oh. My. God.

The thought was like a clash of cymbals in her head as she finally took in the fact that he was stark naked and heavily aroused. Very heavily, very largely aroused.

The stiff, dark flesh rose from between his thighs, much bigger and thicker than she'd imagined. Much more than she'd imagined. The toys she'd used to practice certain acts hadn't been nearly that size.

As she watched, Zack lowered his hand, his fingers gripping the tight flesh just below the head as a bead of clear fluid seeped from the tip.

There went the air from her lungs again. Her heart was suddenly beating in her throat as it tightened, and she really needed to swallow. Her mouth was dry, then watering for a taste of him as she unconsciously licked her tongue over her lips.

"I'm not running, sugar," he assured her, lust throbbing in his voice. "I never was. I was just waiting on you to find your courage and come looking for me."

Find her courage? She should be jumping from his bed and running for her life. There wasn't a chance in hell she'd ever take all of him.

"Yeah, that courage thing," she muttered, breathless.

"Teasing time is over, Grace." His voice was a demand now rather than a sexual croon. "Are you going to run and hide or take what you want?"

Take what she wanted?

Her panties were wet at the thought of taking him—meanwhile, her head was screaming at her to run, to put as much distance between herself and the intimidating flesh she couldn't take her eyes from.

"Need some help making up your mind?" A growling demand should never accompany a question, she thought, disconcerted as she felt his fingers curve around the back of her neck, pushing her head down slowly.

She licked her lips again.

"Do that to my cock, baby," he groaned. "Lick that pretty little tongue over the head and show me how hungry you are. Then I'll show you how hungry I am."

She'd bought a vibrator and imagined she was pleasuring. But she was so out of her league here.

His fingers slid down the shaft, gripped the base of the heavy flesh, and angled it to her lips. "Show me how good you are, Grace, then I'll show you how good I am," he promised.

Grace whimpered, but still, her lips parted, her tongue swiping over the bulging crown as she collected the little bead of moisture awaiting her. The flavor of it sank into her taste buds and made her instantly hungry for more.

No, she wasn't hungry; she was ravenous.

She wanted more—now.

And she really wanted him to show her how good he was. . . .

* * *

Ah, fuck!

Zack's head slammed back into the pillow, one hand fisted in the blankets next to her, the other tensed, the effort it took not to tighten on her fragile neck straining his control. She didn't just lick over the sensitive, engorged head of his cock; she sucked it inside her mouth, and devastated his senses.

Her tongue swirled, it investigated the flared curve, tucked itself beneath the ridge, then found the hypersensitive spot of flesh below it. She sucked at it, drew her lips over it, and when he stared down at her, the combination of shy curiosity and sensual wantonness had him gritting his teeth to hold back his release.

"Son of a bitch," he cursed, jerking his hand back from her neck to clench the fingers of both hands in the sheets beneath him.

It wasn't that she was doing something no other woman had ever done to him. She wasn't. Why the pleasure was this extreme, didn't make sense. He didn't want it to make sense. He wanted to luxuriate in it.

In the feel of her sucking at the wide, painfully hard crest, the way her fingers stroked the throbbing shaft, the flush of arousal in her face, and the green of her eyes—so dark, they looked like summer moss.

And she was his. He'd always known she was his. Some primal sense had locked on her the moment he saw those pretty eyes, and whether he was meant simply to protect her as he had tried to do when she was younger, or hunger for her as he'd done the past few years, a part of him had always known she belonged to him. Even when he hadn't wanted to admit it.

"Damn, Grace." The words tore from him, strangled

and hoarse from the effort it took to hold back his orgasm.

She stroked along the shaft to the tight sac of his balls, caressing and stroking, the pads of her silken fingers rubbing against the sensitive spheres as her mouth tightened on the throbbing head, taking more of him.

His thighs tightened violently, his jaw clenching until he could feel his molars threatening to crack as he watched her take him. She didn't hurry. Oh, hell no, not Grace. Each sensual draw of her mouth on the head of his cock, each stroke of delicate fingers along the wide shaft, each caress to his balls was done with exploratory relish. With devastating curiosity.

There wasn't a chance in hell he could hold on to his control much longer. He hadn't anticipated her taking him up on his dare. He never imagined she'd do more than run for her virtue once he challenged her.

Sweet, shy little Grace? Tactful, polite, she was the epitome of genteel southern femininity. That gentility was currently sucking his dick like a favorite treat and enjoying every second of it.

And he was loving it, too. Loving it so much that he didn't hear missed the ping on his phone next to the bed. He didn't know anything past her mouth on his cock until the sound of Jazz's voice on the stairwell interrupted the incredible pleasure she was giving him.

"Zack, get the hell down here before I come looking for you!" Jazz called out again. "Now! I just got a report trouble's headin' this way, and we have some plannin' to do."

Grace jerked her head up, shocked at the sound of

Jazz just outside the bedroom door. A gasp left her lips before she jumped from the bed and raced for the bathroom, ignoring Zack's curse.

Oh God, what was she doing?

How would she survive what he would do to her when it was over, the danger gone and the traitor apprehended? She'd be broken inside, because losing Zack after giving herself to him would destroy her.

And it would be all her fault.

chapter eight

Grace sat at the marble-topped dining room table, her hair still a little damp, a cup of half-drunk coffee at her elbow. Dressed in jeans and a tank, her feet in white sneakers, she carefully went through the hard copy files Zack had put together, which she'd spread out before her.

The amount of information Zack had gathered regarding his parents' and her father's activities before their deaths was impressive. According to several sources within the Kin as well as at the Brigham Agency, her father, Benjamin Maddox, and his lieutenant, John Richards—along with John's wife, Andrea Nicole Brigham Richards—were investigating the possibility of a traitor within the Maddox family.

An inventory of Maddox–Kin mountain strongholds showed missing supplies—weapons, ammo, several maps of the most heavily guarded footpaths across the mountains. More worrisome, though, had been the evidence of tampering done to steel chambers that had been thought tamperproof and held not only gold but also geographic coordinates for Kin escape routes in the event of foreign occupation and less traveled paths through the mountains, as well as Kin patrol rotations across those routes.

One less critical chamber had also been breached, with a large amount of the cash hidden there taken, along with maps of a particular sector of the mountains that was considered one of the hardest for the Kin to patrol.

That sector had shown evidence of trespassing on many occasions over the past two decades by small groups attempting to hide their presence. In one case, several years before, individuals dressed in Middle Eastern clothing had been glimpsed by a mountain hunter. By the time the hunter had made a cell phone call to Cord and a team was deployed to the area, the trespassers had disappeared.

The hunter, an old friend of Vince's though not part of the Kin, had been found not far from where he'd called, his throat sliced. A thorough canvassing for several miles in all directions resulted in only a few tracks. Tracking dogs followed the scent trails to a mountain stream where the hunter had died, only to lose all trace of it.

The area was difficult to traverse even at the best of times. Sharp cliffs, hidden ravines, and unbridged passes made it treacherous. The intruders weren't Kin, and evidence had been found that they were armed and that someone was using that sector of the mountains to lead possible homegrown or foreign terrorists toward D.C. or New York, maybe both.

Benjamin Maddox, along with Zack's parents, had quickly gathered all the information in the remaining chambers, stored the data in digital files, then caused all trace of the hard copy to disappear along with a vast amount of gold before attempting to slip from the county to D.C. to report their findings to the Brigham Agency.

They died before making it out of the county, their truck exploding on one of the less traveled mountain roads.

After twenty years, an extensive ongoing search for the information Benjamin had secreted away and for the traitor he'd identified turned up nothing. Not even a suspect or a hint of where her father might have hidden the digital files he mentioned in a letter that arrived to his brother the day after his death, in which he listed everything he'd taken and why.

The letter was short, to the point, and in Grace's estimation, hurriedly written.

"He knew the risk of trying to get out of the county," she muttered. "He knew who was behind it, or at least suspected it—and they had to have known he was on to them."

She'd been only five when her father died, twelve when her aunt Sierra died, and now at the age of twenty-four, she felt as though her entire life had been a lie.

"Why didn't Uncle Vince tell me any of this?" Lifting her head from the papers, she stared at Zack where he stood next to the glass wall looking out into the backyard.

"To protect you," he stated, never glancing back at her or shifting his position, leaning against the glass, arms folded across his chest. "As you grew older, Vince seemed to think you'd attempt to take up your father's investigation. The rumor they put out that your father and my parents were attempting to hide the missing Brigham daughter and her son was already in play, so he let it continue. No one knew who my mother was when Dad brought her to Loudon. She'd changed her hair color, wore colored contact lenses, and rarely dressed in the style she'd used before they married."

It was no wonder her uncle hadn't encouraged her interest in Zack. He'd known she would learn the truth if she pursued him.

Zack had never been the focus of the traitor's interest.

Her aunt Sierra was suspected of knowing the location of the files, according to Lucia during interrogation, and she was killed when she refused to give that information up. Sierra's daughter, Kenni, was tracked for over eight years in the belief she might know where it was as well.

Now, after Luce swore her daughter was not only working with her but also knew where the files were hidden, the focus was on Grace. The eight-week investigation by the Brigham Agency into her mother's accusations found no evidence to support the claim or disprove Grace's innocence, which resulted in the order to have her brought in for interrogation.

"Hurt someone enough, and they'll tell you anything," she whispered aloud sadly after reading the particulars of the interrogations, knowing the pain the subjects must have suffered. Especially Luce. She was still her mother, and the thought of the questioning she underwent left her heart heavy.

"It's not just the pain." Zack shifted his shoulders

before straightening and turning to face her. "Hallucinogenics created to ensure the subject reveals memories, thoughts, anything tied to the subject they're being questioned over, are used. There are milder forms of hypnotics that ensure the subject responds to any question while remaining lucid. Those drugs can be more painful than a beating, more dangerous than electroshock.

"The Clans created to protect the back roads and inner sections of the country from infiltration and terrorism, both homegrown and foreign, are vital to the protection of the United States. They're all under threat if that information gets into the hands of the traitor suspected to be in the family of the main Clan. It could destroy the second-phase defense of the country. That second phase is the last hope if we're invaded."

And national security trumped innocence every time, she remembered her cousin Cord stating with mocking disdain.

When Vince had learned that Grace knew his daughter was alive and hiding behind the identity of kindergarten teacher Annie Mayes, he said that Grace was far too inquisitive for her own safety. There had been little amusement in his tone, and now Zack knew why.

Grace wasn't just inquisitive; she was also damned nosy, and she put things together far too swiftly. As she'd been going through the files, Zack was able to see how quick she actually was. While reading information from one file, she'd mutter a connecting bit of information she'd seen maybe two or three files back.

She was like her father.

Benjamin had possessed an uncanny ability to solve

a certain kind of puzzle. Interlocking information, Vince had once called it. Benjamin could work on several mysteries at a time, and as each detail came through, he would file it away in its proper place until he could form a perfect, precise reconstruction of events.

Many of those missing files were ones Zack's father had kept hidden as Benjamin's second.

That talent had most likely been what led him to inventory key store chambers and determine that vital information was being stolen. Once Benjamin had copied and hidden the information that had yet to be compromised, Vince suspected his brother knew the identity of that traitor or at the least had a solid suspicion, and rather than fighting it out on home ground had tried to make his way to D.C. and the Brighams instead. Grace's father had suspected a close relative or key Kin member as the traitor, but he hadn't revealed a name in that letter.

"No one knew your mother was a Brigham?" Grace asked, then lifting her gaze from another file. "Did Dad know?"

"He had to have known," Zack assured her. "He and my father were too close, as close as brothers, I suspect. I know Vince knew. He suspected someone from the Brighams was involved, since they were headed to D.C. first, so he jerked me out of sight and placed me with Toby Rigor. I wasn't even aware my mother had any family until I was eighteen and introduced to Alexander Brigham."

And boy, had that gone over well.

Stiff, angry, and so full of himself, it was insulting, Alexander Brigham had glared at Zack and informed him he looked too damned much like his father.

Any association with the other man would have ended there if Zack could have made the choice. Unfortunately, Alexander Brigham demanded a certain amount of time be spent with the family; otherwise, both the Maddox and Rigor families would be sanctioned for hiding his sister's son during the years after her death. And thus Zack learned exactly why his mother had been so desperate to escape her family.

"It's like trying to untangle a ball filled with knots," Grace muttered then, shifting between files. "There's over twenty years of information here that I was never given." She glared at Zack. "There was no reason to keep me in the dark."

Nosy little minx. No wonder Vince had refused to allow her to know any of it until now.

"Not my decision, talk to your uncle," he suggested with a tight smile.

"You knew." She flicked him an angry look before returning to the file. "You could have told me, Zack. Don't try to convince me otherwise."

"Could have," he agreed. "Maybe I wanted to protect you." He used one of Jazz's *maybe*s to keep from looking too deeply into why he hadn't told her, even knowing she'd had the right to know.

A delicate little snort sounded from her before she pulled another faded file from the stack and opened it over the one she'd been reading. "This could take weeks," she bit out, her irritation obvious. "I don't have weeks to figure this out, do I?"

Zack glanced at the clock on the opposite wall, his eyes narrowing on the hands. No, she didn't have weeks at all. Alexander and his team had landed in Memphis less than thirty minutes before. The Brigham family patriarch and his eldest son, Madden, daughter Victoria, and two of his best agents were already en route.

Vince, his three sons, and Slade would arrive about half an hour before the Brigham brood made it to the house. Jazz would return about the same time.

"You have about two hours, if I'm guessing right." He finally shrugged. "If you come up with anything new before then it would definitely help."

Grace became perfectly still, her expression incredulous before she lifted her head and stared back at him. "Two hours? What fantasy world are you living in today?" She asked the question with a now serious expression.

"One generated by a Maddox–Brigham fuckup twenty years ago," he pointed out with another tight curve of his lips. "Alexander, Madden, Victoria, and two Brigham agents are about two hours out if my information's right, as I said. A little breakthrough wouldn't hurt any of us when they arrive." It sure as hell wouldn't hurt his position once he faced Alexander Brigham.

The bastard had a hard-on for the traitor who had not just created havoc in the organization for two decades, but also murdered the baby sister Alexander claimed to love—and if the information they were all searching for got into the wrong hands, it could destroy not just the fabric of the Maddox Clan but also others scattered across the United States.

It would detail each and every location supported by the second-phase defense network. Families—entire

Clans, in some cases—whose main job was to search for and locate individuals, possibly foreign operatives, traveling through their designated territories. If the identities of those families were revealed, they'd be picked off one by one, and there wouldn't be a damned thing that could be done about it.

Without those Clans, America was just too vulnerable to any group or groups of individuals attempting to slip terrorists into the nation or to overtake it. The military-trained family groups were effective in stopping the spread of violence because they or their locations were kept top secret.

"You should have given me all this information last night, Zack!" she snapped, the irritation even more apparent in her voice now. "There's no way in hell I can sift through all this in two hours." Her hand slapped onto the files, anger glittering in her emerald eyes, a frown creasing her brow.

His own brow arched. "It took a minute to hack the systems I knew some of the information was contained on." He finally shrugged. "I didn't finish until after six this morning. I'm not a miracle worker, baby."

"And I'm not your baby!" she snarled back at him. "I have two hours to find something to keep those bastards from taking me? Just wonderful." There was an edge of fear to her voice now, one he hated.

"No, I said you had two hours to, hopefully, find a new lead to make our positions stronger. But they won't be taking you either way I promise you that."

The Maddox males and his foster brothers would be inside the house with him, but trusted, loyal Maddox commanders would have his home surrounded within the tree line, just in case. He wasn't taking anything for granted or leaving anything to chance when it came to her life.

"Madden and Tory's presence indicates this is no more than a meeting to hammer out details, but the original reason for this little visit was to take you into custody for interrogation." He wasn't going to lie to her. The lies were over as far as he was concerned. "Madden and Tory were included last minute, so hopefully, Alexander has changed his mind."

Grace believed she, Tory, and Madden were friends. As far as Zack was able to learn, the two Madden children had gotten into a screaming match with their father over any attempted interrogation of Grace, and Tory had even gone so far as to refuse the order to travel to Loudon with a team sent to collect Grace after the attack. All the Brigham offspring had more or less been raised socializing with Grace and the Maddox family. But so had Alexander, so who knew what the hell was going on.

"He's trying to use Tory against me, then?" Disillusionment colored her tone as her attention seemed to turn back to the files. "That shouldn't surprise me."

"No, it shouldn't," he stated harshly. "He has the position as head of the agency for a reason, Grace. Because he has ice in his veins and a glacier for a heart. Remember that. And his children aren't far behind him in that regard."

She didn't say anything, just continued to sift through the files, but he could see her expression. Hurt flashed across it before that damned stoic look came over her face once again. "I'll keep everything you've said in mind," she promised, her voice quiet. "Now, if I have only two hours to do this, leave me the hell alone so I can concentrate."

Evidently, keeping peace between the Maddox and Brigham families was dependent on learning something, anything, before the Brighams and their agents arrived. There were more than thirty files stacked on the table. It would take weeks of work to detect any linking threads between them. If she could even find anything. Her skills in deciphering such subtle information weren't nearly so well developed as it was rumored her father's had been. He'd been a master at solving such puzzles.

How the hell had she landed in this position? Why in God's name had her mother decided to throw her only child to the wolves? Her innocent child, at that.

Quickly scanning the printouts in the folders, some of which were an inch or more thick, she fought to find any thread of information not contained in the main file that itemized the clues gathered over the years. Not just the recovered files found on her father's computer but also interrogations of those suspected to have been involved in the treason with Luce, those interrogated and found guilty of other crimes, as well as rumors, suppositions, and associations.

The sheer scope of the information boggled the mind.

There were also the pictures, many of which were taken by her father and by Zack's parents. Groups and gatherings of Kin members as well as social events attended by the Maddox and Brigham families and some occasions that included the Kin, the Maddoxes, and the Brighams.

As she came across them, Grace began separating the

snapshots according to the players involved. Pictures of events and gatherings that included the main Maddox family and in-laws, as well as several stacks that at first seemed to have no connection to the others in any way.

Threads. Every bit of information was a thread—she just had to unravel certain ones to find a common denominator. Unfortunately, that common denominator was leading right back to the members of her family.

"That can't be right." She shook her head, mumbling in frustration at the bigger picture she was seeing.

The main family consisted of her uncle Vince, the only Maddox member not included in the majority of the pictures, and his twin, Benjamin. Then there were four other brothers and their wives as well as a younger sister and her husband. Secondary family members would be in-laws, first cousins, nieces and nephews, and so forth, but no familial connection more removed than that of first cousin or husband and wife to such.

"What do you see, Grace?" There was no sense of urgency in his tone; anyone else would have detected only mild curiosity.

Pulling several pictures aside, she turned back to the first files she'd laid aside and began scanning them again. "Ties," she muttered.

There were always ties. Whoever was behind this had managed to pull Luce in to the extent that she'd been willing to aid in the murder of her own husband as well as her only sister.

Grace frowned at that thought before grabbing the stack of miscellaneous pictures and pulling them to her. Riffling quickly through them, she found the one she was searching for: Luce along with the brothers sent to kill Kenni just after she moved in with Jazz. One, Kenni had killed with an antique corkscrew to the heart; the other was killed the next day after he was dropped off alongside the road outside Loudon. The Kin patrol waiting for him hadn't let him get far.

Photographed along with Luce and the two brothers were two high-ranking Kin team commanders and several of their lieutenants. There were other pictures taken of the same men and other lower ranking Kin. Some of those within the group besides the brothers were already under suspicion by her uncle. But three others hadn't even been suspected.

She stared at their faces in each photo, noted the defensive stance of their bodies, expressions, how they held their arms and seemed to be keeping a careful eye on those who came close to their group.

Something about the groups themselves had a thread of memory tugging at her, but she couldn't follow it.

"Look at the men in these groupings with Luce." She slid the pictures toward him, then quickly pulled free the reports on those who had already been questioned. "In all the photos, there're a total of ten men. Only five are proven co-conspirators with Luce." She said the remaining five men. "That leaves five more not even under suspicion."

"They look damned suspicious in those pictures," Zack murmured, confirming her earlier thoughts. "Why weren't the others questioned?"

"Their names just hadn't come up." She shrugged, frowning as she tried to remember. "And we can't send them to be interrogated simply because they're in the same group photo, Zack."

"No, but an investigation can be opened," he told her. "Each of the men you've pointed out is tied by blood to those who have been proven traitors. That gives us a starting point."

She kept staring at the pictures. There was more to this; she knew there was more. "Uncle Vince has files listing each Kin member and their commanders as well as their team members. I'll need those, but the only access to them is via a closed system he uses. I'll have to go to the office, but I'll need these."

After pulling the pictures free of the pile as well as the reports on those members already proved to have been working with Luce, Zack began stacking the other files.

"I was still working," she snapped, staring up at him in confusion.

"Your uncle and cousins will be here within ten minutes, with the Brigham brood less than twenty minutes behind them. I told you I hacked several systems to get this information. No one knows about the files until we're finished with them, or we won't get to keep them."

She sat back in her chair and glanced at what he'd left behind. She'd had no idea she'd been working so long until she tried to relax and realized how stiff her back had become.

"And how will you explain having the pictures and reports?" she asked.

"The pictures were actually in my father's files, the reports on known coconspirators and the men involved in the attempt on Kenni and her mother's death were given to me by Vince. They're not a problem. Most of the rest of the information could become a problem, though." His smile was tight and hard once again.

A shark's smile, deadly, predatory.

Grace nodded slowly. "Okay, then. Need any help getting them out of here?"

"Got it." He placed them in two large file boxes, stacked the boxes together, then lifted and carried them through the living area to the stairs.

They were stashed in his bedroom, and he was back downstairs within minutes, just in time for the doorbell.

Never let it be said that dealing with her uncle and cousins when they were in "warrior" mode was easy. Add to the mix Zack's foster brothers, Jazz and Slade, and the tension in the air became thick enough to cut with a knife.

The Maddox males and Rigor foster sons were two perfectly balanced forces, each group having enough power within the Kin that should they come into conflict, it could potentially tear the Tennessee sect of the Kin in half. Thankfully, that had yet to happen.

The moment Alexander Brigham, along with his son Madden and daughter Victoria, entered the house, followed by the agents they'd brought with them, that tension became smothering.

Alexander Brigham stood just inside the door, and like Vince, he was in excellent shape for his age. A little over six feet, dressed in a charcoal gray silk suit, a blue and light gray striped tie lying perfectly against his white shirt. His son, on the other hand, had a more laidback style this trip. No tie, white shirt with the top two buttons undone, sleeves rolled back to his forearms, and jeans and boots rather than expensive slacks and dress shoes. Amusement gleamed in his brown eyes when he caught her gaze, though the rest of his face was as implacable as ever.

Victoria was Victoria, no matter whether the setting was casual or formal. Her long, cobalt black hair fell down her back like a thick, living ribbon. Piercing amber eyes were ringed with dark blue, while her expression was frankly disgusted. Dressed in a short gray silk skirt, white sleeveless silk blouse and four-inch heels, she looked like a very professional little pixie.

The two agents with them were tall, dark, but not nearly so dangerous looking as the Maddox men or Zack and his foster brothers.

Jazz, Slade, and Zack wore their customary jeans, T-shirts, and boots. The color of the shirts might vary, but the style rarely did. Though Zack was known to wear neatly pressed shirts, sleeves rolled back, and dressier boots whenever working at the office of the construction company the three men inherited from Toby Rigor.

"Stand your people down, Vince," Alexander suggested after a moment spent sizing each other up. "I'm not here to take her. This just a meeting, nothing more."

Like they believed it, Grace thought, glancing at her uncle's expression before examining Zack's. There was little trust here. The headway she and Victoria had been making over the years was in danger of dissolving with one wrong word.

From the corner of her eyes, Grace watched Victoria give a mocking shake of her head though her normally smiling lips were tight with anger. Then Victoria turned to face her directly.

"Grace, let's you and I visit while these men have their little testosterone powwow," the other woman announced with an edge of cynicism. "I don't know about you, but I'm in danger of choking."

Yeah, Grace could also feel that noose tightening around her neck a little more the longer she stood there. "I know Zack has coffee," she told the other woman as she pushed through the wall of men. "I'm not sure about tea."

"I brought my own." Victoria waved the comment away as she shifted the large leather bag she carried on her shoulder. "Let's go before I do choke out here, trying to deal with them." Blunt to the point of abrasiveness, Victoria was ready to explode with opinions they didn't want to hear. If she exploded, the entire meeting would go straight to hell, and they both knew it.

Grace's luck was actually with her where tea was concerned. She led the way to the kitchen and found a teapot on the chef's stove, ready for use. Filling it with water and turning the gas on beneath it, she turned and watched Victoria reaching up for the teacups she'd found in the cupboard.

"Tall men never think about the fact that a lover or wife might be shorter than they are," she snorted. "Let alone company." Cups and saucers were placed on the marble counter, individual blue and violet silicone tea bags filled with peach herbal tea were placed in each cup before she turned back to Grace. "They're so stubborn," Victoria muttered, her expression turning mutinous as she leaned against the counter, her arms crossing beneath her breasts. "My party's coming up soon. I told Dad he didn't need to do this, but does he ever listen to me? He doesn't even listen to Madden," she bit out. "We've argued with him over this continually since Zack left the house after learning of your attack."

After learning of her attack?

"Zack left the house when he found the orders to have me brought in for interrogation on your father's desk, Tory," Grace informed her. "He learned of the attack as he was driving out of the estate."

Tory's lips tightened, her amber eyes glittering with a promise of retribution. "He lied to us, then. I shouldn't even be surprised, should I?"

Remembering Zack's observation regarding Alexander, Grace murmured, "The position he holds requires he make the bastard decisions. Like Uncle Vince. I don't always agree with him, but I understand his reasons behind it."

For a second, grief flashed through Tory's gaze, but just for a second. "Yeah, well, I've always said you were too soft for this life," Tory reminded her as the teapot began whistling. "Pour the tea before I begin bashing heads."

Bashing heads actually sounded like a good idea. No doubt by time the males of this little meeting were finished, she and Tory would be plotting their demise again.

Carrying the tea to a glass-topped table across the room, Grace bit back the urge to curse as she heard her uncle's voice from the living room, his tone confrontational, though it was only matched by Alexander Brigham's.

Fragrant, steaming peach tea filled Grace's senses as she and Tory sat down; the ritual of chilling out after dealing with her father or older brother always involved tea for Tory.

As Grace was sipping at the steaming liquid, her eyes fluttered in pleasure at the taste.

"How you drink it that hot, I have no idea." Tory shook her head in amusement as she watched Grace. "My tongue would stay blistered."

"Says the woman who eats raw jalapeño like a cucumber," Grace laughed. "I'd much prefer the hot tea over the volcano spice."

Sipping at it again, Grace could feel the easing of the tension that had kept her knotted up inside since learning her mother had accused her of aiding in murder and treason.

"I'm sorry about this, Grace," Tory sighed, her arms braced on the table.

Tory would whimper if she had to sip her tea before it cooled sufficiently.

Drinking more, Grace could feel that slow, steady relaxation simmering through her, pulling the tension free but giving her an otherworldly feeling. So much so that her brain began to feel numb, her limbs weak.

The sound of glass breaking was a distant one, instantly followed by Tory's cry for Zack and then a cacophony of male voices rising like waves, crashing discordantly before easing and rising again.

She couldn't move.

Fear tore through her, an animal-like whimper echoing in her ears, though she didn't know who made it.

What was wrong? . . .

She couldn't move, couldn't process information, her brain wasn't working and neither were her muscles.

"I have you, Grace," she heard Zack's voice from a distance. "It's okay, baby, I have you."

chapter nine

"What did you do to her?" Zack snapped at Tory, his tone deadly, the need to kill surging hot and fast inside him. "So help me, Tory, you'll pay for this."

The other woman stood back from the table, her face white, her amber eyes wide in fear and shock. "Daddy?" disillusionment and confusion filled her voice as the little girl inside her reach out; a plea that she hadn't been used as she obviously had been, as tears glittered in her eyes.

"So help me God, Dad, this is it," Madden snarled, turning on his father, enraged. "You swore you weren't pulling anything here." His fists were clenched at his side, fury enveloping his expression.

"I didn't order this." Frustrated bemusement filled Alexander's face, and his gaze locked on Grace.

She was so still, her breathing erratic; the fear in her eyes was killing Zack.

"It's one of the drugs we use for interrogation," the agent flanking Alexander stated. "I notice the signs. It has a covert delivery system with hot liquid, coffee or tea—the caffeine aids in the quick delivery of the drug into her system."

Zack gathered her closer to his chest, his hands rubbing at the chill in her arms.

"The drug will be active in approximately thirty minutes," the agent continued. "Then it will begin easing from her system."

"You used me!" Tory screamed at her father. "How could you do this?"

"I didn't do this," Grace whispered, the question activating an overriding need to answer whatever inquiry she heard posed.

He was going to kill. Zack could feel the urge racing through him as accusations and protestations of innocence became a war of words between the others.

A war that was going to turn into questions at any minute, and once the questions started, Grace would attempt to answer them whether she understood the questions or not.

Zack lifted her against his chest until she was cradled in his arms and then strode from the kitchen, livid, the need to beat his uncle senseless resounding through him. Damn him, he had to be behind this, it wouldn't have happened otherwise. Alexander had complete control over his section, and he used it ruthlessly.

"Where are you going, dammit?" Alexander burst out as Zack carried Grace past him.

"I don't know," Grace answered.

"Get fucked, assholes," Zack snarled back, the wooden tone Grace used to answer the question enraging him further.

Let them fight it out, Maddox and Brigham. He was aware of Jazz and Slade following him through the house, then up the stairs. The only safe place for her would be his bedroom, safely behind closed doors, where the bastards couldn't get to her.

"Zack," Vince called out as Zack's foot lifted to take the first stair. "I hate like hell what they've done, but let them question—"

"Go to hell!" The snarl that ripped from his throat resonated with fury and the need for violence. "She didn't consent to it, and I'll be damned if I'll allow her to be fucking mind-raped for a Brigham's convenience. And by God, you should feel the same way."

He didn't give anyone else a chance to protest. Taking the stairs two at a time as he cradled Grace closer to him, he wondered at the rage building inside him. Yeah, he should be pissed, sure—outraged for her, even. But the killing fury trying to envelop him was far stronger than anything he should be feeling.

"Baer and Banyan are moving in on the house." Slade spoke softly behind him as they entered the bedroom. "Max and Beau-Remi are right behind them. A word of warning, Beau brought that fucking gator of his with him."

"I hope it's hungry!" Zack snapped furiously as he laid Grace on the bed and then sat next to her, brushing her hair back from her face.

The fear in her eyes was still killing him.

"Someone drugged you, baby," he whispered. "It was

ing a sharp cry from her lips even as Zack moved, drawing her closer to him and kneading the knotted muscles.

The feel of his hands on her back, pushing against the painfully drawn flesh, working it free and warming the chill rushing through her, was incredibly relaxing. Within minutes, the pain eased, leaving her breathing heavy but not so labored as it had been.

"I'm going to kill someone," she croaked, only then realizing how dry her throat had become.

"Get her some water," Zack ordered whoever stood behind him. "Just a minute, sweetheart, it'll get better."

"Better be," she muttered, "or I'm killing Brigham myself."

Alexander had to have been behind it; the question was, had Tory been behind it as well?

God, she'd never drink tea again. At least not anything made by anyone else. Commercial tea bags were wonderful things, she decided, and they tasted just fine, too.

"I want to talk to Tory," she whispered as Zack pressed a cup of water into her hand and helped her ease it to her lips.

"We'll talk about that later," he informed her after she'd finished drinking. Turning, he placed the cup on the nightstand.

"I talk to Tory now. Or the minute I catch your back turned, I'm having all of Dad's old antique furniture moved in here and I'm redecorating the entire house."

*　*　*

Zack stared at her for long, silent moments, their gazes locked, neither blinking. For a single, horrifying moment, he'd almost agreed to the redecorating over allowing Tory anywhere near her.

"I don't like wood furniture," he gritted out, the thought of having his home look as dark and dreary as the Brigham Estate sending a shudder up his spine.

"I'm not arguing with you, Zack," she sighed, weariness pulling at her. "It's either–or. Tory or wood furniture, take your pick."

She was exhausted, she had to be, he knew. The drug created to compel the truth from Kin and Brigham agents alike wasn't easy on the system.

Slade or Jazz snickered from the other side of the bed.

"You want to see her after she drugged you?" he bit out furiously. "Did you lose your mind somewhere, Grace? Is that drug that damned powerful?"

Her lips thinned. Brushing her hair back from her brow with a shaking hand, she gave him a look that demanded he give in to her. That emerald gaze didn't even flinch, despite his glare. That look reminded him of Vince when the other man was at his most determined.

"She's dangerous!" he snapped. "For all we know, *she* drugged you. Dammit, Grace."

Grace turned to Jazz and Slade. "Have any old, heavy wood furniture you want to get rid of?"

Slade turned his back and rubbed at his neck, though his shoulders seemed to be trembling with laughter.

"They wouldn't dare . . ." Zack growled.

"Well, hold up there," Jazz protested. "If she asks Kenni to get in on it, then I might not have a choice.

Kenni can get testy sometimes, and when she does, she goes and visits her family. For a long time." The frown on his face indicated his displeasure.

Kate and Lara were looking on with no small amount of amusement.

Zack narrowed his eyes on Grace. "I'll spank your ass if you dared."

"And I might like it." She wrinkled her nose back at him, though the argument was seriously getting old at this point. Firming her lips and lifting her chin, she stared up at him, far more determined than he could have imagined. He didn't want to dictate to her. "Don't turn this into an issue between us, Zack," she sighed, shaking her head, too tired to continue arguing. "Stay in the room if you want, but I will talk to her, whether you like it or not."

There was a glint to her eye that had a chill of unease working down his spine. She might or might not be joking about changing the house, but even if she was joking, he had a feeling that too tactful, supposedly sweet-natured Grace was far more trouble than he'd suspected.

"Lara," he said between gritted teeth, his gaze still locked with Grace's.

"Uh, yeah, Zack? Want me to go get Miss Brigham?" She was laughing her ass off at him; he could feel it.

"If you don't mind," he growled. "And no one else. If anyone tries to follow her, you call for me."

"Got it," she agreed cheerfully. "Most men don't fuck with me when I get mean, though. Or at least, not for long," she announced as she strode quickly from the room and into the hall.

Silence filled the room.

"We're going to discuss this," he promised Grace. "In depth."

Sure they would, Grace thought, holding back a yawn. All she wanted to do at this point was sleep. He'd have to wake her up first. Before she could sleep, she had to talk to Tory, though, had to make her friend understand that she didn't blame her for something someone else had done.

Who had done it, she wasn't certain. Whoever ordered it would have known of her and Tory's habit of drinking tea together. Grace liked hers steaming hot, while Tory waited until hers was merely good and warm. Grace always took the violet tea bag while Tory took the blue. It would have been so simple to ensure it was Grace who drank the doctored tea rather than Tory.

Moments later, Tory entered the room. Her face was pale, evidence of crying still spiking her black lashes. Her expression was composed, even chilly. Tory had on her stoic face, the one she used to deal with the difficulties that often arose as part of life with her father.

She came to the side of the bed, her hands clasped in front of her, her shoulders tense and straight as she stared down at Grace. "I'm sorry this happened . . ." she began.

"Tory, sit down and stop acting like you have to take the blame for what you believe your father did," Grace ordered her with an exhausted sigh. "I'm too tired for this."

Tory's lips quivered once before she turned her head

away, but she sat down at the side of the bed, staring toward the windows emotionlessly.

"I don't believe you drugged the tea or allowed it to be drugged. I don't even believe your father did," Grace stated.

Tory swung her head around, surprise flashing in her gaze. "Who else?" the other woman demanded. "Who else would have a reason?"

That was harder, but Grace knew the family, knew the agents who worked within the home, two of whom had accompanied Victoria, her father, and her brother to Zack's. "If I had to guess, then it was Peters." Grace frowned. "His sole purpose is to protect your father at all costs. He could have had it done, and one of the agents who came with you would have been there if by chance your father demanded I be questioned despite the deceit. He'd done things before without your father's direction."

Rubbing at her arms, Tory nodded slowly. "Better to seek forgiveness than to ask permission," she murmured. "Peters's favorite motto."

Grace nodded, aware of Zack watching her and Tory closely from the other side of the room with Jazz, Slade, and the two Blanchard sisters, Kate and Lara.

"Don't say anything to your father, though he's likely figured it out. We'll take care of Peters when I arrive next week for your birthday party."

Shock turned Tory's face blank for a moment before her eyes began to sparkle in delight. "You're still coming to the party?"

"After the amount I spent on that damned dress and

those shoes?" Grace snorted. "Zack would be risking his life keeping me away from it."

"Grace." Victoria shook her head then. "How can you be so certain I wasn't involved in this?"

"You would have slipped in a few questions before calling for help." Grace grinned. "If you believed I'd betrayed our families and our friendship to the extent that I'd help Luce, then you would at least have asked that question and claimed you had just taken advantage of what someone else set into motion. You were too shocked and frightened when that drug kicked in."

Tory shook her head, her brow tightening with the anger still rushing through her. "I'll kick Peters's ass myself."

"We both will," Grace promised, smothering a yawn. "As soon as I get there."

Covering Grace's hand with her own, Tory gave it a firm squeeze, her version of a hug. Tory hadn't been hugged a lot, not as a child or as an adult. She'd grown used to Grace's hugs, but giving one on the spur of the moment was something she hadn't yet mastered. "Thank you for being such a valued friend, Grace," she whispered.

"No thanks needed." A yawn slipped out, barely covered as Grace hurriedly lifted her free hand to her lips. "Sorry."

"You're tired." Tory shook her head. "No apology needed. I'll clear everyone out now and I'll see you tomorrow."

"Tomorrow," Grace promised, feeling the weariness crashing inside her as the edges of sleep crept closer.

"Lara, you and Jazz take Tory downstairs and tell that mess to get the hell out of my house," Zack ordered.

"If they're still there when I come down, then we're going to have problems."

"Madden wants a moment of your time before we leave," Tory stated, her voice quiet as Grace felt her lashes lowering, exhaustion crashing over her now. "He told me to tell you he wasn't leaving without speaking with you first."

What Zack said in reply, Grace didn't have a clue. Giving in to the pull of the darkness crowding ever closer, she allowed herself to sink into it and let the comforting tendrils of sleep wrap around her mind.

She had a feeling she'd need all her strength to convince Zack she must attend that party. It was more imperative than ever.

She thought she was going to attend that damned party?

She really thought he was going to let her so much as get out of the damned county after this?

Raking his fingers through his hair, Zack could feel the pounding fury mixing with an overload of frustration where Grace was concerned.

How did she actually manage to get past every instinct he had to protect her? He should never have let Tory upstairs. Hell, he'd known better. He'd known that the friendship she thought she had with Victoria Brigham would become a damned problem.

Stomping down the stairs after leaving Kate to watch over Grace, Zack could feel Jazz and Slade at his back, the two men no less pleased with the results of this meeting than Zack himself.

There was no way to convince Grace of the danger involved in attending that party when someone was obviously out to destroy her. She'd crashed the minute she finished speaking to Tory. She'd wake up, though. In a couple of hours, she'd be completely recovered and ready for the objections Zack intended to unleash on her. Until then, he could expend part of his frustration and fury on Madden Brigham.

And he was damned sure looking forward to it.

chapter ten

Zack wasn't in bed with her the next morning when she awoke. Grace was equally relieved and disappointed. She'd at least expected him to be lying beside her, but if she was going to be to work on time, then it was better that he wasn't.

She showered quickly before blow-drying her hair and dressing in a beige skirt, silk cami, and three-inch heels. Her leg was feeling much better, and thankfully it was high enough on her thigh that it didn't show beneath the above-knee cut of the slender skirt.

A quick application of makeup, a pair of hoop earrings, and a slender gold chain around her neck, and she was ready to go. She might have just enough time for coffee.

After grabbing her purse from the dresser and checking that her cell phone was still in it, Grace left the bedroom and hurried downstairs for that cup of coffee before having Zack drive her to the farmhouse. She'd see about getting her car later.

Zack was sitting at the counter with a steaming cup of coffee and a newspaper, his head lifting as she entered the room. She would have said good morning if his expression hadn't instantly snapped into a glare.

"Don't give me your grouch face this morning," she ordered him. "What the hell's your problem, anyway?"

She really wasn't in the mood to deal with his arrogant-know-it-all opinions, and she had a feeling she knew exactly which direction those opinions were going to take.

It was too damned bad he looked good enough to take a bite out of as he sat there, too. That domineering expression, his overnight shadow of a beard, shaggy hair. Suddenly, he wasn't Rigor's accountant any longer. He was the bad boy every woman dreamed about. That rough-and-tumble lover who would give no quarter and damned sure wouldn't ask for any.

A dark gray shirt, the top two buttons free, sleeves rolled to his elbows, the bottom tucked into jeans that rode his hips like a lover's legs, and that wide leather belt. The belt buckle would be plain, but the bulge beneath it wouldn't be.

"Please tell me you don't intend to go to your uncle's this morning," he sighed, shaking his head—probably because he knew better than to ask. He sounded just as put out as he looked.

Did he believe she dressed like this to deal with him? There wasn't a snowball's chance in hell. Denim and steel-toed boots, maybe, but never a skirt and heels. "Why else would I get all dressed up?" She held her hands out to her side as she faced him before turning to pour her coffee. "Besides, there are some files I need to look at, and they can't be copied or taken from the office. That's the only place I can look at them."

Her uncle's closed system, kept locked in his office, didn't permit anyone to print or send information across the Internet; Vince had made certain of it. The information he kept there could put every man with the Kin in danger, along with their families. Those files spanned information from generations of Kin. Family affiliations, Kin bloodlines, commanders and each man assigned to them, routes never used by Kin but accessible to them. Political and social contacts, who donated funds to the agency's coffers for the Kin and who Vince considered enemies.

"Trust me, Vince would find a way to get them to you without you going into the office," he informed her, his tone deceptively casual, his expression implacable.

Yeah, right. And Zack was going to sprout wings in the next five minutes and begin flying. There wasn't a chance her uncle would copy even one of those files. Even Alexander Brigham had no access to them. Hell, as far as Grace knew, Zack's uncle wasn't even aware of them.

"I actually enjoy my job," she told him firmly rather than revealing the depth of the secret of those files. "Now, come on, drive me to work. And I want to bring my car back here tonight." She hated the inconvenience of not having her own ride, even if it wasn't advisable at the moment to use it too much.

"No." His answer was short and to the point before he turned his attention back to the paper.

Grace frowned at the answer, anger uncurling inside

her. "No, I can't bring my car back, or no, you won't drive me to work. Because I can always ask Uncle Vinny for a ride. He'll come get me himself, trust me."

Her uncle hated looking for the simplest thing in the office. He'd be pulling his hair out before morning was over and screaming over the fact that she wasn't there. She knew him. And by time she got there, if she was too late, then her office as well as his would be a shambles from his search for whatever he was looking for.

No thank you. She'd rather risk Zack's temper than risk her careful placement of information and data. It was simply too hard to replace anything that got destroyed or went permanently missing.

"Both." He turned a page lazily. "Vince will get by just fine without you for a while. Your safety's more important."

"And you don't know Vince!" she snapped back, unable to believe he'd dared tell her no, as though she were a child. No explanation, no reason. Just no. "And I'll be damned if you have the right to make decisions for me, Zack."

She wasn't a child and she wasn't going to allow him to treat her like one. If the danger level had increased, then he could discuss it with her but he would not arbitrarily just tell her no.

He laid the newspaper down carefully, finished his coffee, and when he moved, she really didn't expect him to move so quickly. She sure didn't expect to find herself sitting on the counter, her skirt pushed above her thighs as Zack wedged himself between her legs until his hips were notched there.

He was aroused. Thick and hard—and she remembered just how thick and hard—his cock pressed against the damp folds of her sex through his jeans and her silk panties.

Her body heated up just that fast.

Grace felt the flush suffuse her from her breasts to her hairline, and between her thighs that dampness began to collect and spill to her panties. Her breasts swelled, her nipples becoming sensitive, aching for touch. And he knew it. Zack was far too perceptive not to know exactly how she was responding to him.

His head lowered, one hand pulling hers back to allow his lips to find the sensitive flesh of her neck, just beneath her ear.

"Why are you doing this?" she whispered, the feel of his lips against her neck sparking such rapid-fire pleasure, she nearly lost her breath.

"Because you make me damned hungry." His voice darkened and rough, a graveled sound of arousal. "It's a hunger I can't get over. One I'm getting sick of denying myself."

The primal intensity in his tone had a betraying shiver racing through her as her stomach clenched in answering hunger. "And you're blaming me because you've denied yourself?" That was rich, coming from him. She'd waited for him longer than any man deserved, and he said *he* was tired of denying himself? She was tired of wanting him and being ignored. That had grown old years ago.

"I didn't need anyone to blame." He stepped closer, lust beginning to shadow his expression. "I didn't need an excuse."

She believed that one, didn't she?

"Then what? What did you need, hotshot? Because

you sure as hell weren't going out of your way to let me know you wanted anything more than a flirt here and there. Did you want me to beg?"

His head lifted slowly, interest and lust gleaming in his eyes. "Would you beg?" he asked, his voice lowering. "I think I'd love to hear you beg, baby."

The fingers threaded through her hair tugged at the strands, sending a flash of pleasure-pain through her senses as a gasp parted her lips.

Grace caught at his forearms, her fingers clenching against the warm flesh, feeling the hard bunch of muscle, the power in his hold as he held her captive against his taller, harder body.

"Why should I beg? Why should I have to?" She could barely breathe. "I'm not so hard up that I can't find a man to fuck me, Zack. Nor am I such a hag that I need to beg for a pity fuck from you."

"Oh, definitely no hag," he promised softly, the hand at the middle of her back pressing her closer to his aroused body. "But I'd still like to hear you beg."

"Go to hell—"

The fierce, furious retort cut off the second Zack's kiss stole the sound. His tongue pushed between her lips, found hers, and then retreated, only to tease her with another hungry thrust.

What were they arguing about?

She knew she should remember what it was they were arguing about; after all, it had been important enough that she became rather angry over it.

At least, until he kissed her.

It didn't seem quite so important now.

This kiss was much more important.

The way his tongue worked between her lips, stroked over hers, played and tasted and encouraged her to do the same was drugging. Pleasure suffused her. The feel of his hard body pressing between her legs, his muscled thighs spreading hers. It was more pleasure than she'd ever known.

The way his hand stroked from the small of her back to her thigh, pushing the silk material of her skirt that last bit, allowing his hand to play with the band of her silk panties.

"Softest skin I've ever felt," he rasped, his lips moving from hers to the column of her neck. "I've been dying to get under this skirt since you walked in the room. Just the thought of it has my cock so damned hard, it's painful."

The rough sound of his voice sent a shiver of pure erotic pleasure racing through her body again. If the sound of his voice wasn't enough, the feel of his hands against her flesh was even better. The feel of callused fingertips. The stroke of work-roughened hands as his lips moved to the scooped neckline of the light, sleeveless silk top she wore.

"I want this off you." He caught her wrists and lifted them, then pulled the hem of the blouse from her skirt. He was whisking it from over her head even as her arms were lowering, only to toss it to the floor, his gaze locking on the quick rise and fall of lace-covered breasts.

She was surprised she could breathe through this. That she could remember how to inhale and exhale. The pleasure was killing her, whipping through her like flames.

"Look how pretty you are," he drawled, running a

fingertip on the upper curve of one trembling mound, watching as he smoothed over the skin to the point between her breasts to the front clasp of her bra.

A flick of his fingers and the clasp released.

Lips parting once again, fighting to draw in air, she watched as Zack removed the material from her breasts before pushing the bra straps off her shoulders and allowing it, too, to drop to the floor.

She couldn't move, and she wasn't about to protest. She needed, ached for him. Her breasts were swollen, flushed, her nipples painfully tight and erect, and she wanted nothing more than to feel his lips, his tongue on the hot tips.

"What are you waiting for?" The dare in her voice had nothing to do with confidence, but with a need that was driving her crazy.

Zack lifted his gaze from her breasts to her eyes with a heavy-lidded sensuality that stole her breath for a moment. "Daring me, baby?" he asked softly

"Hmm. Dare?" She questioned his interpretation as she shook her head. "That's not a dare, Zack," she assured him. "A dare is reminding you that I showed you how good I could be the other day. You made the claim that you would then show me how good you are," she pointed out. "All I've seen so far is how good you are at talking about it. . . ."

Zack wanted to laugh. Not in amusement or to mock the obvious innocence and need in her expression as she stared up at him, aching to be touched, to touch in return. She was tired of waiting for it as well.

It was a dare, plain and simple, by a fledgling at the game.

He was a master, and he'd waited a long time to practice all that experience he'd gained over the years on
this one woman's delicate little body. He'd waited too
long, and there were moments he worried that the dark
need he kept under control could slip its leash with her.

Keeping his gaze locked with hers, Zack lowered
his head, aware of the fine tremors that cascaded through
her body. She was trying to keep her lips from trembling, steeling herself as she watched him, as his lips
parted just over the flushed, pebble-hard flesh of a
nipple.

"Sure you're ready, baby?" He cupped the swollen
flesh and let his thumb rake over the tip.

What her response did to him should have been terrifying.

Heavy dark lashes fluttered over her dark green eyes
as a tremulous moan passed her lips. Her breathing was
hard, harsh. The force of it pushed her breasts higher,
brushing her nipple against his lips, the velvet-and-silk
texture such temptation.

A whimper left her lips.

Slender, delicate fingers buried in his hair as Grace
arched to him, the berry-firm tip of her nipple burying
between his lips, and he felt the leash slip.

The things he wanted to do to her, the ways he
wanted to taste her, take her, sent his senses blazing
with hunger.

Grace was certain she didn't mean to cry out; after
all, she'd told herself she was going to stay cool as long
as possible. She needed to at least pretend a little more
experience than what she actually had, right? Instead,
the second his lips surrounded her nipple and he sucked

it inside the heat of his mouth, the sound tore free from her.

She felt herself shudder in his arms, felt the heat and need flooding her before more dampness spilled between her thighs.

Oh God, he had to take her this time. He had to finish it. Surely he would.

Where he'd been playful before, watching her with teasing lust, at the sound of that cry, his gaze flared, darkened, and what had been male hunger became devastating male greed. His mouth tightened on her nipple, his tongue lashing at the tip and at the same time he lifted her from the counter and carried her quickly to the couch in the other room.

Guiding, supporting, he settled her against the cushions before leaning over her, his lips and tongue sending maximum pleasure tearing through her senses. The folds between her thighs were swollen, heated, needy. . . . She was so needy. . . .

"Zack." Her back arched, the plea, cry, demand for more spilling from her lips.

But when his hand cupped her pussy and the pad of his palm ground against her clit, she felt sensations overwhelming every part of her. Any protest, any uncertainty she might have felt was forgotten. Her hips arched, the heated spill of her moisture beneath the thin material of her panties quickly dampening them further.

And it was so good.

The callused rasp of his thumb caressed her sensitive flesh and pushed her to an edge of need she'd never known. The wetness spilling from her eased his way, gave his fingers a slick path to the emptiness tormenting her, the aching flesh hidden just below the nub of flesh he was stroking with such devastation.

It was like a storm of sensation without respite. It swirled faster, building by the second, intensifying as his mouth switched from one hard nipple to the other.

The suction of his mouth pulled at the tender tip and locked it within the fiery moisture. The lash of his tongue was a heated caress of painful pleasure. It was a pleasure past bearing, and it kept building until she found herself writhing beneath him, desperate for more.

"It's so good." The words tore from her as she felt his teeth, felt them grip her nipple, tug, then the fiery drag and pull of his suckling mouth driving her higher. "Oh God. Zack."

Her thighs parted farther at the feel of the callused rasp of his fingers raking deliciously over her clitoris for a second. Over it, around it, he stroked, teased, and kept her trying to arch closer, to get the touch she needed to leap into the chaos of bliss awaiting her.

Just a second.

It wasn't enough.

Bending her knee and spreading her thighs even wider for him. Arching, gasping, broken moans spilling from her lips as a kaleidoscope of sensations began swirling through her overly sensitized body.

She was close . . . so close. . . .

"Fuck." He tore away from her, shocking her, leaving her to stare up at the ceiling in confusion, need pounding through her senses.

He'd stopped?

Just like that, he'd pulled back when she was poised at the edge of an orgasm.

Well, now, she hadn't seen that one coming, had she?

Humiliation raced through her. The heat of it spread from her bare breasts, along her neck, and straight to her hairline as Grace pushed herself from the couch, rushing back to the kitchen to find her bra and blouse.

And to hide her tears.

Tears? She was going to cry over him?

Zack had always been teasing, but until now, he'd never hurt her enough to make her cry.

She dressed hastily, refusing to look at him as he stood with his back to her, hands braced on the table in front of the window as he stared out at the front yard.

"We needed to talk," he bit out, anger pulsing in his voice.

They needed to talk?

"I don't particularly feel the need to talk to you right now," she informed him, her voice shaking as she pushed her fingers through her hair and tried to restore order to it.

She couldn't remember a time when she'd felt less like talking.

"Dammit, Grace, don't turn this into a confrontation." Turning, his arms folding across his muscular chest as he stared at her with a brooding frown, he presented an imposing sight.

Unfortunately for him, he didn't intimidate her much.

A little, maybe.

Sometimes.

"No confrontation," she agreed, smiling tightly as she waved one hand, the mockery clearly present. But it hurt—oh God, how it hurt. "Unfortunately, my patience for your bullshit is rather low right now. So I think it would be a good time to take me to work. I'm already late, and Uncle Vince will tear my filing system apart if I don't hurry and get there."

"We need to talk, Grace. Now." The expression on his face would have sent a chill of foreboding up her spine if she weren't so damned pissed off.

"The last thing we need to do right now is talk," she ground out, hating the brittle tone of her own voice, hating the tears she was forced to hold back. "You can drive me or I'll walk."

Zack's first impulse was to put her over his shoulder and take her to his bed, exactly what he should have done instead of trying to be noble. Instead of trying to make sure she knew the rules before she gave herself to him.

Until he saw the tears.

Those tears had his chest tightening so hard, so fast, he found his breathing growing heavy and a sense of failure sweeping over him.

Failure?

How the hell did her tears constitute failure, anyway?

"Please, Zack. Now." Her voice trembled between one breath and the next before she managed to conquer it. Her back straightened, her expression became smooth, though her eyes, like bruised emeralds, stared back at him and betrayed her firmness with the glitter of moisture she hadn't been able to suppress.

He could make sure she was safe in the office, he knew. Just as he knew Vince, now that he was on guard, would ensure only his most trusted men were anywhere near the house. He couldn't imagine Vince being as destructive with files as she described, but maybe Grace needed to feel like her uncle needed her that much. With Kenni's return and her mother's betrayals, she had to be feeling lost, confused. That hunger to be needed could be relentless, he knew.

She would be safer here at the house with him, though. Every inch of the outer perimeter of the house was wired for heat, video, and sound. If a bird shifted on a branch, then he knew about it. If anything larger moved, then the silent alarm on his phone was instantaneous.

He pushed his fingers through his hair restlessly, arousal still pounding through him, the need to have more of her pushing at him, aware that she'd give in to him, that she'd give him more of the lush sweetness he'd only tasted so far.

That insane urge he'd had to make her understand that once the traitor was found, the affair would be over, to warn her not to fall in love with him had him mentally kicking his own ass now.

"Forget it, I'll walk." Evidently fed up with waiting on him, Grace turned and stepped to the door.

"Grace." He caught her wrist and then instantly released her when she froze and gave a desperate shake of her head. "I don't want to hurt you," he whispered. "That's why I stopped, so we could figure this out."

"I thought it was women who overthought every damned thing." She flashed him a disdainful look. "Don't worry, Zack, I won't try to claim the heart you don't have. I'm not completely stupid. If I had no chance at it before, then I damned sure don't have a chance at it now. Right?"

Dark emerald eyes flashed with a hint of grief before

she managed to rein in emotions he might have wanted to understand better.

"Don't bother denying it." A husky laugh hinting at pain more than amusement parted her lips. "Just take me to work, if you don't mind. I don't want to discuss emotions that don't exist and rules that go with fucking you. Better yet, I think that's a discussion we need to table for a very, very long time."

chapter eleven

Grace entered the office before coming to a stop, her gaze alighting on her uncle as he dug through the file cabinet. Several files lay haphazardly on top of the cabinet, another on the floor, and she could only imagine what the inside of the drawers looked like.

Dressed in silk slacks, a short-sleeved shirt, and dark leather boots, he looked like an executive pretending to be a farmer. It was a look he swore garnered trust in some of the political figures that used the Maddox hunting cabins and lodges for safe houses and "bigwig meetings," as Cord had once called them.

There were six two-room cabins and three two-story lodges in the mountains, built on Maddox property and patrolled by Kin. Those cabins and lodges were the public face of Maddox financial security, though most people were unaware of who used them. The farm was secondary, with covert funds coming in for the surveillance and security of the mountains they covered.

The files her uncle was going through held nothing even remotely connected to Kin activities, so the rule was, he was to stay the hell out of them. He made a mess with files. He might remember whatever his filing system was, but no one else could make heads nor tails of it. Not even Grace.

"Weren't you banned from my file cabinet?" she asked, keeping her voice firm as she made certain the heels of her shoes snapped against the hardwood floor while she moved toward him.

Her uncle froze, head lifting like a deer caught in headlights before he glared at her. "You're two hours late!" he snapped, slamming shut the drawer he was pilfering through while gathering up the files he'd pulled free.

"I'm not exactly on my own schedule anymore, Vince," she informed him, blaming Zack for the good hour it was going to take, if not more, to straighten out the files her uncle had no doubt made a mess off. "Yell at Zack."

"He looks like Cord after having dealt with the Blanchard girl," Vince sniffed after looking up at Zack. "I think I'll leave him the hell alone."

Her brows lifted at that comment. "You're not distracting me." No doubt he had some gossip to impart this morning concerning Cord and "the Blanchard girl," God knew which one.

"I'm not trying to distract you." Scratching his head, her uncle frowned down at her, trying for sincerity and displeasure in a single look.

It wasn't working for him this morning.

The look would have been intimidating if she hadn't spent the years since turning eighteen dealing with it.

Shuffling through the half dozen files she took from his hand, she could only shake her head. "What are you looking for?"

"Estimates on the new hunting cabin that came in," he groused, peering over her shoulder at her desk for a second before seeming to give up on the idea of messing it up as well. "I was going to have Zack go over them and tell me what he thought."

"Did I put the estimate together?" Zack asked in a faintly querulous tone before Grace could answer.

He hadn't, Grace knew. Vince had never used Rigor Construction for any of the projects on the Maddox holdings.

"No, but you can still look at them!" Vince snapped, his expression bordering on frustrated anger. "Besides, I might change my mind. Jazz is almost family now."

Almost family?

Grace wanted to laugh at the comment. Jazz and Vince's daughter, Kenni, had scheduled their wedding for March just before Vince projected to have the new hunting cabin started. Jazz had loved Kenni since before her disappearance, though. Loved her to the extent that he'd never had a serious relationship until her return.

"I'll give you an estimate on what you want built, but I'm not going to go over anyone else's estimates, Vince, you know better than that," Zack snorted. "Now I'll leave you and Grace to discuss her files. I need to talk to Cord for a minute."

"Yeah, you do that," her uncle muttered, casting her a wary glance that almost had her laughing at him. "He's gonna become a pain in my ass."

She didn't comment—she knew better, and she had too much to do to become involved in the debate she knew would follow.

"The file for the estimates is in your office, Vince," she reminded him as the door closed behind Zack. "I don't get the file until you've approved it." And he knew that. It was a system they'd used for years.

"Well, I can't find the damned thing. . . ." Vince destroyed files. He didn't lose them, they never left the office, but he could spend hours searching for one because he so hated the hard copy system and because Grace had given up on learning his filing system. He was forced to use hers, which meant if the file was put in the cabinet, she put it there. Once she found it.

The age of the Internet was, in Vince's opinion, a godsend. All his files in once place, a closed system he didn't have to worry about losing a page from. Scan the hard copy into it, deposit the physical pages in a box to be stored, and it was over and done with. Until he needed it. Or he needed to show someone else a file not as sensitive as the others on the closed system he used. Then it could take hours, sometimes days to go through all the boxes stacked in the fireproof room beneath his office.

After getting the file her uncle needed from his office, she handed it to him and watched him stalk to the door leading into the house. When he reached the hall, he called to Sawyer and Deacon: "Keep your asses wherever Gracie goes." Seconds later, the two younger cousins were sprawled out on the couch across from her desk and watching her a little too thoughtfully.

That look was always guaranteed to give her a headache.

"Turn on the TV, amuse yourselves with a magazine or whatever, but don't harass me," she ordered them. "Your father, the file-destroyer, has made a mess and I'm none too happy."

Deacon snickered. The twins seemed to have rediscovered their jokester sides after finding their baby sister alive. For a while, Grace had worried she'd never hear Sawyer's deep laughter again, or watch Deacon play his little pranks on the family or on the men who worked around the farm.

"Sleep late, did ya?" Sawyer drawled from where he slouched back in one corner of the couch.

"No, I didn't." She turned her back on them and went to work on the file cabinet, more so they couldn't glimpse the reason behind her lateness in her expression. "Zack had to debate all the reasons I shouldn't come into work. Then I had to argue all the reasons I should. It took a minute." Or so, she amended silently.

She could almost feel those two fiends as their minds worked. She knew Kenni had worried so much about the missing gaiety they once possessed that she'd started playing pranks and pushing to reignite that male humor. When they were practicing on someone else, it was funny as hell. Not so much when they were practicing on her.

"Minute man, huh?" Deacon murmured.

Her face flamed.

Giving herself a moment to collect her composure, she turned her head and gave them the bland, no-nonsense look she'd had to learn to adopt with all the Maddox men and certain Kin commanders. "Really, Deke?" she stated in disappointment. "Am I known for being so easy that all a man would have to take is a minute with me?"

She was known for being completely unattainable, and she knew it.

"Yeah, but you've been hot for Zack since you were eighteen," he snorted. "And I know the signs of a man that's just as hot for some woman. That boy's been known to leave a gathering within an hour of your arrival simply because one of us had to punch him in the gut for the way he looked at you."

She was shocked. She'd had no idea her cousins ever did such a thing. "Why would you do something so idiotic?" she asked in disgust.

Sawyer rolled his dark green eyes in amusement. "Sweet cousin, every man you've went out with has gotten a punch in the gut and a warning not to play with you. Hell, it's the only way to keep men like that in control. If they really liked you, they would have come back."

Where the hell had they gotten that idea? She could only stare at them in disbelief, amazed that they had come up with something so infantile.

"For more torture? Who would be that stupid?" That was insane—no wonder she'd had so few second dates. She'd assumed it was because she wasn't willing to just hop into bed with them.

"Zack," they answered at the same time, looked at each other in surprise, then snickered before Sawyer followed it up. "That boy's brains have been in his pants since you come of age, Gracie. Everyone knew it but you."

She was calling bullshit on that one.

She couldn't deal with these two today. What had ever made her think she missed their boyish high jinks? There had to be a way to distract them.

"Did you see the email from our DOD contact?" she asked as casually as possible. "He has a few toys he thought you might be interested in."

Toys being military hardware the Kin had access to through their affiliation with the Brigham Agency.

"We got it," Sawyer drawled. "Stop trying to distract us. Come on, Grace. Tell us if he needs his face bruised. If he made it past first base, then we're definitely bruising his face."

She paused in the act of returning a file to its proper place before sighing heavily. This was going to get old fast.

"He doesn't need his face bruised," she assured them, lying through her teeth.

"Did he make second base?" Deke inquired with no small amount of interest. "That's two punches in the gut."

God help her.

"Leave." Turning on them in frustration, she pointed to the door. "Now."

"He made second base," Sawyer assured his brother. "Look at the blush on her face. Both of us get to hit him in the gut and in the face."

Carefully, she stepped across the room, her eyes narrowing on them as they suddenly deserted their slouched positions to sit up straight, tensing as she reached the couch, where she sat between the two of them slowly.

Reaching out, she gripped each cousin's knee and

gave a little squeeze. "Do you remember when you made the last mistake in teasing me over Zack?" she asked as she crossed one leg over the opposite and gave them each a tight smile. "I still have the pictures. Should I share them?"

Sawyer's eyes widened. "The doctor said those pictures would never be seen by anyone!"

"But he handed me the camera when he stepped outside your bedrooms to get the bag I'd brought up for him," she informed them gently. "It was so easy to steal them." And she was lying through her teeth again.

And though she hadn't been the cause of the doctor's visit, she wasn't above taking credit for it. It tended to make them more wary of her.

The poison ivy that had somehow gotten into the insides of their jeans had created havoc over the course of a day. By the next morning, as she'd heard her uncle laughing uproariously, it had created havoc in their male parts.

"And you know, you never know when it might happen again—accidentally, of course," she sighed patiently. "That stuff just spreads like wildfire outside the house unless someone keeps up with it." Her eyes widened as she glanced at the two in turn. "Maybe I need to do some weed control for Jack." The aging gardener would appreciate the help. He always did. Even while laughing at the probable reason for the help.

"You little gremlin," Deacon growled. "That's just wrong, Grace."

"No." Bracing herself on each of their knees, she pushed up from the couch and turned to face them. "Just one bruise on Zack, no matter the reason, is uncalled for. And teasing me about my personal life is right up there with it. So be warned." She smiled with sugary sweetness. "I do know how to get back at you. One way or the other." She turned her back on them and went over to the files.

"She's the reason I had to start wearing damned underwear again," Sawyer bit out beneath his breath, though she caught enough of the statement for a smug grin to shape her lips.

"No kidding," Deacon half groaned. "Try boxers, it's better protection. . . ."

She ignored the little debate that rose up over boxers versus briefs and concentrated on the files. She still had to get her uncle to unlock his computer to access the files there. It was a request she rarely made, but she had to have the information she knew was contained there. She could feel the puzzle pieces of information she'd gone through the day before. Once she went through the files Vince had, she could return to Zack's, make the notes pertinent to what she was searching for, and begin laying everything out in order.

If she'd only known sooner, she thought wearily, perhaps other lives could have been saved. Not her father's or her aunt's, but those of friends who had begun to suspect Lucia's activities and suffered the consequences.

What else had they begun to suspect? she wondered. And how hard would it be to get information on that as well? A thought began to slowly form.

She frowned at her cousins. "We haven't had a family reunion since Dad died, have we?" she said softly. "Do you think we should have one?"

Their silence was telling, first blank stares and then

both of them standing up and heading for the door. "Hang on there, cuz. We forgot to take care of something—we'll be right back."

Her mouth nearly dropped open at the bizarre response. That quickly, that suspiciously, they were gone.

And they thought they were getting off the hook that easily?

She so didn't think so.

Grace was adamant that she needed her car. Why she needed it? That one Zack hadn't figured out yet. It wasn't as though he'd be crazy enough to actually let her get out in it by herself, especially with the top down.

The sporty little black cherry Volkswagen sat in the garage, to all appearances as secure as a babe in its crib. Until Cord had checked the vehicles after a ten-minute lapse in the security feed earlier that morning.

Suspicious by nature, even bordering on paranoid, Grace's cousin had checked the vehicles, first thing. Finding the danger to Grace's car wasn't easy, but gut instinct and a belief that his cousin was seriously in danger had his training kicking in. Cord had found the problem hidden in the intake box: a small, powerful explosive rigged into the speedometer to detonate at a certain speed.

They were still waiting on a bomb detail already on quick egress out of Memphis to the farm. The squad was still about twenty minutes out, though.

The experience and training needed to set an explosive in so small a window of time indicated they weren't dealing with an amateur. This was professional.

"This isn't good, Zack," Cord sighed as they stared

at the small explosive. "All we'd have found of her was ashes."

"Shut the fuck up," Zack muttered, crossing his arms over his chest, never taking his eyes off the vehicle's motor.

He'd already imagined what would have happened to Grace if the explosive had triggered, and the thought sent chills racing down his spine.

"Someone's serious about this," Cord growled, pacing around the car. "Why kill her if the objective is the information Lucia said she has?"

He'd considered that question closely himself, since the first attack against her. Why kill her if that information was so important?

"Someone's afraid it's going to reveal who's behind the attempted thefts of information and what was behind it twenty years ago," Zack murmured. "That's all it can be. She's potentially more dangerous alive if that information is found by any of us. Or in their eyes, if she gives it to one of us."

Cord was silent for long moments, his expression icy. "How far would they go to kill her?" her cousin asked then.

"They'll put a sniper on her next," Zack predicted. "I want her out of here, Cord. I want her back at the house, where she'll be safer."

The windows of his home were bulletproof to a certain degree, but the electronics installed in them would help in keeping thermal sights from getting a bead on her. Keep the windows closed and eyes and ears open in the mountains, and they might have a chance.

"She's determined to go to Tory's party," Cord pointed

out as he stepped back from the car. "She'll fight being hemmed in."

Would she? Grace wasn't suicidal, she'd see the danger she was in now, and he didn't think she'd fight the steps to protect her. As long as she wasn't kept ignorant of the investigation, he didn't think she'd fight as hard as Cord obviously thought she would. And if she did?

If she did, then he'd see to it that she was too tired to fight him.

"Let me get Sawyer and Deke out here." Cord breathed out heavily as he reached up to activate the ear-bud he wore. "The bomb team will be coming over the mountains any minute now. I'll have them put Baer and Banyan with Grace."

Zack shook his head. "I'll get Grace. Get a team ready to move out in my truck, and Grace and I will follow in yours. I want her back at the house, Cord. Now. We'll meet there and consider our options." He gave the other man a hard look. "And check the other vehicles before we leave. Let's make sure Grace's was the only one they got to."

chapter twelve

Sawyer and Deacon hadn't run out of the room because she'd mentioned anything about a reunion; they left because Cord had ordered them to on a private channel that linked into the tiny earbuds they wore for ease of communication in the event of problems.

A channel separate from the one Grace herself wore.

And they'd been called out because her car contained a bomb.

If everyone was so damned convinced she held vital information, then why kill her? It didn't make sense. Even if the information contained evidence against a traitor, then it still didn't make sense. If she had such a thing, then Vince would already have it in hand.

Unless she intended to sell it, as Luce would have done.

Huddled on the couch in her office, she nibbled at her thumbnail, frowning at the problem she faced. Richard

James had believed she was trying to help Luce betray the killer, which was a killing offense.

Where would her father have hidden a Microdrive? A place that hadn't been searched? Perhaps a place she should be able to remember?

Dammit, she'd only been five when he died, and though they'd been close, she hadn't even been aware of what he meant when he said *Kin*. She'd thought he meant "family," the usual definition when the word *kin* was used.

The door to her office opened quickly, revealing Zack as he moved to her. "We're rolling. Let's go," he ordered, gripping her wrist and helping her from the couch before one arm went around her shoulders.

"I needed to check the files—"

"Later." His voice was harder, colder than she'd ever heard it before as he led her into the hall. "Let's get you to the house first, then we'll discuss everything with Vince and your cousins. I want you safe."

She tried to object again. "I'm safe—"

Stopping in the middle of the hall, he swung Grace around, his head bending until he was almost face-to-face with her as he gripped both her shoulders firmly, holding her still. "Now is a really bad time to argue with me, Grace." Icy rage filled his tone and burned in dark, slate-colored eyes. "We're going, and we're going now, before someone has time to stop us."

She didn't have a chance to respond before he was pulling her along again, once again holding her close to him as though shielding her. . . .

Shielding her from a bullet. She was suddenly sick

at the thought. And waiting at the door were her cousins and several Kin. Sidearms rested at their hips, and in their hands they held powerful automatic rifles.

God, this was so bad.

Tears filled her eyes as they surrounded her and Zack and accompanied them quickly to Cord's black pickup. It sat between Zack's, which was almost a replica of it, and another behind it.

After lifting her into the backseat, Zack slid in beside her, while Cord and his most trusted commander, Que, slid into the front, with Que driving.

The black-haired SEAL was one of the most aloof and, Grace had always suspected, most dangerous of her uncle's men.

"We're rolling!" Cord barked, obviously using a private channel on the earbud. "Keep a car length between each vehicle, and let's move fast."

The three trucks tore out of the driveway and hit the main road before increasing speed and racing several miles along the twisting two-lane road before hitting a narrower, less well cared for road.

They were taking the back roads and trails rather than the main roads, with Cord snapping out turns just before coming to them. Before long, even Grace was uncertain exactly where they were, but the bumpy, twisting lanes became little more than dirt trails for a while before the vehicles hit the main road less than a mile from Zack's home.

The drive took longer than a straight route would have, but she knew the reason for their detour. In case of a potential ambush. They wouldn't be expected to move along the back roads, especially if she was in her car, which would have exploded soon after leaving the house.

"Get her in the house with me, then roll out!" Zack ordered as they turned into the driveway. "I'll expect you back tonight, covert cover, one at a time. And bring that fucking computer so she can go through those files. I'll be damned if she'll risk herself by going back to that damned office anytime soon."

The trucks came to a hard stop, and the method they'd used to get her to the vehicle was repeated to get her into Zack's house, where she was pulled to a stop.

"Stay right here," Zack ordered. "Sawyer's with you." He gave her cousin a hard look and nodded toward Grace. "We'll check the house, then you can leave with the rest of them."

Pulling the pistol free of the holster at his hip, Zack was moving through the house along with Cord, Deacon, Que, and Que's second, another SEAL, Garret.

The higher-ranking Kin commanders were part of the mountain force Grace rarely saw. They were normally on security detail at the cabins or lodges scattered over the mountains, and rarely at the main house.

"It's gonna be okay, cuz." Sawyer moved closer, obviously using his larger body to cover her as the others moved through the dark house. "We just want to make sure you're safe."

"By risking yourselves?" she whispered painfully.

Could she survive if Zack or one of her cousins or any of the men who followed them gave their life for her? Could she live with that blood on her conscience?

She couldn't. She knew she couldn't.

Thankfully, the shadowed foyer allowed her to hide the tears she could feel welling in her eyes.

"Look, we wouldn't really hit Zack, you know?" Sawyer told her softly, for what reason she wasn't certain. "We know how you feel about him, Gracie. But, he's hard, ya know—"

"Stop." Lifting one hand helplessly, she could only shake her head at him. "I don't want to talk about this, Sawyer."

She couldn't joke right now; there wasn't anything light enough inside her to allow laughter.

"This is serious," Sawyer protested. "Don't love him, Grace. He'll hurt you. Then we'll have to get mean and take the consequences when you get pissed. Because he knows not to break your heart. If he does, then anything we do is on him, not you."

A teardrop fell. "My heart will break if he's killed because of me," she whispered, the pain so tight, she had to press a hand to her stomach to hold it back. "My heart will break if a single man loses his life for me. Who will pay for it then, Sawyer? I'd gladly have it shattered because he walked away from me instead, don't you know that?"

"But, Grace, you're our sister, the same as Kenni. And we'll do whatever we have to do to protect you, no matter who or what the pain is."

She knew that tone of voice. There was no talking to him. She'd seen Sawyer when he came home after taking a bullet in the shoulder during the four years he'd spent in the marines. He'd laughed about it, joking that the kid he'd taken the bullet for was still in shock. He felt it was his duty, just as Cord and Deacon did, to protect those who were weaker. To protect those they loved. And Zack was no different; he'd proved that when he covered her body with his own while moving her through her uncle's house.

"Clear," Cord called from the kitchen. After the announcement, each man called his own out, upstairs and down, with Deacon exiting the basement Grace had yet to see.

They met at the foyer once again, lights still out, though the sunlight spearing from the windows in the ceiling lit the house beautifully despite the tightly closed curtains.

"We'll be back after dark, cuz. I think Jazz and Kenni are bringing groceries. I put in an order for submarine fixins, if you're in the mood." Cord's trademark cocky grin was in place as he bent and laid a kiss on her forehead. "Be good till I get back, now."

Slipping out the door, followed by the others, Cord left the house. Surprisingly, Que gave her a little nod and a compassionate look before following them and leaving her alone with Zack.

"I think I need to lie down." Her voice was too rough. She could feel the tears, so close to spilling.

She had to get away from him before that weakness showed itself and she completely broke down. She wasn't certain if that break would spill her rage or her pain, though. A combination of both would be simply disastrous.

"Keep the curtains closed. A sniper can't get a heat signature from you as long as you keep them secured. I'll be up later," he promised, his tone rough but quiet.

"There's no need for you to come up, Zack. I'll be

fine," she stated, staring up at him, the thought of what would happen to her if she lost him ripping her to shreds.

Would it even affect him if she died? Other than the general grief of having lost someone he knew? It wasn't as though he would be grieving for someone he'd loved. Her family would grieve, but despite what Sawyer had said, she wasn't a sister to them. She'd always known that.

And in that second, she realized she'd spent so long waiting for Zack that her passing wouldn't be noticed by any man who'd loved her. She didn't have her own family. Her parents were dead—one before she'd even been aware of what the loss meant—and her mother must have truly hated her to put her in this position.

But this man? It would kill her to lose him, it would shatter every corner of her heart, there would be nothing left for anyone else.

Who loved her to that extent?

"Why don't we just stop this charade now," she told him, her voice hoarse. "I'll go to the spare room, and you can sleep alone. There's no sense in making this situation worse for either one of us."

"And what the hell do you mean by that?" He grabbed her arm, holding her in place when she attempted to break free.

"Exactly what I said!" she cried out, fury and pain both escaping. "Six years of waiting for you and being teased by you as though I were no more than a teenage crush that amuses you? Do you think I want in your bed now? That I want to play some kind of damned game just to convince someone else you finally deigned to

come off your fucking high horse long enough to realize I was alive?"

And she could be dead tomorrow.

"Dammit, Grace, that's not the only reason you're
there," he growled, not that the snarly, rough sound
didn't have the power to intimidate her at the moment.

"Like hell. It's exactly why." She pointed her finger
at him, furious at that knowledge. "And it's the only reason, or I wouldn't have lain up there for the past two
nights while you slept like a damned baby. And I won't
do it anymore." She was shaking, horrified at herself and
at the rage exploding from inside her. "No more, Zack.
From here on out, I sleep somewhere else."

"I wouldn't attempt it if I were you." The harsh rasp had
her pausing as she started to turn toward the stairs.

"Really?" she drawled, flicking a glance over him
and taking in the impressive erection those jeans were
doing little to hide. "If you were me, Zack, you'd know
that staying and dealing with the bullshit wasn't in your
best interest." She made certain her smile was anything
but polite. "Perhaps later."

Or next week.

Or next year.

Sometime after she managed to forgive him for leaving her hanging and reneging on that promise he'd made
to show her how good he could be. She should have
known better, she scolded herself. Men rarely kept their
promises; she should have learned that lesson by now.

"Perhaps we ought not tempt my patience," he warned
her rather than letting her go.

Perhaps they ought not tempt his patience?

She stared back at him, feeling that crack in her self-control widening as her anger surged past her common sense. "Your patience can go straight to hell, Zack," she informed him, lips curling in contempt, heat flooding her face in waves. "Better yet, you and your patience can fuck yourselves, because I'm tired of dealing with both of you!" She turned and stalked to the steps, trembling with the anger, fear, and furious, ever-present sexual heat.

His patience?

She should worry about his patience?

He should worry about her baseball bat connecting with his—

She was swept off the floor, tossed over his shoulder with enough care not to pull at the stitches in her leg, but firm enough to hold her in place, and before she could make sense of exactly what he was doing, he was striding up the stairs.

"You bastard . . ." Her fist struck his muscled ass.

His hand connected with her bottom, and the sting should have enraged her. It did enrage her. Sure it did. Right after it went straight to her clit, slammed into her belly, and stole her breath.

Shock.

Excitement.

Maybe anger.

Anger, she decided, as soon as she figured out why the hell that slap had excited her with a dark, burning heat, to leave her trembling and all too aware of the fact that they were heading for his bedroom.

chapter thirteen

They needed to talk, Zack tried to remind himself as Grace bounced on his bed, her flushed, furious expression only fueling the lust he was fighting to hold back.

Damn her. He could have lost her today. He could have lost that bright spot in his life that he always looked for and tried so hard to protect. From him, from the truth. And she had no idea what truths he still hadn't found a way to tell her.

It was like that first break in a dam.

The pressure was just too much, the need pushing against that fracture in his control, slamming against it, determined to be free.

Going over to her before she could lift herself into sitting position, Zack had his nose within inches of hers, the weight of his body straddling her on the mattress as he braced his hands next to her shoulders. "Stop pushing me, Grace," he warned her, feeling desires he'd refused

to consider with her. "You will not like the consequences."

Sweet, unimposing, tactful Grace glared up at him
rather than dropping her eyes and avoiding this particular confrontation.

He should have expected it. He should have known
he'd never be this attracted to a woman he could easily
control, even in bed. But sweet heaven, this just wasn't
a situation where she wanted to assert her own stubborn
willfulness.

"No doubt!" she snapped back, pushing at his shoulders. "Considering the fact I'm beginning not to like
you." The dark ire burning in her gaze was like a red
cape to a bull in rut. Son of a bitch.

They needed to talk. He needed to explain what was
going on, at least prepare her for what might be coming
before he took her into his bed and tried to quench the
lust tearing through him. At this rate, he'd end up fucking them both stupid rather than explaining a damned
thing. And stupid wasn't where he needed to be once the
subject of the true extent of the danger surrounding her
was broached.

"Let me up, you overgrown oaf!" She pushed at his
shoulders again, snarling up at him when he refused to
move.

"Overgrown oaf?" He glared down at her. "That's
what you call those morons your girlfriends run with."
That much he knew about her. The few friends she had
rarely dated men she didn't call morons.

Her smile was so damned mocking, it set his back
teeth on edge.

"Well, now, that should tell you something, shouldn't it?" she snarled up at him, displaying her teeth much the same way her pet did. With a little curl of her lip and the promise of retribution in her eyes.

It told him that Grace was far less cautious where he was concerned than she should have been in this particular situation.

"Grace . . ." he tried to warn her.

"Do you know, Zack, I think I'm just entirely sick of dealing with you and your damned hot again, cold again attitude," she informed him, despite the feminine lust burning in her eyes. "And I'm really sick of being teased like some damned schoolgirl virgin. Get off me or fuck me already, because I have things to do."

Grace wasn't certain what she'd expected.

Hell, she didn't even know what made her say something so outrageous.

It was the truth, though. She was tired of being teased by him, sick of having him pull her toward him only to have him push her away again. She was beginning to feel like a damned yo-yo.

She didn't expect the sudden rending of the silk blouse straight down the front, though, or the lash of white-hot sensation that burned through her senses as Zack brushed the edges of the shirt aside and with a flick of his fingers released her bra.

"Teasing again?" she asked, trembling beneath him. "I don't have time for it—"

"Make time." His voice was harsh, a rasp of primal male lust and intent.

Before she could reply, his lips were covering hers, his tongue parting them and surging inside in a kiss that claimed, that branded her and left her reeling.

Sensation washed through her body as his hands stroked and caressed, removing the rest of her clothes, removing his own as his lips worked over hers and drugged her with a dark, greedy hunger she had no idea how to control.

She didn't even know if she wanted to control it.

Once he had her naked, the fact that she was bare beneath his heavier, harder body didn't register. Self-consciousness had always plagued her when contemplating sex with anyone else. The thought of being naked, of having their eyes on her always bothered her. The thought of being naked now, of having Zack's hands on her only amplified the sensuality washing through her.

Just as it gave rise to a curiosity about his body that she'd never felt before. She wanted to touch him.

The feel of the powerful muscles of his back shifting beneath her fingers was incredible. She could feel the tight, lust-taut ripple of movement beneath his flesh and let her nails scrape over it.

His kiss deepened at the caress, pulling a whimpering sound of pleasure from her lips that she knew she'd never made in her life. Pleasure surrounded her, infused her. The feel of his larger, harder body covering her sent a feeling of feminine, sensual weakness surging through her, and it went to her head like a narcotic.

"God, Grace." His lips slid from hers to her jaw, where he spread stinging kisses down along the column of her neck as his tongue licked against her flesh. "Keep touching me, baby. Show me how much you like it."

Her nails clenched against his back involuntarily. Arching to his wandering lips as they stroked from the curve of one breast to the other, she could feel her nipples growing harder, more sensitive as his lips moved closer.

"Like it a lot, do you?" he asked, the guttural tone of his voice another caress to her senses. "Talk to me, Grace. Let me know how you feel."

Let him know how she felt?

She was supposed to think? To actually form words? She didn't think she could—

"Should I stop?" he questioned her, his lips pausing just above one hard, aching peak.

"No!" Grace shook her head, desperate now. "No. Don't stop."

She arched beneath him, the feel of her nipple stroking over his lips—or was it his lips stroking over her nipple?—had another of those whimpering little sounds spilling from her lips.

"Tell me how you like it," he demanded again, and this time, the heated stroke of his tongue over the tight point was a deliberate promise of pleasure. "I wouldn't want to do anything you don't like."

The suggestiveness in his tone was simply wicked. Dark, demanding, the assurance he would stop if she didn't find a way to speak—

"Oh God!" The cry tore from her as his teeth captured one hard bud, exerting just enough pressure that the wave of pulsating pleasure that rushed through her and left her breathless. "I like that. I like it. . . ."

"Hmmm." A low sound of approval vibrated against the bundle of nerves with a lash of added sensation.

"Good girl." He kissed her nipple, licked over it. "What about this?"

Grace's hands jerked to his hair. Moist, brilliant heat surrounded the pebble-hard bud and sent fingers of such violent sensitivity racing through her that she found herself suspended within the lush promise of complete ecstasy.

"So good," she moaned, her head grinding into the blankets beneath her as Zack held her arching hips to the bed by lowering more of his weight between her thighs.

She loved it. Loved feeling him so close to her, restraining her as she fought for pleasure.

"More." Instinct guided her, formed the words, and made the sounds. "Harder, Zack. Do it harder."

His tongue lashed at the painfully hard tip before the inner heat of his mouth began sucking at her with firm, hungry pulls that sent those fingers of electric sensation to race harder, faster straight to the clenched depths of her womb.

Mewls of pleasure spilled from her as his lips moved from one hard nipple to the other, torturing each with the steadily building tension and rapid-fire arcs of sensation whipping through her.

"No. Don't stop." Desperation filled her voice as the hard, fiery draws of his mouth were suddenly gone. "Zack—"

"It's okay, baby." He caught her hand with his and drew it to her breast. "Let me see you do it. Work those pretty nipples for me, Grace. Let me see how good you like it."

Her thumb and forefinger found the aching point of

one nipple before he caught her other hand and made it do likewise.

"Show me, baby," he demanded, voice harsh. "Work those tight little nipples, and we'll see how good I can work that hard little clit with my tongue."

Sensation detonated in her stomach, jerking her tight with such an increase in erotic need that she could barely breathe. Her fingers tightened on her nipples, the sharp pleasure tearing a moan from her lips as Zack began kissing his way down the center of her body.

"How do you like that pretty clit touched, Grace?" The sandpapery sound of his voice pulled her deeper into the dark, brutally sensual storm gathering through her. "Come on. Tell me how you like it."

How did she like it?

She was supposed to know how she liked it?

"No one—" She jerked as a whisper of breath stroked over the swollen bud. "Wouldn't let anyone . . ."

She was shaking, so eager to feel his lips there that it was all she could do to keep from screaming with the agonizing hunger for it.

"You wouldn't let anyone?" Low, vibrating with lust, the question whispered around her. "Why wouldn't you let anyone?" Callused hands parted her thighs further, pushing them wide just before she felt the first touch of his fingers against the bare, saturated folds of her sex.

"Why, Grace?" he questioned again. "Why wouldn't you let anyone eat this sweet, pretty pussy?"

"I thought of you . . ." she panted, shudders of pleasure tearing through her. "I kept thinking of you—"

Her hands slapped to the bed.

Her fingers curled into the blankets, and a cry of

agonizing need whispering past her as lips suddenly surrounded her clit, drawing on it with hungry demand and burning through any resistance that might have remained.

There was no thought of resisting him, though. No will to do so.

Nothing existed for Grace but this. Nothing else mattered.

Her fingers moved of their own volition, stroking and tugging at her nipples, creating rapid-fire blasts of pleasure-pain to add to the stimulation of her already violently sensitive clit.

Just when she thought she'd explode, when she was certain the tight, hungry draws of his mouth would throw her completely into orgasm, it was gone.

She couldn't protest, couldn't demand more.

His tongue slid through the heavy layers of slick moisture to burrow between the swollen folds. He rimmed the entrance, licking at her with hungry strokes and short, teasing dips into the clenched tissue of her vagina while his hands cupped her buttocks, lifting her to his mouth and giving himself greater access.

"Tell me!" he snapped, momentarily halting the assault against her senses. "Tell me how it feels. What you want. Tell me or by God, I swear I'll stop. . . ."

Zack was tortured. The dark excess of need whipped through him, breaking free of the bonds that normally controlled it. The hungers he'd always tried to keep reined in spilled through him and focused on the too delicate, far too innocent young woman he'd sworn to himself he'd never release them on.

Lowering his head once again, he let his tongue take the swollen flesh, licking through the plump folds and the sweetest feminine cream he'd ever tasted. It spilled from her pussy like nectar, slick and hot. His cock throbbed between his thighs, the taste of her swelling the already hard flesh.

"More," she finally cried out in response to his demand. "More with your tongue . . . fuck me, Zack . . . with your tongue . . . please . . ."

Her hips arched, and he lifted her and sent his tongue thrusting inside the clenched, rippling entrance, the taste of her inner juices drugging his senses. She was tight, hot. Her inner flesh tugged at each licking thrust as her cries of pleasure spurred the brutal hunger ripping through him.

"Yes . . ." she hissed as he drew his tongue back and began working two fingers inside the clenched sheath, groaning at the snug grip surrounding them.

Licking, tasting her, Zack moved back to the swollen bud of her clit, feeling it throb beneath his tongue as he surrounded the responsive bundle of flesh with his lips and drew it into his mouth once again.

She was coming apart beneath his touch. He could feel her beginning to unravel, feel the tension growing inside her, perspiration building on her flesh as she arched into each rapid thrust of his fingers into her pussy.

Too tight.

Ah fuck, she was so tight. And his cock had never been thicker, never been harder than it was right now.

Never in his life had Zack been so primed and ready to fuck or so aware of the fact that the flesh he would be fucking into was so damned tight.

Not yet, he ordered himself, his tongue stroking the rapid throb of her clit, feeling it pulse and tighten as she grew closer to orgasm. Let her come first, let her body adjust. Sweet God, let him get a handle on the hunger tearing his senses apart.

"So good," Grace cried out as he added another finger to the first two pushing inside her. "Zack." Her hips arched, aching need filling the whimpering cry. "More. Oh yes, more . . . It's so good. So good, Zack . . ."

Ah hell, he was losing it. He could feel it.

Control was sinking beneath pure lust-crazed pleasure as her pussy rippled around his thrusting fingers and her clit pulsed against his tongue. And in that second, a low, agonized cry tore from her lips as he felt her orgasm slam through her.

Her hips flexed in rapid little thrusts against his pumping fingers as her vagina clamped down and the heated wash of her release slickened the inner flesh further.

Pulling his hand back, he released her clit from the suction of his mouth and rose between her thighs, the fingers of one hand gripping the base of his erection in a desperate grip.

"Look at me," he growled, lust becoming a frenzy of need as he fought to hold back just enough to keep from hurting her. "Watch me, Grace. Watch me fuck that pretty pussy."

Dazed, heavy-lidded, her gaze fell between her spread thighs, and then her eyes widened at the sight of the thick crest parting the glistening folds.

"Are you sure?" Some inner demon had to open its

mouth and voice that question. "Be sure, Grace. Once I start burying my dick inside you, it's going to be too late to say no."

Fiery, slick, her juices spilled over the engorged crest, the lash of sensation overriding the last fragile thread he was holding on to reality with. His hips jerked, the flared head of his cock surging inside her, parting her, and rocking his senses with the heat and brutal pleasure that suddenly surrounded the too-sensitive crest.

Grace couldn't breathe.

The sudden explosion of pleasure-pain tearing through her senses stole her ability to draw in air, to think, or to reason. Her neck arched, eyes closing as sensation overwhelmed her, drawing her muscles tight as spirals of ecstasy began racing through her body.

Her sexual experience was limited, her ability to process such an overload of pleasure nonexistent. Each push and retreat of the thick flesh invading her was like a lash of burning ecstasy. Each thrust took him deeper, stretched her further, and stole more of her mind. Nothing mattered but taking more of him, taking him deeper and experiencing more of the destructive power building inside her.

"Fuck, Grace," he groaned, his lips lowering to her ear as she fought to breathe, to survive the sensations overtaking her. "You're so fucking tight, baby. So sweet and hot . . ."

Her body responded to the added pleasure of the harsh declaration by spilling more of the slick moisture as he pushed deeper inside her. Each forging thrust stretched her inner flesh, sent those rapid-fire shots of fiery sensation to tighten further through her body as the brilliant pleasure-pain built with each hard stroke.

"That's it, baby," he groaned, nipping her ear. "Tighten on me. Milk my cock just like that, Grace. Fuck, you're killing me."

He was killing her. He was destroying her with the building rapture.

Each stroke inside her too-sensitive inner flesh, each stretching, painfully intense thrust seared her senses, until with one heavy, powerful lunge, he was buried to the hilt, the rapid pulse and throb of the engorged crest vibrating in the very depths of her.

Grace shook in the grip of the pleasure tearing through her now. She was stretched so tight around him that pleasure and pain mixed and mingled until she didn't know which was which. She didn't care. She just wanted more.

And Zack was more than willing to give her more.

As if finally burying his full length inside her loosened some restraint he'd imposed on himself, a strangled groan rumbled from his chest as he pulled back, pausing as the head of his cock slid partially free of her, then thrusting hard and deep inside her again.

Her breath caught again, the storm whipping through her nearly violent in its intensity. Her entire body was sensitized now, the tension deepening with each thrust and tearing her further from herself and into ecstasy.

"That's it, baby." He pushed faster, harder inside her. The sound of flesh moving against flesh and his voice becoming deeper, darker were all she knew as she felt herself unraveling.

"Zack . . ." Her hands gripped his shoulders, fighting to find some hold on reality causing her nails to dig into his flesh.

"That's it, baby, let me have you," he groaned, the pace of his thrusts speeding up. "Let me have you, Grace. Come for me, baby. Ah, fuck . . . come for me, Grace . . . Now."

Now.

The firestorm building inside her exploded. White-hot, blinding, her hips jerked into his, taking his cock deeper, harder, a fiery pulse of heat echoing in the depths of her vagina. She was lost in the violent eruptions of ecstasy detonating through her senses.

Shudders raced over her, through her.

She was jerked into a place of such rapture, of sensations that were both pleasure and pain, hot and cold. They merged, blended, until Grace could do nothing but hold on to Zack and let the storm rage through her.

As Zack fought to catch his breath, to pull his senses back from the savage pleasure filling him, he knew he'd made a grave error where Grace and his response to her were concerned. He should have known that years of hunger, of unrelenting need for one woman could be destructive. He should just have fucked her years ago rather than remaining at the periphery of her life, hungering for her like an animal that had never known warmth or caring while she represented the last hope for it.

Even now, letting her go, moving away from her, took an amount of effort he didn't think he'd manage to conjure up. The fact that he was able to lift himself from her and ease his still sensitive flesh from the grip she had on it amazed him.

Rolling to her side, he was preparing to lift himself from the bed when she slid easily against his side and snuggled in, a little shiver racing over her. Automatically, Zack tugged the comforter over her and held her to him, frowning at the gesture. It wasn't like him to let a woman cuddle after sex. It made them get strange ideas. Ideas that they could stay, that more than sex might hold them together.

With any other woman, he would already have been out of the bed and in the shower, cheerfully easing himself out of his lover's home. Because he had never, at any time, fucked a woman in his own bed.

The guest room, a few times, though not often. He much preferred their beds, because escape was easier and less messy. So what the hell was he doing lying here with his arm wrapped securely around Grace and allowing her to slip deeper into sleep?

Going crazy was what he was doing, he admitted. Because holding her to him and allowing her to sleep against him weren't his first mistake. They weren't even the worst mistake. Hell no, he'd committed a far graver error by allowing himself to slip inside the fist-tight grip of her sex without a condom. Then he'd compounded that error with each violent eruption of his semen inside her.

He stared up at the ceiling with a frown. And he wasn't even shaking in fear or going through any of the other responses he would have expected when doing something so insane.

He'd never spilled himself inside a woman. Never had

he taken the chance that an innocent life could pay for his sins. Until now.

Until Grace.

The fact that he was complicating his life no longer escaped his notice, no more than he'd missed the fact that he'd made sure they landed in his bed rather than in the guest room.

The fact that it took so long for the act to register only elicited a resigned sigh.

He'd search for his sanity after Grace woke. Until then, he could probably use a nap himself. Keeping up with Grace while keeping her safe wasn't going to be easy. It wasn't going to be comfortable. And keeping the emotional aspects of it out of the mix wouldn't be easy at all.

It was Grace, after all.

She was nothing if not emotional, it seemed.

She inspired emotion, even in him. Emotion he was definitely going to have to guard against.

No matter the consequences.

chapter fourteen

He was dressed when she awoke.

Like a cat burglar.

Black pants, shirt, and boots. Leaning against the wall, with the low light on the bed table casting long, sinister shadows around him as he stared at her silently. The expression on his face was pensive in the low light—brooding, perhaps.

"Well, I'm going to guess the postcoital bliss has passed," she stated, sitting up in the bed and staring around the darkened bedroom.

The fact that she was still naked, not quite awake nor entirely focused, wasn't lost on her.

But he was entirely too focused now. And that wasn't a good sign.

"Something's come up—I have to leave the house for a while."

Something came up, huh? More like someone was desperate to run.

"Then go." She waved him to the door. "Why wait until I woke?"

"Que and Garret will be in the house, along with two Brigham agents, Calli and Lobo. You'll be safe until I get back." And his expression never changed.

Sawyer had warned her not to love Zack. He should have warned her years ago.

"Fine. Why are you waiting, then? Just leave already." So she could cry or rage or shower or something. So she'd be alone to process this emotional roller coaster.

Instead, he was just standing there.

"What, Zack?" she demanded, keeping her voice low. "What are you waiting for?"

"I forgot to wear a condom," he told her, the unemotional tone of his voice giving little clue to how he might feel about it.

She was guessing he wasn't pleased by that tidbit of information. And she'd be damned if she knew what to feel about it herself.

"I see." She cleared her throat uncomfortably. "I gather that doesn't happen often?"

She should have guessed, she told herself. It was okay to fuck a Maddox, but the risk of a lifetime connection to one was quite another story. Especially a connection involving a child.

"First time," he admitted, sliding his hands into the black slacks he wore, his gaze revealing little.

She nodded, holding the sheet to her breasts as the ache in her heart refused to abate. "Well, isn't it a good thing I don't leave it to my partners to keep me from getting pregnant." Flipping the blanket back, she slid her legs from the mattress before rising. "No worries at all.

Though I'd do something about that faulty memory of yours. It could end up getting you in trouble at some point."

Zack watched as she strode from the bedroom—chin lifted, her expression composed despite her anger—and restrained a sigh. Not that he could blame her for being offended. Wasn't that what he'd intended?

"True." Straightening from the wall, he followed her from the bedroom, unable to keep from staring at the bare, sensual curve of her ass.

She did have a pretty ass. Perfectly curved with just enough plumpness to tempt a man's hands and his common sense.

"Stop staring at my ass, Zack," she ordered as she paused at the dresser, pulled open a drawer, and removed a pair of sexy silk panties and some outfit that looked soft and far too loose for her delicate frame.

"You have a nice ass," he pointed out. "It's hard not to stare."

"When you're letting all those prick tendencies of yours out to play, then you can keep your eyes to yourself," she ordered once more, striding to the bathroom. "Close the door on your way out to your meeting or whatever." Pausing at the doorway, she turned and shot him a hard, mocking smile. "Have fun."

His brow arched. "Your cousins will be there—the best I'll get by with is not getting hit."

"I wouldn't bet on it," she muttered as she turned away and entered the bathroom, closing the door behind her.

If he wasn't mistaken, she locked it as well.

He'd wanted the distance between them, hadn't he? So why did he feel like a complete ass? It had worked better with other women, so what happened this time? Because she wasn't just a little put out; she was frankly pissed off. No, she was hurt, and he knew it.

He hated it.

His dick wasn't happy with him either.

Surprise, surprise.

Son of a bitch, he'd come like fireworks. He should have been drained at least until morning.

Shaking his head, he turned and left the room, closing the door behind him. Downstairs waited Kin militia members Zack trusted implicitly, Dylan and Eamon, who were also Navy SEALs. They were dressed in black, armed, and ready to leave the house.

The two agents he was most wary of, though not for security reasons, waited as well. Lobo was better trained than most Kin, and Calli, though years younger, could hold her own even at eighteen. They were seated comfortably in the living room, Lobo sprawled out in the recliner, feet up, while Calli glared at him.

She spent a lot of time glaring at Lobo.

"She's taking a shower," he told the two as Dylan and Eamon waited at the door.

"You tell her you were leaving?" Calli asked, her expression knowing as she stared back at him mockingly. Short black hair framed her delicate face while pretty grayish blue eyes watched him knowingly. The eyes and hair were her mother's; her features, though delicate and feminine, were much like her father's.

"She knows I have a meeting, that's all. And she better not learn who it's with."

She rolled her green eyes at the deceitfulness. "Really, Zack?"

"Really, Calli," he assured her warningly. "If she comes down, she better not know a damned bit more than she knows now."

"Fifty bucks says he pissed her off enough to ensure she probably remains in her room," Lobo drawled without opening his eyes. "Bad Zack. Very bad. I'm ashamed."

"I'm heartbroken," Zack grunted, nodding to the other two men. "We'll be back in a few hours. You met Kate and Lara. They should still be in the kitchen with Garret. Que and the rest of his team are patrolling the grounds."

Calli just shook her head at him as Eamon opened the door and Zack left the house.

Fine, he should have told Grace the truth by now. Hell, Vince should have told her. He'd planned to. Until he began to suspect she'd start demanding answers to questions he didn't want her asking. And once Grace decided there were questions to be asked, no one was safe.

Yeah, avoiding that was pretty damned important.

"Cord, Sawyer, and Deacon are on the move," Dylan reported as they neared the Jeep parked away from the house. "Looks like they're heading toward Kingston."

"Keep track of them," Zack ordered him. "Let me know when they head back for the meeting here."

And they would change direction, he knew. Cord wasn't heading to Kingston, and Zack knew it. It would be interesting to see where the Maddox brothers were headed, though.

Starting the Jeep, lights out, Zack put the vehicle in gear and headed along the dirt road leading into the mountains around them.

"Tech says they have a tail." Dylan relayed the report from the technical genius working the drone flying above the Maddox vehicle. "Black van, no plates, running lights out."

That sounded like a tail to him.

"Can the drone get close enough to identify the driver?" he asked the other man.

"Tech says no, not without revealing the hardware," Dylan answered.

"Let's keep the hardware hidden," Zack drawled. "I'd hate to lose the only advantage we have. Keep tailing them, make sure they're not doubling back."

"Clyde's going to get curious about that tail," Eamon pointed out as he leaned forward. "You know how he gets."

Yeah, Zack knew how he got. His uncle was incredibly nosy.

"Then don't tell him," Zack ordered. "He doesn't have to know everything."

The problem was, Clyde invariably managed to learn everything, though, just as Alexander did. Zack just liked Clyde better.

"Don't mean he won't find out," Eamon chuckled. "Probably already knows . . ."

No doubt, Zack thought fatalistically. That would be just his luck, now, wouldn't it?

Grace paced the floors, worried, fumed, and silently cursed while waiting for the sound of the vehicle to return. A Jeep, she guessed when she'd first heard it, just after stepping into the hall in time to see Zack leaving.

Dressed in black and armed, just as the other two

men were. And he hadn't even been nice enough to tell her where he was going.

She didn't let it disconcert her when she went downstairs for a late snack and found the couple—armed and a bit surprised by her appearance—as they lounged in the front room.

The other woman hid her grin and rose to her feet, one hand resting on the holster of the handgun strapped to her thigh. "Zack's umm . . ."

"Not here." Grace nodded. "Yeah, I heard him leave."

The couple exchanged glances. The man gave a little grunt, leaned his head back on the chair, and closed his eyes again.

"You're a lot of help," the girl muttered before turning back to Grace with a wide smile. "I'm Calliope, but this mess over here calls me Calli." She grinned, gesturing to the dozing man. "He's Lobo. We're friends of Zack's."

And for all her friendliness, Calli, as she called herself, didn't care much for Grace's presence there, evidently. But it wasn't the typical jealousy of an interested woman for a man she couldn't have. Because Zack would never take a teenager to his bed. No, this was different. It was equal parts curiosity, anger, and fear.

Grace wasn't a threat to Calli. Calli considered Grace a definite threat for some reason, though.

"No doubt," Grace sighed. "I'm going to go see what he has in the kitchen for a late supper. Hungry?"

Lobo's eyes opened quickly, the mention of food giving his gaze an avaricious gleam.

"He's always hungry," Calli snickered, and shrugged. "Sure, supper sounds great. I'll help if you like?"

"Let's just hope Jazz and Kenni actually made it here with the food," Grace suggested, heading for the dimly lit room in question.

"Sure they did, but Zack does actually keep food in stock," Calli promised with a little wave of her hand, sauntering past Grace with a smile. "Hard to believe, huh, with all those hard muscles?"

Grace stopped just inside the kitchen and stared at the young woman knowingly.

Another bright smile curled the Cupid's bow lips as Calli faced her, the cheerful innocence in her expression so false, it was sickening.

"He's a prick, too arrogant for his own good, and before he and I part ways, I intend to castrate him with one of his own kitchen knives," Grace stated conversationally. "After that, do with him as you will." She looked to Lobo's bland face, then back to the laughter in Calli's gaze. "So, since you evidently know where everything is, what's for dinner?"

The laughter in the other girl's slowly widening eyes stilled instantly as her expression filled with amazed distaste. "I'm not the one who mentioned food." Calli shrugged her slim shoulders. "But I wouldn't get too cozy here—Zack doesn't keep women for long, you know."

"Good, I won't have to stay long," Grace assured her. "Anything else, you'll have to take up with Zack, not me." All Grace cared about at this point was something to eat, not some starry-eyed crush this kid had.

"A real woman fights her own battles," the younger woman muttered as Grace walked by her.

Pausing in her tracks, Grace couldn't help but laugh

at that statement. "No, honey, a real woman doesn't play such childish little games to begin with," she told Calli gently. "You care for him, I get that. And I'm sure you're none too happy with the problems I've brought into his life, neither am I. But I'm not his enemy, nor am I yours. Now, if you'll excuse me, I'm really starved."

Something flashed in the other girl's eyes, something almost envious and conflicted. "I really don't like you," Calli breathed out, glaring at Grace now.

Calli didn't dislike her, not really; there was a difference between that and not wanting to like someone. Calli didn't want to like Grace. She didn't want to be polite and nice; she had something to say, but it was something she had no intention of saying, if the tension at the side of her lips and eyes was any indication.

"And that really breaks my heart," Grace assured her. "But I'm still going to eat, if for no other reason than because I haven't eaten all day and I need a sandwich."

"You're really cold, huh?" Calli asked then, ignoring Lobo's warning mutter to "shut the hell up."

"You know." Grace remained relaxed, watchful, her arms at her sides, her feet firmly planted. "This has been a really shitty week for me. I don't know you, so I don't have to consider whether or not you have any qualities I might deem likable, and first impressions are everything. So get the hell off my ass or I promise you, I won't let your obvious youth or your no-doubt-justified animosity stand between me and the very grown-up asswhipping I'll give you. Are we clear?"

Calli gave a triumphant little smile before doing something really dumb. "Lobo? Aren't you going to do something?" Calli turned to her partner or whatever the hell he was as though he were supposed to defend her.

He watched the confrontation silently, his dark gray eyes narrowed, his expression thoughtful despite Calli's anger and Grace's chastisement before saying. "A real woman fights her own battles, remember?"

Grace only shook her head. "My aunt Sierra once said the mark of a true lady was the ability to accept when she's wrong—"

"I never claimed to be a fucking lady, now, did I?" Resentment filled the girl's expression and her tone when she turned back to Grace.

Whatever she was holding back, whatever animosity or supposed slight she thought Grace had dealt her was on the edge of her lips, ready to spill amid the clash of anger and pain in her expression.

"At least you're not a liar." Grace shrugged. "Yet."

Calli's lips tightened further, and a war waged in her gray-blue eyes. "What, your father never gave you any advice? Just your aunt?" Calli drawled, watching Grace closely. "Mine always told me to avoid vipers. Like you."

Grace didn't speak. She just watched the younger girl, took in the signs of secrecy and hurt. There was nothing left to say now, nothing that could ever change what had already come out of Calli's mouth.

"Calli." Lobo said her name softly, with apparent gentleness despite the warning.

"She started it when she made Zack feel like he had to protect her." Calli turned to him, her hands propped on her hips, glaring at Lobo now. "And I don't like her threats."

Grace kept her emotions at bay, simply watched Lobo and Calli now. The man was much better at hiding his emotions, but Grace was able to identify the small signs of emotion he did display. There was that tiniest hint of regret and compassion in the lines next to his gray eyes.

"Sorry, baby." Lobo shook his head, his expression firm. "It's not a threat. She's tougher than you think she is. Besides, you attacked first. Now, let it go."

Calli didn't even argue. Her lips thinned, her expression setting into lines of complete stubbornness and determination. Turning on her heel, she stalked from the room.

Silence filled the kitchen for long moments as Lobo watched Grace then, those calm, dark gray eyes assessing but lacking condemnation. Stepping past him, she continued her search for food.

"She's a good kid," Lobo stated behind her, his quiet voice causing Grace to turn back to him slowly. "Zack's a good friend, and she worries."

Yes, Calli was very worried, very resentful, and the other girl obviously didn't like feeling that way, but neither did she know how to handle it.

"As you said, she's a kid," Grace agreed. "Which doesn't explain why she's here, a gun strapped to her thigh and murder in her eyes. She's involved in something that could get her killed. Is that what you want?"

For some reason, the thought of someone so young facing the choice of killing a man with that gun she carried or being killed herself was so damned saddening, it just pissed Grace off.

"That part actually worries me the least," he admitted with a weary quirk of a smile. "I'd trust Calli to protect my back over many others. But she can get a little emotional over friends."

In other words, the fact that Calli was too young to play such dangerous games was none of Grace's business. And he was right; it wasn't her business. Grace told herself she needed to keep it that way.

"As long as she keeps that gun in place where I'm concerned." Grace stalked to the refrigerator, shaking her head at the man and at the young woman playing adult in ways she shouldn't be. "Hell, who knew Zack had such a complicated life? I haven't even heard rumors of strange military types and teenagers with guns running around, protecting all his muscles like some sister with a brat complex," she muttered to herself. "I should shoot Cord for not warning me."

"Cord and Zack are actually a lot alike," Lobo drawled.

Grace pulled cold cuts, mayo, and mustard from inside the fridge and carried them to the counter, where a wrapped loaf of bread sat. "Too much alike," Grace agreed. "They should be best friends rather than casual enemies."

She'd thought that many times over the past years. And she even suspected that at one time, they might have been—

"They were, as kids." Lobo's revelation had Grace freezing as her thoughts and his statement collided. She waited, drawing in a deep breath before she turned to where he was leaning against the counter several feet from her.

"I didn't know that either," she sighed, turning back to the food to hide the confusion she felt.

"When they were boys," Lobo told her. "Until the night Zack's parents were murdered. He blamed the Maddox family for a long time, and that included Cord."

That was where the conflict began, she guessed. Another mark against her.

"I know he once believed my family was somehow responsible for it," she breathed out roughly, regret a bitter taste in her mouth. "Is that why their friendship ended?"

Crossing his ankles as he leaned against the counter, Lobo contemplated the tips of his boots for long moments, frowning, she suspected, over what to say at that point.

Grace made her sandwich, saying nothing more and guessing the answers might be more than she wanted to hear at the moment.

"There are a lot of secrets in this area," Lobo finally said softly. "Connections and bonds no one could imagine, and tragedies that would break even a hard man's heart. Those secrets, though." He paused for a moment. "They're just as deadly now as they were when they began. Just because one doesn't know certain parts of the past they're part of, or their parents' pasts, doesn't mean it can't endanger them."

She slid a sandwich to Lobo, left one for Calli, then picked up her own before facing him. "I'm very well aware of that," she said wearily, watching him closely, making herself pay attention, making herself catch those little signs that feed suspicion and pull the truth from the subconscious. "Stop beating around the bush, Lobo. It doesn't become you."

"That bush might save my life, though," he admitted

with a rather sexy little wink meant to distract her. "I hear you're a smart young woman—figure it out. And stop just accepting what you're told. Always look beyond the obvious. It might end up saving your life."

It wasn't the first time she'd heard such advice.

Lobo bit into his sandwich, watching closely as Calli reentered the room.

"Zack's returning," she informed him with none of her earlier animosity; instead, there was a little hint of remorse. Remorse and trepidation. "We need to meet him outside."

Lobo tore off several paper towels, wrapped one around his sandwich and then another around Calli's before nodding to Grace and leaving the room.

Calli waited until he disappeared into the other room before meeting her gaze. "I apologize for my earlier attitude." She propped her hands on her hips and gave a frustrated sigh. "I care for Zack. I worry."

Grace stared back at her, feeling those threads, suspicions, and connections she wished she could ignore. "Good enough." Grace nodded. "Consider it forgotten."

Calli nodded, too, fidgeted for a moment, then met her gaze once again. "I've heard a lot about your aunt Sierra," she said somberly. "You remind me of those stories. From what I understand, she was a very good woman. A compassionate woman, but tough as hell. And so are you."

Tears flooded Grace's eyes before she blinked them back hastily and gave the other girl a thankful smile. "She was the best," Grace whispered, clearing her throat. "I miss her."

Calli nodded again, rubbed at the back of her neck,

then turned and strode from the kitchen without giving voice to whatever she so longed to say. Moments later, the sound of the front door closing signaled that she and Lobo had both left.

Her uncle Vince always said her strength was in her ability to see and hear things others didn't catch, or weren't really on guard for. It came naturally to her. So naturally that the suspicions now beginning to form couldn't be immediately pushed aside as coincidence.

She doubted they could ever be pushed aside as coincidence. The implications of what she'd seen and what she'd heard in the shifting tones of voice and the flash of certain emotions in both Calli's and Lobo's expressions bothered her far too deeply.

Could the betrayals from those she loved go so far? . . .

She was being used as a pawn; she'd known that all along. Now she just had to figure out why.

Just as she had to figure out how to deal with the pain of those betrayals.

chapter fifteen

Zack listened to Lobo's report and felt a disappointment he hadn't wanted to feel. As Lobo spoke, Zack turned to Calliope, his gaze meeting the painful, conflicting emotions in hers. The remorse and pain in her eyes weren't going to get her out of trouble, though. He'd warned her before he ever allowed her to play a part in protecting Grace.

In the past few years, Calli had developed an animosity for Grace that made no sense, considering the fact that Calli had never been in the area until now. Her parents were at a loss for the reason why, and Calli never explained it. She had promised him it wouldn't interfere in her job, though, and he'd believed her.

His mistake, Zack acknowledged; he wouldn't make it again.

"She realized she was wrong, Zack," Lobo stated, his voice low. "She made it right."

She made it right, had she?

Lobo was always quick to defend Calli, just as he was quick to inform her when he thought she was wrong. The problem was, Lobo was beginning to develop a problem with others letting her know she was wrong.

"Don't look at me like that, Zack," Calli whispered, distressed as he simply stared at her. "I should have had more control—"

"Should have had more control?" he asked her carefully. "Is that all you can say, Calli? Is control all you lacked tonight? If that were true, then I wouldn't be nearly so concerned about it."

Her lips thinned, jaw clenching as she turned away from him and shoved her hands into her back pockets, refusing to hold his gaze. "I'm justified . . ." she finally protested, still refusing to look him in the eye.

"Justified?" Zack blinked down at her in shock. "Where, Calli? Where is the justification? How can you even excuse your actions?" He was mystified by her attempt to excuse her actions and blame Grace instead.

"Because I know what happened now," she whispered painfully, finally looking up at him. "None of you wanted to tell me, but I know. I've known for years."

Rubbing at the back of his neck, Zack glanced at Lobo, wondering if he knew what the hell Calli was talking about. Lobo's answer was a flash of confusion in his gaze and a negligent shrug.

"What the fuck do you know, Calli?" Zack shook his head, wondering where he'd managed to miss important information where Grace was concerned. "What did she do?"

Tears shimmered in Calli's eyes. It wasn't often he

was reminded of how young she was, but now he wondered if perhaps he should have fought her parents harder over the decision to let her join Lobo's team.

"She told them where he was," Calli hissed, surprising him once again. "That night, she told them where Dad was, Zack, and you know it. That's how they found him and how they found your mom and dad, because of her."

The past was a dirty fucking bitch chained to his ankle with no hope of escaping her.

"No one knows that for sure, Calli. But she was a kid," he snapped. "A child with no knowledge of what was going on. He shouldn't have told her, if that's true. But none of it can be blamed on her.

Calli couldn't even look him in the eye, but he glimpsed the tears in hers. That sheen of moisture she rarely freed, rarely acknowledged.

"She's your sister, Calli—"

"No." Calli turned on him, fury erupting and escaping the tenuous hold she had on it. "She's one of them . . ." she bit out between clenched teeth.

"For God's sake, so are you." He wanted to shake her, to make her see what she was feeling wasn't hatred or dislike or even animosity.

Confusion and fear were emotions Calli always had a hard time facing. Just as Grace did.

Calli's arms crossed over her breasts, and she stared off into the darkness, refusing to discuss the issue further.

"Do you want me to tell you what's going to happen when she realizes how she's been lied to?" he asked her carefully.

He knew, Zack thought. He knew Grace and he knew this would destroy her completely. Everything she knew about the past and her father's and his parents' supposed deaths was a lie. Realizing that lie, realizing Ben had left her alone and escaped only to make another family, to father another daughter, would rip her soul apart.

"Come on, Zack," Lobo protested, disgust filling his voice. "Don't do this. Let it go for now."

Zack flicked the other man a hard look before returning to Calli. "Answer me, Calli. Let me tell you what's going to happen. For about five seconds, she's going to be that five-year-old little girl who idolized her father. She's going to stare at him with so much joy that you'll think she'll never give a moment's thought to the fucking lies she's had to eat for so many goddamned years." He stepped closer as her chin trembled for just a second. "Then you're going to see all that joy die at the very moment she realizes he left her. He fucking left her to a cold-assed traitor of a mother and a family living under the shadow of a killer. He left that child who sobbed inconsolably for him for months . . . who fell asleep on his fucking grave as she cried for her daddy . . ."

He remembered it. He'd been no more than a boy, a teenager who haunted the mountains when he couldn't sleep. And that night, he'd wished he stayed in his bed.

"Stop," she protested, her voice ragged.

"And she's going to think, and rightfully so, he left her for his lover and the child they later had. Walked away from her when she would have willingly walked with him—"

"Enough—" She flinched, jerking away from him, one hand lifting in a gesture of finality before stalking away from him and jumping into the Jeep she and Lobo had arrived in.

"Think I haven't tried that?" Lobo snapped furiously. "Think that's helping, Zack? It's not. You're only hurting her more."

Zack turned on him, the burning lash of fury erupting inside him. "Then you better figure out what will help, real fucking fast, Lobo," he ordered his cousin. "Because Ben called me directly tonight. He caught wind of what the hell's going on here. He knows everything now, and he's on his way here, along with Calli's mother. The past is getting ready to fuck us all up the ass, my friend, unless we find some way to fix it before the family descends on this damned place like a plague. You got me?"

Lobo watched him with dawning realization for long moments before his head jerked to the side, his gaze finding Calli. "They'll both be hurt," Lobo breathed out heavily.

"Exactly!" Zack snapped. "There's no saving Grace's heart, and I'll be damned if I want to see Calli savaged by this because her parents refuse to explain what the hell happened. So you better find a way to talk to her, or she'll end up hurting herself more."

Lobo strode away from him, leaving him with Dylan and Eamon to join Calli and her anger. Zack would have much preferred Calli's anger to what faced him once the family arrived. He had three days to tell Grace that everyone she had loved most in the world had betrayed her, lied to her, in the worst possible way.

Him included. Because he'd known for years that Benjamin Maddox was still alive and living with the lover he'd taken just before the attempt on his life, on hers, and on the child she'd carried, at the same time trying to uncover the identity of a traitor.

Lucia had been a conspirator, not a leader.

And until the head of that traitorous nest of vipers was found or Ben finally remembered the events of that year before the explosion, not Grace nor Calli, Ben or the Kin were safe. But they'd known that for years. And every step Zack had taken since he was eighteen in his own investigation had led back to the same answer.

The traitor was a Maddox.

Not an in-law.

Not a soldier.

It was someone old enough to have orchestrated Zack's parents' deaths, Sierra's murder, and the attempt on Kenni, as well as the attempt on Ben.

The traitor was part of Grace's family.

"Tech find that van yet?" Zack breathed out, his voice rough as Eamon shifted in the Jeep behind him.

"Not yet, boss," the other man answered quietly. "It up and disappeared on them. The family's ETA is actually forty-eight hours now, though your uncle has promised they'll take covert protocols for another forty-eight. It's still gonna get bad."

Yeah, it was going to get bad, Zack admitted. There was no way to stop it, no way to soften it.

"What about your brothers?" Dylan asked as he leaned against the back of the Jeep and stared out at the night around them. "You haven't told them yet, either. Have you?"

Zack could only shake his head. He'd have to talk to them, tell them; there was no way to keep any of it a secret now. When he did, Jazz and Slade wouldn't hate him or desert him, but there was a chance they'd use their fists on him. Some things could only be dealt with during a good old-fashioned brawl, Jazz was prone to explain when they all ended up in a fight.

When he looked up at Grace's bedroom balcony, he saw her then, behind the patio doors, staring down at him before stepping back, the curtain falling into place once again.

Grace wasn't stupid. She might not be trained to strap a gun on her thigh and race into danger, but the instincts he knew she possessed were just as important. If not more so.

He had possibly four days to figure out who had spent over twenty years methodically weakening the Kin from the inside out. Whoever it was, they were smart enough to get rid of anyone who could identify them. . . .

His gaze narrowed on the balcony doors.

It made more sense now. He couldn't figure out why Lucia had accused Grace of helping her betray not just Kenni, but also Kin secrets. She did it to get rid of Grace, obviously, but Zack hadn't been able to figure out why. Even Cord and Vince seemed genuinely confused by what was going on.

Because everyone overlooked what Grace was best at, piecing together the truth through suspicion and those little nuggets of information people were never aware they were giving away at the time. They overlooked it because Grace kept far too much to herself.

Zack, like Grace, was a watcher, and he'd spent a lot of time watching Grace. Just like her father, she solved the puzzles no one else could and did it with such instinct that he doubted she even paid attention to the process.

Over the years, Zack had picked up on her ability because he had also watched Ben do it, saw the process, and questioned the other man on it. Once Ben explained it, Zack had been able to recognize Grace's ability as well.

Benjamin Maddox had nearly died because of that instinctive gift. To the world, he *was* dead.

For some reason, whoever wanted to get rid of her couldn't kill her as easily as they'd tried to kill her father. Instead, they thought they could use the agency to kill her, wire her car to scare her into giving what they thought she had, and keep Zack running in circles. It was a more impersonal strategy, and one that implied some affection for her.

An affection they hadn't felt for Ben.

Affection or not, they still thought they could get rid of her. They thought they could isolate her, bring the agency in, and have her murdered during interrogation, like Lucia.

When that never happened, they resorted to wiring her car. Whoever was behind this wasn't stupid. They knew that car would be checked thoroughly before Grace got near it.

The night hadn't given him the answers he was looking for; the Kin he'd met with hadn't come to the meeting empty-handed or without much-needed information. Information that included the movements certain family members were making.

The fact that Cord, Sawyer, and Deacon as well as Cord's personal security team had headed out in the dead of night as well was quite interesting. Tech had lost track of them in Knoxville, when they managed to get outside the drone's view. But Zack knew Cord. The other man was running his own investigation, and so far, no one was even whispering about it.

For all appearances, Cord's search for Grace's attacker wasn't letting up. He was out there, running down leads and supposed sightings as they came in, but he was also meeting with certain members of the Kin who no one was aware had ties to them. And he was making other stops, talking to other informants while doing so.

The fact that Cord was doing all that was interesting, to say the least, and opened a whole other can of questions as far as Zack was concerned. Questions he'd have to get answers to.

"Dylan, you and Eamon get some sleep," he ordered the other man. "We'll be busy tomorrow."

Zack now had a direction to move in, at least. Four days wasn't going to be nearly enough time to figure out what the hell was going on and neutralize the threat to Grace and the rest of the family, though.

Ben had given Clyde an ultimatum after Lucia's death. Neutralize it, or he was returning himself for his daughter and his sons. All of his sons. If the NOLA twins got involved in hiding Grace, then she'd never fucking be found. Those two, Zack didn't even want to deal with. The fact that they'd shown up only minutes after learning Grace's car was wired made him damned nervous. They were in the mountains somewhere, probably close, with a fully grown gator just waiting to pounce. One of these days that damned monster was going to pounce on one of the Bayou brats and take a limb off.

"Got it," Dylan acknowledged. "Team two will be in place in an hour. We'll stay here until then."

Zack nodded and stalked toward the house and Grace. She was awake and waiting for him, and he had no doubt her suspicious, puzzle-solving little brain was already beginning to compute all the subconscious little clues she'd picked up for the past three days and then added them to what she'd detected from Calli and Lobo.

There were few people who could hide from Grace. It was one of the reasons he'd kept his distance from her. Once she put two and two together, the realizations of the scope of the betrayals from those she loved would destroy her. And it would destroy any bonds she had with those who'd lied to her.

Zack included.

Grace heard the bedroom door open and then close softly.

She had no idea where the files he'd had the day before were located, so that left her in the bed alone, with no buffer if Zack decided to join her. And it seemed he'd made that decision. Now, if she could just figure out how she felt about it.

Rolling to her side, she watched as Zack stood just inside the room, the hard, stubborn set of his expression and the lust burning in his eyes only igniting hers further.

Oh yes, she wanted him, to the point that saying no to him would be impossible.

That didn't mean she had to like it, and it sure as hell didn't mean she had to submit to him. For some reason, he thought he could push her aside and just take care of whatever the hell was going on in her life, without any input from her whatsoever. And she completely disagreed with such an idea. She wasn't going to sit back with a smile on her face when people she cared about were risking their lives for her.

She hadn't figured out exactly what was going on around her yet, but Grace could feel the pieces of the puzzle coming together. Just as she could feel the lies she'd been unaware of before emerging. Years of lies, sleights of hand, deceptions practiced with the ease of long familiarity and the belief that quiet little Grace wouldn't protest even if she did catch them deceiving her. Only her uncle and cousins really knew her, but even they were prone to hide things from her.

Moving from the door to the chair placed several feet from it, Zack sat down, then bent and removed his boots. His gaze locked with hers, though whatever answers swirled in the stormy depths were hidden by the shadows that filled the room.

Grace sat, sliding the blankets from her before turning, rising from the bed, and drawing her white cotton robe from the bottom of the mattress. Pulling it on over the matching floor-length gown she wore, she kept her back to Zack, uncertain of his mood, but even more uncertain of her own.

"This isn't your bedroom," she stated, keeping her back to him as she fastened the decorative ribbons on the robe beneath her breasts.

"You elected to leave my bedroom," he pointed out,

his voice holding a hint of remorse beneath the natural arrogance he'd been born with.

Turning slowly, she faced him. She wished they'd been able to come together differently, without the danger chasing her, without her suspicion that he would never have taken her otherwise.

The need had always been there between them, a knowledge both of them accepted. But he'd waited, watched, and he didn't take her until that hunger had grown out of control and her presence had become inescapable.

And she hated it.

"You would never have touched me if you hadn't found yourself in the position where you had to protect me, would you?" she asked, her fists clenching in the pockets of her robe.

Zack's brow arched in surprise. Leaning back in the chair, his arms resting comfortably at the sides of it, he watched her for long, quiet minutes. "You don't know that," he finally retorted, a hint of amused resignation tilting his lips.

He suspected the same thing. She could see it, even in the shadows that darkened his expression. Pressing her lips together to hold back the fiery accusations burning inside her, Grace glared back at him. "And you're not denying it." But she'd known he wouldn't.

He chuckled, shaking his head at her slowly, the knowing amusement that filled his expression causing her teeth to clench in anger.

He thought he knew her. She could feel that knowledge coming together now. He thought he knew what she would do, what she would say in any given situation.

That he knew what she was thinking. What she was feeling.

"When are you going to start saying what's on your mind, Grace?" he questioned when she didn't argue the statement, the jeering tone of his voice scraping across her raw nerves. "You never do that. You bite your tongue, keeping your lips pressed tight together, and keep it all buried inside you." He shook his head at the thought. "Don't you get tired, baby? Don't you ever just want to tell everyone to fuck off?"

More than he knew.

"And what would it accomplish?" she asked instead. "If I burn all my bridges as I cross them, then it could get rather difficult should I need to find my way home again."

A low, dark chuckle vibrated from his chest. "So you just let us walk all over you so you don't have to worry about how you'll get back to a place you probably wouldn't want to return to anyway?" he grunted mockingly. "Hell of a way to have to live, ain't it?"

"You know better than that." She didn't bother to hide the disappointment in her voice. "If you've walked over me, then you were careful to ensure I was unaware of it at the time. It's your own guilt haunting you now, not my refusal to slap anyone down whenever you feel they deserved it. Or that I'm not slapping you down at the moment, as you no doubt deserve."

He frowned at her, obviously uncertain how to broach that particular accusation. She could almost see him sifting what she knew, might know, and could suspect, categorizing it, and deciding which to confront.

"This is because I left the house earlier." He remained sitting, but the tension that emanated from him likely made it incredibly hard to do so, Grace thought. "I'm not going to figure out what the hell is going on by sitting here on my ass." His lip curled at the thought. "And I'm sorry Calli was rude to you." She could see just enough of his expression to see the minute tightening of the muscle beneath his jaw to indicate he was hiding far more than he was telling. "She's still young—"

"This isn't about Calli," she assured him. "So don't try to distract me by making it about her."

The worst thing she could do right now was face him as he lied to her. If she saw a lie pass his lips, she wouldn't be able to bear it.

"Then what the hell is it about?" he growled, surging to his feet and pulling the black shirt he wore over his head before tossing it to the floor. "Better yet, forget it!" he snapped. "I don't want to know what it's about. All I can think about right now is fucking us both silly before daylight so I can get a few hours' sleep without the need for it torturing the hell out of me."

Muscles rippled across his chest, his biceps bunched, power building around him like an invisible skin he wore, along with the sheer arrogance and determination that it took to use it.

"And of course, you think I'm just going to lie down and say, 'Yes, please.'" She waved her hand to the bed with a mocking little roll of her eyes. "Really, Zack? You couldn't even tell me you were leaving earlier until I awoke. Even though you didn't say where you were going, or why you were going. You did everything you could to make certain I didn't know you were leaving. Had I not woken when I did, I'd still be clueless."

His lips thinned. "You're not my wife, Grace."

No, she wasn't his wife, and wasn't he just prick enough to point it out to her?

"And you're not my husband," she informed him. "So far, you're no more than a one-night stand with control issues. Tell me, Zack, what makes you think I shouldn't know what you're doing or where you're going, when it involves my safety or the danger threatening me? This is my life!" she cried, the pain and anger slipping free as her arms fell from her chest, one finger pointing back toward herself. "My life and my safety, and I have the right to know."

"You have the right to know if I find out anything," he amended. "Which I haven't."

She stepped back in amazement, eyes widening. "Is that really what you think?" she snapped, bitterness flooding her at the knowledge that he could think anything so idiotic where she was concerned. "Wrong, Zack. I have the right to know who you're meeting with and why. I have the right to know anything you intend to ask whoever you're meeting, and if I disagree with your questions, I have the right to that as well. I have a right to oversee every damned area of an investigation that so far, I have no idea if you're conducting or not. Because it's my life and my right, whether you like it or not."

He began loosening the belt cinched around his hips as he walked around the bed, his expression taut with hunger now. And beneath those pants, the fact that he was fully aroused couldn't be mistaken.

"We can debate that one later, too," he growled, a rumbled sound of a man only growing more aroused by the moment. "Right now, the only thing on my mind is fucking you. If you disagree, say no, and I'll walk right out of here and see how much sleep I can get instead."

Those were her only options? Well, now, wasn't that nice of him to give her a choice?

"Do you really think I'm in the mood to pamper your need to fuck right now?" she asked in furious disbelief.

His gaze flared as the vulgarity slipped past her lips, the lust burning brighter as he focused on her mouth. "Damn, Grace, I'd love it if you'd pamper my need to fuck," he assured her as his lashes lifted, his gaze moving to hers. "More than you can imagine."

She glared back at him. "Try sleeping instead," she suggested, her lip curling with the contempt she felt with regard to her so-called choices.

He loosened his pants, moving closer. "You didn't say no, baby," he pointed out, his voice rougher now. "You have to actually say the word tonight, not play lip service to it." His lashes lowered with wicked sensuality. "Though, I wouldn't care a bit if you want to play a little lip service of another sort to me."

The teasing, suggestive tone of his voice had her heart racing, her senses suddenly chaotic as he reached out and pulled at the end of the ribbon holding her robe closed. The bow slid free, the material parting easily.

He removed his pants then, tossing them to the side of the room, his cock rising, thick and fully engorged. "I couldn't wait to get back to you. Couldn't wait to feel you wrapped around me like hot silk as you were earlier." He pushed her robe from her shoulders, leaving her in nothing but the thin gown she wore beneath it.

"Zack . . ." She couldn't give him the denial he required to stop the course he'd set.

Didn't even know if she wanted to deny him, and herself. Despite her knowledge that he wouldn't have taken her otherwise, her certainty that he didn't love her, didn't need her as she needed him. Still, saying no was impossible.

He placed two fingers against her lips. "I'm too hungry for you, baby. Too damned hard and all too aware how sweet and tight your pussy gripped me earlier. I simply don't have the control for anything else right now."

chapter sixteen

Wild.

Untamable.

When Zack gripped the back of her head to hold her in place for his kiss, Grace glimpsed the intense hunger in his eyes. Half a heartbeat later, that dark need met burning curiosity and exploded out of control. Out of both their control. The need became something more, something they could no longer do without. They couldn't deny themselves, and they couldn't deny the arousal building crazily out of control.

Zack's lips slanted over hers, his tongue pushing possessively past her lips to taste hers with teasing flicks and licks. Rough, greedy, his kiss consumed her as she fought to consume him. To hold on to this moment when nothing else mattered but the pleasure they could find in each other.

Grace knew her world was changing. She could sense

it, could feel the destruction looming. For this moment, right here and now, she wanted to steal this pleasure, steal the heady, untamed sensations Zack incited in her body.

"That's it, baby," he groaned against her lips. "Don't think. Just feel how good this is. Fuck, you're so damned good."

Her fingers tightened in the back of his hair, tugging hard as a rough chuckle whispered through the air just before his lips covered hers again. His hands were at her hips, her back, stroking and caressing as he pulled her gown slowly up her legs, then to her hips.

"Lift your arms," he demanded just before taking a nip from her lower lip. "Now."

Her arms lifted and the gown was whisked over her head and tossed aside, leaving her naked and arching closer to him as he backed her against the wall.

And he felt good.

He felt so damned good.

Powerful muscles clenched beneath her hands as she gripped his shoulders and flexed against her swollen breasts as he held her against the wall. His lips moved over hers, kissing her deep, with a hungry demand she could only accept and meet with her own.

His teeth nipped at her lower lip again.

"Look at me," the rough, erotic sound of his voice sent a shiver racing over her as her lashes lifted and she stared up at him in dazed fascination.

"That's it," he crooned, his hands cupping her rear, tightening then slowly lifting her. "Put your knees against my hips, hold on to me baby." The stiff length of his cock slid between her thighs, drawing a gasp from her lips. "Keep watching me, Grace. Watch me while I take you."

Watch him?

The thick, flared crest pressed between the swollen, slick folds of her sex, parted them, and began pushing slowly inside her.

So slowly.

Stretching her, creating a heated, ecstatic sting that had her lashes fluttering in pure pleasure.

"Keep them open," he growled, his tone serrated now. "Watch me, Grace. Let me see your pretty eyes, see how good I can make you feel."

Holding her between him and the wall, his eyes locked on hers, his hips flexing, pushing his cock deeper, retreating, thrusting back inside her by slow degrees. Each shallow thrust parted sensitive tissue, the iron-hard width creating a slight pleasure-pain that bordered ecstasy.

Slick moisture spilled along her vagina, met each thrust, and heated her sex further as pleasure ricocheted along her nerve endings and caused the sensitive flesh to tighten further around the invading shaft.

Male dominance filled his expression, tightened the flesh over his face, and darkened his eyes until the stormy gray was nearly black.

"Hold on to me, honey." Wicked, hungry, his expression became more sensual, bolder. "I'm going to give you all of me now."

All of him.

In one bold, fierce move, he thrust inside her, burying to the hilt and shattering her senses with the intensity of the pleasure that erupted inside her. Her muscles clamped around the thick penetration, rippling over it as he drew back, only to push inside her again as her thighs tightened at his hips, her arms around his neck, and she drove herself harder onto the fierce impalement.

She couldn't be still, couldn't stop the desperate need to take him as well, to meet each thrust, her vagina tightening around him as she felt the pleasure racing over her flesh.

"Damn, Grace," he groaned at her ear as her head pressed into the tight muscles of his shoulders, her breaths panting from her chest. "Ah hell . . . that's it baby, take me . . ."

Take him, hold him. She wanted to stay right here forever, lost in the sensations storming through her, searing her heart and mind, and marking her soul. And she couldn't stop it from happening. Couldn't stop each wildly spinning spiral of ecstasy as it tightened through her, couldn't stop the need that built with each touch, each stroke of his shaft inside her intimate flesh, each nip of his teeth and heated kiss at her neck.

"There you go, fuck me, Grace," Zack groaned, his hands clenched at her rear, kneading the flesh, adding to the sensations tearing through her. "You're almost there, baby. Almost ready to come for me, aren't you?"

A mewling cry escaped her lips as he whispered the words against her heart, his voice rough, grating with his own pleasure. The explicit words only inflamed her further and had the instinctive movements of her hips and thighs accelerating with his.

She drove herself onto the iron-hard shaft and tried

to scream with the need shattering through her each time she felt his cock stretch her, burn her with his need.

Rippling contractions milked at the stiff intrusion, fighting to hold him inside her even as she lifted herself at his retreat, teasing herself and unable to stop the madness.

"Damn you. Ah hell, Grace, that's it, milk my dick, baby," he rasped as he pistoned inside her, the sound of their bodies coming together, the feel of his thrusts and pushing her to a brink she was certain she couldn't survive.

"That's it, ride my cock, Grace. Ride me, baby . . . so fucking tight." He nipped her ear, his muscles bunching as the sensations torturing her began to tighten, to amplify until they were racing in ever-increasing arcs of agonizing pleasure.

She couldn't control the storm, couldn't control her own body or her need to move harder, faster, to meet each thrust inside her and take more of him.

"Zack . . . Zack . . ." She gasped his name, fighting to hold on to him, to find some anchor to reality as her senses abandoned her to rush for the edge of rapture surging higher, twisting faster inside her.

"Come for me, Grace," he demanded, the hard, controlled ferocity of his tone snapping through her as the storm raged out of control. "Give it to me, damn you. Come for me, baby, all over my dick . . ."

She exploded, wailing his name, certain she was screaming out for him as she felt the first wave of brutal sensation steal her mind. From that point, all she knew was the mind-numbing excess of completion as it slammed inside her.

She jerked against him, the hammering thrusts of his cock increasing the already violent explosions of ecstasy as her body trembled and shook, her muscles locking her place, her pussy clenching around the shuttling flesh shafting harder inside her.

Until she lost herself.

Between one explosion of brilliant sensation and the next, her senses disintegrated in the catastrophic storm that tore through her.

And still, Zack was moving inside her, his body slick with sweat, his groans echoing in her ear as the world spun around her, braced her, cushioned her, held her as the chaotic swirls of release finally eased and she found herself lying back on the bed.

Her thighs were splayed over Zack's as he knelt between them, staring down at the point where he now moving slowly inside her, his expression savage with lust, jaw clenched as he watched his possession of her.

"Zack . . ." she whispered, her voice weak, strained as she fought against the return of such violent pleasure so soon.

"We're not finished yet." Guttural and intent, his voice grated over her senses as he pushed slowly inside her once again. "Fuck, Grace, you're so tight, it's like having a silken vise clamped around my dick," he panted, his gaze lifting to hers then. "Let me have it again, baby. Let me feel that hot little pussy coming for me again."

Her stomach clenched, convulsed, and sensation went racing over her again, pulling her into the sensual, erotic hunger he'd awakened within her.

"That's it, Grace," he crooned, one hand clenching

her thigh, the other finding the swollen, highly sensitive bud of her clit. "Spill all that slick heat around my cock, baby. Give it to me." His gave lifted to hers again. "It's my turn to ride now."

He was a man possessed, and Zack fully admitted to it. Lost in a pleasure so fucking extreme, he couldn't bear to let it go just yet. And so damned dangerous, he knew the cost he'd pay for allowing himself to take it could become impossibly high.

Why the pleasure was so extreme with this woman, he didn't have a clue. She wasn't the first to challenge him, she wasn't the first to make her own demands. But she was first he'd ever taken quite like this.

The first who had ever made him feel adrenaline-dazed, pumped so high on sheer excitement that he didn't want it to end.

Staring down at the bare folds hugging his cock, the heavy layer of slick, feminine dew glistening across them and coating his hard flesh, he was fucking amazed at how she took him. The stiff width of his cock looked like a club as he retreated, the delicate folds flattened around the dark erection as her pussy rippled and milked him back in.

And inside . . . ah hell, inside was so tight, so fucking hot and tight, sucking at the unbearably sensitive crest, holding on to it and rippling around the shaft demandingly. It was so damned good, he didn't want it to end. Not now. Not ever.

He'd never get enough it.

Even now, his balls were drawn painfully tight to the base of his cock, the need to come shooting arcs of electric sensation straight to the base of his skull. First, he wanted to feel her orgasm again. Wanted to feel the wash of her slick cream over the head of his cock, feel way her pussy clenched on his cock, ever tighter before milking the head with deep, internal spasms of her own release.

He could become addicted to that particular pleasure. He could spend his life trying to figure out why he was addicted to it even as he reveled in each instance of it.

And she wasn't content to just lie beneath him and accept what he gave her. Not Grace. Even panting for breath, weak from the intensity of her earlier release, her hips lifted and fell with each hard impalement and withdrawal inside the flexing grip of her pussy. Her thighs tightened against his, splayed open as he knelt between them, watching her feminine flesh, tracking each change as he pushed her closer, pushed them both closer.

Her juices spilled from the snug grip each time he drew back, then pushed free of her to slicken her further with each inward thrust. Her clit was a dark, flushed pink, glistening with moisture and engorged with need.

As he watched, slender, graceful fingers slid to the aroused button, easing alongside it, and began massaging it with slow, delicate strokes as her hips lifted and fell to each pumping stroke inside her.

The head of his cock throbbed, a wave of pleasure dragging a groan from Zack's chest as he felt the warning pulse of release. He was bare inside her again, nothing separating, nothing protecting either of them from the destructive pleasure gripping them.

Holding her thighs, careful of the tender, wounded

area, Zack held her open, his attention focused on her fingers, watching as she stroked herself, felt the combined sensations from her manipulation of the swollen little bud and his shafting cock as they attacked her pussy.

The cries spilling from her lips intensified, broken whimpers of sexual need spurring him to push inside her faster, harder. To fuck her to hilt with each impalement as shudders began racing up his spine.

Damn her. He couldn't hold on like this.

With each increasing level of pleasure she experienced, she tightened further on him, her cunt rippling around his cock, sucking at it, gripping the sensitive crown and working around it with destructive rapture. And as she pushed him closer, all he could do was hold on for the ride and watch those pretty fingers masturbate her clit in tight, furious little circles.

"How fucking pretty," he groaned, holding on to her, slamming inside her, glimpsing the furious pace of his cock as he fucked her harder. "God, yes, Grace . . . tighten like that, baby . . ." Strangled, the breath leaving his chest, he felt her body jerk again, felt her pussy clenching so tight on his dick, he cried out himself as she arched violently, jerking beneath the orgasm overtaking her as he felt his own wrench through him.

Brilliant color attacked his eyesight, he swore his heart stopped for blinding seconds, and complete brutal ecstasy slammed into him as his release shot from him. Pulse after heart-jamming pulse of semen exploded from his dick as her pussy clenched and sucked at the throbbing release. Each ejaculation amplified the plea-

sure until he cried out her name, as lost in her as he
knew she was lost in him. When it was over, all he could
do was catch his weight as he leaned over her, his head
burying beside her neck, his lips pressing into the flesh
beneath her ear.

His heart was racing in his chest, perspiration drip-
ping from his hair and the sensation sizzling along his
nerve endings as the violence of his release slowly eased.
Boneless, exhausted beneath him, Grace was breathing
was just as heavily, faint little cries spurred by the af-
tershocks of her release fell through her occasionally.

Pulling from her, Zack clenched his teeth at the rush
of pleasure he could still feel even after such a powerful release. Still half-erect and far too sensitive, he was
certain that if he could muster the strength to move, he
could fuck her again.

Just the thought of the pleasure awaiting him had him
wishing he could make his muscles cooperate. Instead,
it was all he could do to drag the blankets back and tuck
them both beneath them. With Grace's head cushioned
on his shoulder, sleep already washing over her, he knew
he was in trouble.

Slade once told him that he'd known before he ever
took Jesse the first time, that she would own him. When
a man was so focused on one woman, the scent of her,
each expression, even the way the wind blew through
her hair, then he should have enough God-given sense
to know she owned him.

Zack hadn't wanted to hear what he was saying at the
time. He'd been watching the wind play with Grace's
dark blond hair, watching her solemn expression and

wishing she would smile, just once, even if it wasn't for him. He hadn't wanted to admit what a part of him had already known. Grace belonged to him.

She belonged to him.

And he'd betrayed her every day since the day across a coffin, lying into her tear-washed face and aching to shelter her from the pain of the loss of an aunt who had been more like a mother to her. Ached to shelter her from the ragged fear and uncertainty and the knowledge that she could be taken from him as easily as her aunt was taken from her.

He'd known and he'd slammed that door as quick as he'd realized it was opened inside his soul. Slammed it so hard and fast that the pain of it had caused his stomach to tighten in rejection. He'd lost enough, he couldn't have survived losing more at the time, and Zack had known it. Just as he'd known that when the teenager became a woman, the need to comfort her would become a far different need.

The need he was feeling now.

The need to keep her.

If he'd done things differently, he thought regretfully. If he had found a way to convince Ben and Clyde that taking her out of Loudon was better than allowing her to stay, then it might have been different. If he'd been old enough, mature enough to tell her the truth once she reached adulthood, then it might have been different.

But he hadn't done any of those things.

He'd stood back, watched out for her, tried to make her smile and tried to keep enough distance between them so that if, when, she learned the truth, her hatred wouldn't destroy him. That the agonizing loss and betrayal she'd feel wouldn't rip his guts into shreds and leave his soul bleeding.

"I'm sorry, Grace," he whispered into the darkness of the bedroom. "I'm so sorry, baby . . ."

The light in the guest room was extinguished, leaving the house dark but for the security lights outside it. The light in the master bedroom hadn't come on, indicating Zack had gone to the guest room where Grace slept rather than stay his own room.

"He on ma bad side, dat boug is," Beau-Remi sighed as Joe's chains clanked from the edge of the water where he lay in wait for any prey dumb enough to come close. "Da poor lil ting, she gonna have da heart broke fer sure."

"English, Beau-Remi. English," Mad grunted from the sleeping bag he rested on, one arm thrown over his eyes.

Fine, he wanted English.

"I'm going to kill that motherfucker Maddox," he enunciated clearly. "Skin him out, then feed his body parts to Joe."

Mad lifted his arm from his eyes and peered over at him, a hint of wariness in his expression. "It's her choice," he was reminded quietly. "She's not a kid."

Mad had been repeating that advice for days, as though trying to convince himself of it as well.

Beau-Remi snarled back at him, his lip lifting in contempt at the reminder. "Dey lie to her," he muttered, reverting back to the colloquial speech of the swamps. It was easier to keep his temper under control that way. "All of dem. Dey keep her from us." He waved his hand between the two of them. "Dey lie to us." Anger threatened to engulf the control he wasn't good at to begin with. "Dey tell us she is safe an' happy, and den we hear da truth." He shook his head at the information they'd uncovered over the past days. "Ah, Mad, dey shame us wit' da blood we carry."

Maddox blood.

Benjamin Maddox's blood. The worst of the liars and conniving bastards who kept their baby sister in danger until it damned near out of control now.

"The mission hasn't changed, Beau-Remi," Mad just had to go and remind him. "She'll never be safe if we just steal her away. We'll just distract everyone from identifying the problem. You know that."

"You know dat," he sneered in contempt. "I know, Mad, dat dey are da reason danger comes for her," he bit out furiously. "Dey are da reason we sit here while dat capon betrays our baby sister, *oui*? When his lies, dey break her heart, what say you den?"

Mad laid his arm back over his eyes. "I say I can't understand a fucking word you're saying," he muttered.

He understood every word, Beau-Remi knew; he just chose not to address them. Mad was one who kept it all inside, refusing to speak of it, refusing to acknowledge the problem until the moment he could use his knife on it.

Mad was damned good with that knife, though. Still, keeping the anger pushed back wasn't something Beau-Remi dealt with very well. Venting kept him in control, he often told his twin.

"Chill out, Beau-Remi," Mad sighed then. "You'll make her hate us before she even knows who we are if you kill the bastard. Besides, the best revenge will be watching his soul being peeled apart, slice by slice, by Grace. She'll not forgive him easily."

Beau-Remi almost rolled his eyes at the statement. "You don' know, Mad," he sighed instead. "Dat girl, her heart will forgive, you see, she won' make him pay."

"Then we will," Mad sighed. "Now, go to sleep, dammit. We have things to do tomorrow, and I'm tired."

Beau-Remi stared out into the darkness instead. Yes, they had things to do tomorrow, things to prepare for. At that thought, the cell phone lying on the ground next to him vibrated. Again. The dim display showed the number calling.

Beau-Remi's lips tightened. "Dat capon, he don' give up," he told his brother despite Mad's admonition to let him sleep. "He done callin' again."

"Good ole Dad," Mad muttered, no more pleased with their sire than Beau-Remi was. "How about you kick his ass when we see him?"

"He gettin' ole enough." Beau-Remi grinned. "Maybe no' as quick as before, huh?"

"Find out for us," Mad yawned again. "If I do it, I'll end up using my knife. Whoremongering son of a bitch."

At least after his so-called death, he'd learned a bit of fidelity. Not once had he stepped out on the little Richards girl. Poor payment for nearly getting her and their unborn daughter killed, though. Her as well as the child she carried, the daughter Ben Maddox had raised, trained, and loved. Unlike the daughter he'd left sobbing for her papa with heartbreaking cries.

"I do no' forget," he said then. "To see her lay on dat dirt, da dark aroun' her, begging her papa to take her wit' him." He shook his head at the memory. "An' to den sen' us away, Mad." He shook his head once more. "Dey lie to tell us to say dey take care of her."

"Go to sleep, Beau-Remi," Mad sighed heavily. "We'll remind them of it. I promise you that."

And they would, but still, that memory, unlike many others, was one he couldn't push away so easily. The night he and Mad had gone to pay their respects to the father they'd believed was dead and found their baby sister lying upon the bare earth, weeping her broken heart to a father who hadn't cared enough even to secure her safety before seeking his own.

Ben Maddox, bastard that he was, might have been lying in a coma at the time, but he'd come out of it, he'd lived, and still, he left little Grace in that nest of vipers.

Would he ever forgive that betrayal of his baby sister? Beau-Remi wondered. It had seared his soul so deep that when Ben showed up, alive and well in the Bayou several years later, and told them of the lover and daughter he was then living with, Beau-Remi had refused to lay eyes on the girl. It had taken years for him even to acknowledge her.

"Stop frettin' over this, Beau-Remi," Mad demanded, his voice harsh despite the whisper of sound. "Go to sleep, because you're only pissin' me off more."

And he had to smile at the warning.

They were twins, that connection as natural as breathing.

Settling back against the wall at the mouth of the small cave they'd found shelter in, close enough to water to allow the gator comfort, he closed his eyes and drifted into that half sleep he allowed himself.

He wasn't back home in the Bayou, where he knew what surrounded him and connected with the land. He'd be home soon, though, as soon as he took care of the threat against his sister and hopefully got to feel his fist against his sperm donor's face.

He could go home happy then, he thought. Or at least as close to happy as he could imagine knowing. After all, he was Ben Maddox's son, and that wasn't a gentle legacy to the male offspring the bastard had helped create.

It was a curse.

chapter seventeen

Nightmares twisted and swirled through Grace's dreams until she awoke, groggy and still exhausted early the next morning. It had been years since she'd dreamed of her father before his death or let herself remember them once she woke.

These dreams refused to be forgotten, though. She could feel the feel tie between the past and her present, and in her dreams what he was trying to tell her was always drowned out by static. But she saw his eyes, saw the pain and regret in them, and as she jerked awake, she'd glimpsed tears.

She'd never seen her father look like that, so somber and sad, desperately trying to make her understand something so painful that it brought tears to his eyes instead. It had never happened.

Her father had always been teasing, playful, even in the face of Lucia's bitchiness or petty rants about their daughter. He'd wink at her and send her from the room, then deal with her mother's temper himself. It had never been allowed to touch Grace, until after his death.

With his laughing green eyes and wide smile, handsome features and strong build, women buzzed around him like bees to honey, it was said. He was more outgoing than his twin, Vince, and found it harder to keep his pants zipped as well.

At last count, there were six sons, all older than Grace. When he married Lucia and Grace was born, everyone thought he'd settled down. There weren't even rumors of an affair with anyone. Grace would have heard about it over the years if so, and Lucia would have found great pleasure in hurting her daughter with that information.

He hadn't been faithful, though.

The pictures. The proof of it was in the pictures Zack had showed her that first morning. There were several of Zack's aunt, Ureana, John Richards's baby sister. She'd visited the summer before the deaths of Grace's father and Zack's parents. And in those pictures, she'd stared at the photographer with shy though unabashed love. The look of a woman who believed the person she stared at loved her. And in those pictures, she was pregnant. Barely showing, but enough that anyone searching for the truth in the picture would find it. Or someone who put puzzles together would see it as a cornerstone to a past she was trying to figure out.

Whatever had really happened all those years ago, Grace could feel its ties to the danger swirling around her now. It wasn't the fact that her father had kept an affair hidden—that was surprising but not worth killing over.

According to Zack, they'd been investigating treasonous activities, even then, she remembered as she showered. Someone had been working to betray the family or the Kin, and her father had found reason to suspect it. He'd drawn Zack's father into it, and the result had been the death of Zack's family and her father.

Whatever Benjamin and Zack's father had been close to uncovering was still thriving, and thanks to Lucia, Grace was in danger because of it now.

Why had Luce believed Grace knew where that information was hidden? What would make her mother believe her father would have trusted her with the hiding place?

That question was still running through her mind as she entered the kitchen for coffee and breakfast. As soon as she saw Zack, he was hauling those damned files and pictures out. Then he could just keep his promise that her uncle would transfer his computer to Zack's house.

Stepping into the kitchen, she came to a slow, surprised stop, her eyes widening as her gaze went around the room.

Kenni and Jesse both sat at the kitchen table, steaming cups of coffee beside plates piled with eggs, bacon, and muffins.

Jazz and Slade stood next to the counter closest to the women, arms crossed over their chests, scowls on their faces. They weren't pleased in the least. They were evidently angry enough that they'd hit Zack. Past rumors indicated that happened only when one of the foster brothers neglected to tell the others something vitally important.

What could Zack have hidden from them that would

cause such a reaction? Grace had a feeling she knew exactly what it was he may recently have revealed.

"Food's on the stove," Kenni indicated the covered skillets with her fork and a smile and a wink of one emerald eye. "There's fresh coffee, too. Help yourself."

Grace's gaze was locked on Zack again, his glare daring her to say a word about the bruise forming on the left side of his face. Or the fact that he seemed to be comforting his side with one hand. Kidney shot, too?

Whoa, they were excessively pissed, it seemed.

She turned back to Kenni and arched her brow in question.

"Some things, we just stay out of," Jesse stated, her smile commiserating as Grace met the rich amusement in her gaze. "We find it much easier on our nerves."

Which meant they didn't know why Zack's face was bruised. Tilting her head, she considered the darkening around his eye and cheek. Jazz went for the hook, Slade for the kidneys, she suspected.

Reaching up, Zack rubbed at the back of his neck, his jaw tightening as his chin lifted with arrogant superiority. For just a second, shocked amazement raced through her as disbelief threatened to pull a gasp from her lips.

Disbelief or not, the unthinkable cemented in her head, pulling her gaze to other clues. The arch of his brow, the narrowing of his eyes.

Oh God, why hadn't she seen it before now?

The tug of pain and slash of betrayal she felt nearly stole her breath as she let the truth slowly form from her first suspicion to the small clues she picked up without realizing she'd done so.

Calli. Calli was Ureana's daughter and Zack's first cousin.

Accusing him would be the wrong route to take, she thought, pulling her gaze from him. She had to broach this a bit differently. Men, after all, weren't the easiest creatures to deal with on a good day, even if they wanted to cooperate.

Better to state the obvious than to voice the suspicion, in this case. Besides, she had work to do before beginning a confrontation with Zack.

With that in mind, she got her own coffee and breakfast and moved to the table with Kenni and Jesse.

"I don't think we have to worry about snipers or a real attempt against my life," she stated after taking a sip of her coffee. "It was a distraction—a very clever one, though. A way to get me back to Zack's and away from Uncle Vince's, for some reason. I suspect it was to keep me out of those files."

"Why would anyone do that?" Zack asked, watching her closely. "That was an explosive, Grace, not a hole in your brake line."

She nodded as she swallowed the eggs she was eating. "And it was very well done," she agreed. "But it serves no purpose to kill me. Killing me would end the game they're playing without collecting the reward. The reward being the Microdrive everyone knows I don't have. What our industrious traitor wants, therefore, is control. To get that, he needs the Microdrive. He needs me scared enough to hurry and try to sell it, remember where Dad might have hidden it, or force someone else who may know to reveal it." She smiled sweetly. "Uncle Vince is fond of me. If he had it but were holding it back for some reason, then such a threat might cause him to take action, especially if the traitor were someone close to him and that traitor believed he knew what was on the chip. Which he doesn't." She shrugged and took another bite of fluffy eggs and bacon.

"So who has it?" Zack asked with a shake of his head.

"Doesn't matter who has it or where it's hid, or who's betraying whom," she told him, meeting his gaze long enough to cause suspicion to flicker in the gray depths of his eyes. Gray eyes, just like Lobo's. Like Lobo's. Somehow Zack was related to Lobo as well. Closely related. No wonder he claimed absolute trust in them.

"It doesn't matter. I don't need to know where the chip is hidden. Only Dad knew that one, no matter what Lucia claimed. But that doesn't mean whoever's behind this hasn't given himself away. I just need to go over the files and pictures again. It will come to me, if I have Uncle Vince's system."

"They'll be here tonight," Zack sighed. "They're taking care of something else today."

Her brow lifted, wondering if he'd tell her what.

She didn't have to wait long.

"They found Richard James's body next to the river just down from your uncle's house," Zack told her gently as Slade's muttered curse was followed by Jazz's.

"Hell, she was eatin' breakfast, dumb-ass," Jazz followed up. "You could have waited." He shook his head despairingly. "I thought I taught you better."

"He nearly killed Magnus," she told Jazz softly. "Knowing he's dead isn't affecting breakfast.

Zack's jaw bunched. Whatever he wanted to say, he couldn't say in front of his brothers.

"Did you get the bruised face and ribs because of Calli?" she asked calmly despite the rush of hurt she couldn't stem.

All three men stiffened, giving her the answer she was searching out. Ignoring them, she ate another bite of food before finishing her coffee.

"What about Calli?" Zack finally asked as she sat at the table between Kenni and Jesse, whose curious gazes watched her with sudden interest.

"I'm not stupid," she told him then. "As soon as I saw the picture of your aunt Ureana in that pile the other day, it began coming together. I took most of the night to figure it all out after meeting her. So how is my baby sister doing this morning?" Grace asked, watching closely as the cup jerked back from his lips and he nearly spat the liquid to the floor. "She still hate me?"

Jazz wheezed on his coffee while Slade, having been smarter than to actually take a drink, merely lowered his head and shook it solemnly.

Grace placed her fork carefully by her plate and watched as Zack placed the cup on the counter, wiped his hand over his face, and stared back at her coolly.

"Lie to me," she suggested, her chest tight with the knowledge that he was considering it. "Go ahead, Zack, make that mistake and tell me I'm wrong."

Kenni and Jesse both appeared in shock as they rose to their feet and walked to their men.

"Let's go, baby." Kenni hooked her arm in Jazz's firmly. "Time for us to go home."

"Like hell." Pure satisfaction and anticipation filled his expression. "I want to watch her kick his ass."

"I want to sell tickets to the event," Slade drawled.

Jesse bent to Grace and gave her a quick hug, followed by Kenni, before leaving.

"Call us if you need us," Kenni whispered. "You know I'm here for you."

Grace could only nod, her chest tightening painfully at the words.

Kenni and Jesse both would be there for her, too, Grace knew, in a heartbeat. But this was something she had to deal with herself, something she had to take care of herself.

Jazz finally let Kenni draw him from the room, and long seconds later, the front door closed behind them, leaving her alone with Zack.

"You should have told me," she accused him painfully as they watched each other cautiously across the length of the room. "This shouldn't have been kept from me."

The memory of her sister's anger and dislike seared her now just as it had the night before. No wonder she'd felt so off balance around the girl, uncertain what to say.

"It was a lot of years before I knew myself, Grace," he bit out, anger darkening his eyes like thunderclouds.

Of course. Ureana had probably done everything she could to hide the fact that her daughter belonged to Benjamin Maddox, especially after his death.

"Dad would have been proud of her," she said, her heart clenching at the memory of her father. Rather than letting the tears fill her eyes, she threw Zack a sharp smile instead. "He was always a little disappointed in me, you know?"

"Ben wasn't disappointed in you, Grace." He shook his head, his voice hoarse, rather resigned.

"Yes, he was. Even as a little girl I knew it, but he still loved me, and that was all that mattered." She stared down at her plate for several long moments. "He wanted a tomboy, but he got this little girly girl who didn't like to go hunting like Kenni did. And I didn't like the sound of the guns firing." The memory wasn't a painful one, but rather a fond one. "But he still loved me," she said, lifting her gaze to Zack once more. "Calli, he would have been nuts for, though." And Grace knew she would have been gently set aside for a delicate little girl who could do all the things her father loved. A princess and a warrior all in one. He would have loved it. "I bet your sister is really proud as well." She nodded, then asked gently. "How did you pull that one off? Keeping her hidden so well that no one suspected Calli existed?"

He stared up at the ceiling with a heavy sigh and shook his head. "I was twelve, I didn't pull it off, I didn't even know about it for several years." When his gaze met hers, she nodded, knowing he wasn't lying about it at least.

"So who pulled it off? Dad?" she asked, wondering if she was succeeding at all in hiding the pain.

He nodded sharply. "Ben, in part. My uncle Clyde did the rest. He took Ureana to stay with him, kept her hidden, took care of everything."

"And left you to foster care?" Anger shot through her.

"He left me with Toby Rigor," Zack amended. "A far better choice. My uncle had Ureana to care for, then Calli. Toby offered to take care of me. Foster care was just a formality to make it look good."

"Lobo's your cousin as well," she guessed, remembering the curve of the other man's jaw, a certain stance as they talked the night before.

"Stop it, dammit! I hate it when you start tying up fucking loose ends and get that damned hurt look on your face," he snapped, anger brewing in his gaze as his arms crossed over his chest and he glared at her as though it were her fault.

Grace's chest actually hurt from the force of the pain she could feel building in it. All these years, and she had a sister.

"Why doesn't she like me?" she asked somberly, needing to know why the other girl had been so vehement, so certain in her dislike.

Wondering why her sister wouldn't want to love her.

Zack wanted to hit something. Or somebody. The unconscious hunger on her face was another nail driven straight to his soul, and the guilt ground it in further.

Why didn't Calli like her? It wasn't that Calli didn't like her or didn't want to like her sister. It was that his niece had evidently picked up some information that simply wasn't true. But he couldn't tell Grace that, now, could he, he thought in contempt.

"Calli has issues to work through," he finally said heavily, wishing he could explain the truth to her. "She'll get there, it'll just take her some time."

A bitter curve of her lips was a testament to her disagreement. "And her issues are none of my business." She gave a short little nod. "Point taken."

"That wasn't what I said, dammit." Fuck, he hated her father right now. As much as he respected Ben's strategic

mind and ability to tie information together, he hated
what he knew the truth was going to do to Grace.

"You didn't have to say it." She shrugged, the
wounded look on her face enough to make him grind
his back teeth furiously. "It's probably for the best, anyway." Her voice was rough as she rose to her feet. "You
should send her home, Zack. She has no business being
dragged into my mess. None of you do."

With that, she turned and walked out of the kitchen.

Zack frowned at the empty doorway. She was just
walking away? Just giving up? Son of a bitch, after
last night, he hadn't expected that. He sure as hell thought
she'd had more fight in her.

This had gone on long enough.

She'd lost everyone, everyone she loved, even the
sister she hadn't known, to whatever malevolent shadow
was determined to destroy the Maddox family. She was
a pawn, she'd been a pawn one way or the other all her
damned life, and she was tired of playing the role.

She was tired of being betrayed and lied to.

Not that she could really blame Zack, and God knew,
she wanted someone to blame. His aunt and Calli had to
be his priority, not the daughter of a traitor, the daughter
of the man that had endangered his aunt by getting her
pregnant to begin with.

Grace couldn't be his priority, no matter how much
she wished she were someone's priority at this point.

He was a priority to her, though, and now, so was her
baby sister. That meant this had to be finished, quickly.
Neither she nor Calli would ever be safe until she figured out why someone wanted her out of the way, and

the only way to do that was to watch, to listen. She couldn't do that sitting on her ass or lying beneath Zack.

She changed from the jeans and sleeveless T-shirt she'd pulled on earlier into a pair of light gray tailored slacks and a silk blouse.

Her camouflage, she thought mockingly. It never failed for everyone to overlook her when she dressed as they expected her to. Put her in jeans, though, and they stared at her as though she were an alien.

Once she finished dressing and pushed her feet into the plain, low-heeled pumps she normally wore, she braided her hair down the back of her head and tied it off with dark, elastic ribbon.

If she timed things just right, she'd arrive at the Maddox home just in time for the monthly family meeting. Four brothers and one sister, all part of the intricate web of the Kin stronghold, each aware of their part in the secrets they kept hidden.

As she secured a gold chain at the back of her neck, Zack walked into the bedroom, his gaze instantly narrowing on her. "What the hell do you think you're doing?" he asked, his gaze moving over her slowly.

"I'm going to the monthly Maddox family meeting," she told him with false cheer. "As I've worked as Vinny's assistant, there are really very few Kin secrets as far as I'm concerned, and I have several questions regarding family matters. The best time to ask them is while all of them are together. They have a harder time lying then." She gave him a tight smile. "And when they do lie, it's much easier to detect when they're all together."

She knew them.

She'd sat in on so many family meetings in her capacity as Vince's assistant that she'd learned the slight nuances that indicated lies, deceptions, and half truths. Though, at the time, those little transgressions hadn't been outside family affairs. But she'd also not been looking for anything outside family affairs. She'd been known to give herself a headache by trying to follow too many threads of suspicions. She avoided it now as often as possible.

Perhaps too much.

"And you think I'm going to allow it?" he asked, stalking farther into the bedroom, his muscular body appearing more powerful as he stared back at her aggressively. "No matter what you believe, Grace, two attempts have been made on your life. Let's not give your assassin another shot."

She gave a low, mocking laugh in response to the question. "I really don't think it's your place to allow it, or not," she pointed out. "As I told you last night, this is my life, Zack. I won't hide in a corner while everyone else is trying to protect me. Besides, whatever's going on is originating from within the family somehow."

She hated to think her aunt or uncles could be capable of ordering their brother or their nieces killed. Lucia was another story, she thought wearily. She hadn't been well liked in or out of the family. Still, she'd been family, and the Maddox Clan had always touted family above all things.

"So you think you're just going to prance into that meeting and know what's going without anyone saying a word?" he mocked her, the dark glower on his face imposing but not exactly swaying her.

She considered the question for a moment, though. "It's been known to happen when my suspicions are aroused." She finally shrugged before trying to explain. "I know them, Zack. I know their expressions when they're lying, when they're hiding something, or when they're just being assholes and pretending to. It's all in asking the right questions and paying attention to my instincts. I might not know what's going on, or know who's trying to get rid of me, but I might be able to figure out which direction to search in. Why do you think Vince's trusted me as far as he did all these years? Because he knew I'd see their lies before he even suspected them."

"No . . ."

"You don't have the right to tell me no," she informed him, holding on to her composure by a fingernail. "You can go with me. You can bring a dozen friends to back you up if that's your choice. But I'm going."

"Not if I tie you to the bed," he growled, stepping closer, his arms lowering slowly to his sides. "You won't be going anyplace then."

And he meant it.

Frustration threatened to push her past the calm she was trying to find, threatened to destroy the hold she had on her fragile emotions.

"And I'll never forgive you . . ."

"But you'll be alive," he snarled, crossing the distance too quickly for her to avoid the broad hands that latched on to her upper arms and dragged her against him. "Do you hear me, Grace. You'll be alive."

"Will I?" she whispered. "How much more do you think I can take, Zack? Everyone I've loved, everyone I want to love, is threatened. And the reasons we're coming up with don't make sense. But my father and my aunt died trying to identify it. My mother betrayed everyone who could have loved her for it. Kenni lost eight years years of her life, and a sister I didn't know I had hates me," she cried out. "I deserve to know why."

She struck out at his chest, her fists slamming against the solid wall of muscle as she nearly lost control of the tears threatening to strangle her.

"I deserve to know why," she whispered, laying her head against his chest and feeling the tentative, gentle touch of his palm as he held her against him.

"And if I can't protect you?" he asked her, his voice quiet as he held her to him. "If something happens to you because I was looking in the wrong place at the wrong time, how do I survive that, Grace?"

She shook her head. "What difference if it's today at Vince's or the day after, or the day after that somewhere else." She pressed her cheek to his chest. "Someone already believes I know something I haven't put together yet, and they want to make sure it doesn't happen. And only the immediate family is aware of the fact that Dad could piece information together and that Vince was hoping I'd learn how to do it. If it's one of them, then today is the only chance we'll have for another month. Because those five rarely come together, and then, only when they have to. And Vince makes sure they understand that once a month, they have to be there."

Because he loved them, she knew. Loved them and regretted the choices he'd had to make that resulted in the endless arguing that seemed to erupt every time they were in the same place at the same time.

And he feared they'd all grow apart somehow, and if they did, then the strength of the Maddox family would fade as well. They were strong, he often said, because they stood strong. They stood together. And he was determined to ensure they always stood together.

Whether they wanted to or not.

She loved her uncles and her aunt Mary. They were an endless source of laughter, warmth, and family dinners at their respective homes. They couldn't get along with Vince, but extended invitations to his sons and to Grace often. They trash-talked their brother, railed about him, but the moment Vince had ever needed them, they were there for him, old feuds forgotten.

The thought that any of them could have a hand in attempting to take over the family and the militia Vince controlled was unthinkable. But Grace didn't just love her family; she also knew them. And she knew any one of them, with the right push, had the potential to turn against Vince.

And all of them were capable of killing.

But were any of them capable of murder? . . .

chapter eighteen

This was a really bad idea, Zack thought as he escorted Grace through the house to the garage where the pickup sat waiting.

Outside, Eamon and Dylan would drive ahead of them with Lobo and Calli behind them and Tech controlling the drone by satellite from wherever the hell he was located. It was all the protection he could give Grace, and it should be overkill. But something was making his neck itch.

Whether instinct or premonition, the hunter always knew when he was being hunted, and Zack had felt hunted for days. That warning that he was being watched, stalked, that a wild card waited, anticipating the best moment to throw a wrench into Zack's plans.

But hell, Grace herself had become a wild card. He hadn't expected her to go to her room and do the dress-for-success thing she'd done while working for Vince. The prissy, tailored pants and silk blouse that made her look like a million bucks and as cool as an ice princess. It made him feel like some lowly knight without a chance of melting her.

It made his dick thicken and throb with the need to feel her melting around him again. Because she might look like an ice princess, but he knew damned well exactly how hot she could get.

Hot enough to burn a man clear to his soul.

The drive from his house to the Maddox home just on the outskirts of Loudon, along the banks of the river, didn't take long, and despite the itch on his neck, they pulled into the Maddox driveway without incident.

That didn't mean there wouldn't be an incident.

One thing you could count on with Vince Maddox and his sons: they were an incident waiting to happen.

When the three black vehicles drew to a stop, Zack breathed out a heavy sigh as he glimpsed dozens of men just inside the tree line bordering the house on three sides.

The front door opened to reveal Cord himself, a scowl on his face as he leaned against the doorframe, simply staring at the truck, his expression closed. Jeans, a short-sleeved shirt, boots, and leather vest with a weapon strapped to his thigh.

It wasn't often he saw the other man so clearly armed.

"What do you think?" he asked Grace as she sat still and quiet in the seat next to him.

Grace watched her cousin carefully, his expression, the way he leaned lazily against the doorframe, thumbs tucked into the leather belt cinching his hips, weapon clearly displayed. He didn't appear to be happy to see them, but he wasn't glaring at them. Weary patience seemed to have settled on his broad shoulders, the temper that could easily explode when tested was nowhere in sight, but it was simmering.

"He expected us," she said quietly. "He's resigned to something, but he doesn't like it. He'll fight it. But he's expecting trouble. He's also anticipating something. Cord likes to stir things up sometimes. He says it gets results. He reminds me a lot of the stories I've heard about Dad."

"You know this how?" Skepticism colored his voice as he gripped the steering wheel, glancing from Cord to her. "He just looks pissed to me."

And he might, to someone who didn't know him as well as she did.

"You're looking at his expression, not his eyes, or the way he's trying to appear relaxed. The tension in his shoulders tells another story. They're straight rather than slouched as they would be when he's relaxed. His feet are firmly planted rather than tilted in with his body. He's ready to react." She knew the members of her family in ways she doubted they suspected.

She'd watched them, studied them over the years, just as she did everyone else she came in contact with. She knew body language, expressions, and even the lack of expressions told their own story. What she hadn't known instinctively, she'd learned by reading. She had known when dealing with personalities as strong as her uncle and cousins that she'd need an edge to keep up with them.

She wasn't confrontational, she wasn't an in-their-face type person, and trying to be such a person only gave her indigestion.

"Possible danger?" Zack asked.

She snorted at the question, amused that he'd ask it. "He'd love to bruise your other eye, but you're not in danger of a bullet, if that's what you're asking."

"What about you? Are you in danger of a bullet?" Something dark and dangerous edged his voice at the question.

"Not as far as Cord's concerned." She shook her head slowly. "He'd neither pull the trigger nor give the order. He's not above playing the game, though. He's after something," she murmured thoughtfully. "I suspect he expected us, and he'll use it."

"Hide-and-seek. Come on, honey, let's go play with them for a little while," he muttered, the words causing her to still, to hold her breath as he opened his door and slid from the vehicle.

Hide-and-seek. Where had she heard that before, in relation to her search for information?

"I'll hide," she said softly as he opened the door.

"I'll seek," he drawled, gripping her waist and helping her down.

He'd keep them distracted enough that they wouldn't watch her as closely as they might otherwise, allowing her to glimpse any unguarded expressions or telltale body language.

He'd ask the questions, she'd wait for the silent answers.

She knew that game. She knew it all too well.

"Afternoon, Zack," Cord greeted them with a drawl, all southern cordial and mockingly welcome.

"Cord," Zack returned the greeting in the same vein as they started up the steps to the porch. "I could complain, I reckon, but would anyone listen?"

Southern male posturing. It was subtle, polite for the most part, but filled with knowledge of one another.

"Gettin' someone to listen is the easy part. Now, gettin' them to do something about it is a mite harder," Cord pointed out as they stepped to the porch. "This isn't a good idea, cuz," Cord stated softly, his gaze softening as she and Zack neared him. "Family night's savage as hell, and you seem to be their favorite topic of conversation tonight. Go back to Zack's and settle in with a movie or something."

"And spoil your plans?" she asked, seeing his surprise that she actually called him on the fact that he knew she'd be there and he'd planned accordingly.

"Only if you stay, sweetheart." Fondness softened his features. "You leave, and I'll cover you, you know that. Stay, and they'll focus on you more than they'll focus on each other."

"Like a pack of coyotes scenting blood," Zack snorted.

"Or sharks," Cord agreed with a sigh before he straightened from the door. "We found Richard James." His gaze locked on Zack's. "Dead. Missin' his innards, too, when we found him. You know anything about that?"

The gruesome act had her stomach churning. Who would do something like that?

"Not me," Zack assured him, though satisfaction radiated from him. "And here I would have just put a bullet in his heart.

Cord's lips quirked, no doubt hearing the echo of disappointment in Zack's voice that Grace caught as well.

"Might as well come on in and let the family see

you're alive, Grace." His smile was faintly sardonic. "Before they save me the trouble and kill each other."

It was a monthly refrain, a monthly threat.

Despite the thoughtful glances her cousin cast her way, Grace didn't acknowledge them, and she didn't speak. She couldn't.

"You know, Grace." Cord surprised her when he paused in front of the doors to her uncle's office and stared back at her somberly. "Sometimes, to protect the people he loves, a man has to give the impression he doesn't care if they're protected or not. Doesn't mean he hasn't done all he can to ensure that protection, or that he wouldn't step in at the last minute if needed."

It wasn't an apology; it was a statement. Cord was trying to tell her he'd done what he felt was best. But he didn't regret the decisions he'd made.

"Enough, Cord," Zack growled. "Leave her alone until she can piece this shit together."

Cord glanced back at him thoughtfully. "Want another fist in that ugly face of yours?"

It wasn't a rhetorical question. Cord wanted a fight, the tension gathering in his body would take the outlet if Zack wanted to accommodate him.

"The two of you aren't twelve anymore," she informed them both scathingly. "Cord, get out of the way. Now."

"Mouthy brat," he muttered, but opened the doors and stepped inside with a cocky swagger she hadn't seen him use in years.

"Look who came to visit," he announced as the four men and their baby sister turned to the door in surprise. "It's Grace and her guard dog, Zack."

Vince sat at his desk, leaning back in the comfortable red leather chair and staring at his family, his face flushed, jaw clenched as each of them leaned over the desk, yelling over the general state of the family and the Kin.

At Cord's announcement, they stared at Grace for long, silent moments, their expressions as unguarded as they were going to get.

"And did you hear? We found Richard James," Cord stated, causing all eyes to swing to him. "Stomach tore open and his guts missing, but it was definitely him." He turned back to Zack and Grace to mutter, "There, I got them all warmed up for you."

Cord had been waiting on something, all right, and he was definitely after something. He was waiting on Grace and Zack and the chance to make his announcement as she watched the family staring back at them.

Shifts of expression, tones of voice, they were often subtle, slight. The answer wasn't always immediately apparent, but Grace knew when suspicion and knowledge were on the same path. As Cord and Zack kept the rest of the family from focusing on who she was watching and when, she kept her lashes lowered, her attention measuring each of them as questions and accusations were thrown like vicious blows among four brothers and a sister who would claim at any given time to love each other. As long as they weren't in each other's company.

The answers were there, as was the guilt. She could feel it. The tension radiating amid the anger and defensiveness slid like an oily residue over her senses. Body language and expression went a long way, and could be learned. Instinct was far different. And that instinct assured Grace that whoever orchestrated her father's and aunt's deaths, whoever was determined to destroy her, they were in that room.

The questions didn't reach into the past. Zack and Cord kept the arguments focused on Lucia and Grace. Who suspected Lucia was conspiring against Vince, who didn't. Who was Lucia seen with, how Richard James had learned of Luce's accusations against her daughter.

Richard was known by each of them. He'd gone to school with Grace, knew her cousins, socialized with them. He'd returned after a single tour in the service and stepped into the lower ranks of the Kin.

Of course, none of them knew if Ray and Lucia had socialized much, except Grace. And she knew her uncles were lying about it. Each of them was. Several times Lucia had mentioned seeing them at this party or that barbecue, kissing up to the agency, Lucia had stated insultingly.

Her aunt Mary didn't deny it in the least. She invited him to dinner several times, and yes, Lucia had attended a few of those same dinners. No, they hadn't seemed overly friendly.

"She was nothing but a whore anyway, it seems," Teague, the third youngest brother sneered, his Maddox looks softened by his mother's side of the family.

"The point they're getting to," the oldest brother next to Vince, Camden, bit out. "Is did we whore with her. And I sure as hell didn't." He thumped his chest for emphasis. "I might cuss him twice a day, but Vinny's still my brother. Fucking prick," he muttered, turning to the brother in question. "So was Ben."

"Point taken," Vince snorted, still slumped in his chair and glaring at his family.

"I might have if she wasn't such an all-fired bitch," Egan, the younger brother proclaimed angrily. "She thought she was better than every one of us, Vinny included." He stabbed at finger at his brother. "Dammit, Vinny, what the hell did you marry that little tramp for."

Grace could feel her throat tightening with tears. It was the truth; she knew it was the truth. Lucia hadn't inspired respect in anyone. But Grace still found it humiliating to hear her uncles speak of her mother in such a way.

"That's enough of that." Mary turned on the three of them, her tone disgusted. "We might not have liked Lucia, but Grace is another matter entirely. At least care enough about her to temper what the hell y'all are saying."

The three brothers turned their glare on Grace.

"She knows the truth," Teague snapped, adjusting the band of his slacks over his thick stomach before glaring back at his sister. "It's not like she's surprised by it."

"You're a moron, Teague," Mary informed him angrily. "How Lana puts up with you, I have no idea."

Teague sniffed at the insult. "I'm a moron? I'm not the one who married my brother's wife, now, am I? I warned all of you then that there would be problems from that, and you didn't want to listen," he snapped, his face twisting with anger and superiority.

"Teague, you, Egan, and Camden can take your asses home and leave me the hell alone." Vince rose angrily from his chair then and stalked to his sister, where he gripped her shoulders and kissed her cheek affectionately, if impatiently. "Go home Mary, I've had enough."

Her brothers were always gentler with her than they were with each other, and Vinny always swore she was the best of the lot of them.

Her expression softened. "I love you, Vinny," she sighed. "But fix this shit, it's getting on my nerves." She shot Teague a fuming look, then returned her brother's kiss, gathered up her purse, and moved to Grace. "Stay away from this place, sweetie," she told Grace, giving her a quick hug. "It's bad for your blood pressure." Mary swept from the room in a cloud of subtly spiced perfume, the office door slamming behind her.

"I've had it, too," Egan declared, his tone heavy with resignation. "I don't know why we even do this every month. Nothing changes, everything stays the same, and I'm tired of having it shoved down my throat." He shot Vince a hard look, contempt flashing for just a moment in his expression. "You should have stepped down years ago or gave one of us Ben's place, Vinny. Because you're jacking it all up."

By now, Vince had his elbow propped on the arm of the chair, his cheek resting against it as he watched them with an irritated frown. Which was normal by this point.

"I agree with Teague," Camden snapped. "You should have replaced Ben—"

"Replaced my twin?" Vince sat up again at that, his expression tightening angrily. "Which of you do you think would have fit the role, Teague? You?" He laughed at that. "I can't spend an hour around you without wishing we'd drowned you at birth. And you, Camden?" He shot his other brother a mocking roll of his eyes. "Really? I'm still not convinced you're even related to me. The only one of you I can tolerate for more than a short span of time is Egan. And he's smart enough to leave. Or Mary. God love her heart, she's just too sweet to be related to any of us. There's no way in hell any of us are related to her."

Grace had heard that said so many times. Mary would always laugh and point out her green eyes and the fact that as much as she hated it, she had her father's nose. And she did, too. It wasn't the most becoming part of her face either.

"I'm like Egan, this bullshit is a waste of time. I could be sleeping," Camden muttered, shooting Grace a glare. "Sorry if I hurt your feelings, girl." He cleared his throat, though his expression didn't change.

Stomping past them, he, too, left the room.

That left Teague.

He shook his head and shot Vince a look filled with disgust. "If it weren't for Cord, you'd have already lost control of everything our family has worked for generations to accomplish. And you risk it every damned day with this bullshit where Lucia and Grace are concerned." He shook his head, the look he gave Grace uncompromising. "I'm sorry, honey, but you don't belong here. You're my niece and I think the world of you, but your daddy was a whoremonger and your momma no more than a tramp. You're bad blood—"

Zack and Cord moved at the same time. Which would have gotten to him first, Grace wasn't certain, but Vince beat them both, the fist he slammed into his brother's face knocking him on his ass.

Where he stayed.

Gripping his jaw, he chuckled at the blow and worked it slowly, his expression resigned as he looked up at his brother. "At least you still know how to do that."

"Banyon!" he bellowed.

Banyon didn't step into the office alone, Baer followed, and neither of her half brothers appeared in pleasant spirits.

"Just make sure he leaves, then call Lana and tell her to have him take his antidepressants before coming back here."

"And be nice to him," Grace spoke up then, staring at her uncle with an acceptance that weighed at her heart.

"Be nice to him?" Baer asked carefully. "Why? He just called you bad blood, dammit. We were standing outside the door, not the other side of the property, Grace. Everyone in hearing distance heard him say it."

Lifting her head, she met his dark, emerald green eyes directly. "At least he acknowledged we were related," she told him flatly. "It's a hell of a lot more than the two of you have ever done."

And it was. She'd been raised with the knowledge that they were her brothers. Raised knowing it and watching them from afar, wishing they'd act like brothers. They had yet to do so.

She turned on her heel and moved slowly for the doorway.

"Grace, for someone who sees so much more than others do, you've been incredibly blind," Baer said sadly.

"No, I haven't," she admitted, turning to stare back

at him. "I've seen the games. I just didn't appreciate being shanghaied rather than invited to participate. Try an invitation next time, I might be more obliging." Then she shook her head, her eyes lifting to Zack's. "On the other hand, maybe I won't be."

She walked slowly from the house to the truck were Lobo opened the door for her, his gaze somber. Of course, she'd forgotten about the communication devices they were wearing that paired to Zack's. Wasn't she the smart one?

"Grace." He touched her arm gently before she lifted herself into the truck. "I'm sorry, girl."

I'm sorry, girl. . . .

"I'm sorry, girl," her father laughed as she pouted when she lost her hold on her kite. "There'll be another time."

"I'm sorry, girl." Her father patted her shoulder gently. "Maybe you can go with me next time. . . ."

"I'm sorry, girl. . . ."

"So am I," she whispered pulling herself into the truck and feeling immeasurably tired. "So am I."

"Well, you handled that one well," Zack stated as he watched Grace pull herself into the truck, Cord and Vince just behind him. "You know, the men in this family are a hazard to the safety of anyone who gives a shit about them, and that's the truth."

"Damn, Uncle Ben used to say that, too," Cord breathed out roughly. "We still don't know who the hell is after her, though. I was hoping she'd see something. . . ." He shook his head at the thought.

"Haven't you and Vince used her enough?" he asked

Cord softly, the anger at he felt at the look on her face burning in his gut. "You've sure as hell hurt her enough."

"It beat burying her," Vince sighed. "That's what we would have had to do otherwise. She was supposed to be with Ben the night his truck went up in flames, Zack. She would have died with him."

He turned to the other man slowly. "She was supposed to be with him?"

Vince nodded. "Ben wanted her to go with him, but Grace was sick that evening and couldn't go."

Ben had intended to take Grace with him the night he'd planned to leave Loudon. The explosion had caught him unaware when he stepped from the vehicle to meet Clyde in his. It had nearly killed him. Had Grace been with him, he'd probably have waited in the truck instead to protect her. And they would both have died that night, along with his parents.

Ben had never meant to leave Grace behind, though. Zack hadn't known that, and he didn't believe his sister knew it at the time either.

"Did Grace know where he was going? That he wanted her to go?" he asked her uncle.

Vince shook his head. "She never knew. And we never told her." He shrugged at the answer. "It would have been cruel to tell her that. Even Lucia hadn't known. Thank God."

Despite Calli's conviction, Grace hadn't known where he was going that evening either. It was a belief she'd obviously held far longer than they'd been in Loudon, too. He'd have to be sure to discuss that particular situation with Ben himself. He wasn't looking forward to the meeting.

"If you think of anything, call me," Zack ordered then, ignoring the veiled looks of disbelief the other two men shot him as he left. "Until then, make sure you show up with that system, Vince. Let Grace do what she does best and piece it together. Before someone takes her out."

And he needed to be with Grace. She looked too damned alone where she sat in the cab of the truck, waiting still and silent, refusing to look toward the house.

"We love her, Zack," Vince said as he stepped from the house. "I know she doesn't believe that now, but we love her."

"Try showing it next time. She'd probably appreciate that more," he advised them, almost wincing at the advice as he walked away from them.

Damn this place, this family.

Damn him.

Grace had been lied to so many times and in so many ways that he doubted she'd ever trust in the word "love" again. And who could blame her?

Sliding into the truck and starting the motor, he looked over at her, praying she wasn't crying. "Back to the house?" he asked softly, seeing no tears on her face nor the damp sheen of recent ones.

She nodded slowly. "That seems the only option, doesn't it?"

He breathed out heavily and put the truck in gear before driving around the curved driveway and heading back to the main road with Dylan and Eamon, Lobo and Calli maintaining their positions.

It was the only option left for her, she'd said.

Zack considered that statement as he drove back to the house, glaring into the late-summer day, wondering why the hell it bothered him so much. It shouldn't. But damn, it mattered. He didn't want it to be her only option; he wanted it to be her choice.

chapter nineteen

Within hours, Cord, Sawyer, and Deacon arrived with the laptop that held the files Grace needed. The fact that her uncle let it out of his home shocked her. The risk he'd taken showed how imperative it was that whatever her father had hidden be found, or at the least that the traitor be revealed.

And like her, Grace suspected, he'd begun to believe whoever had been pulling the strings for the twenty-odd years was someone in the immediate family.

Luce had always said that the lives they lived were nothing but lies and subterfuge, and Vince and Ben Maddox had perfected the game but their brothers had perfected using it against them.

The age of technology, terrorists both homegrown and abroad, and their ability to cause such destruction had necessitated those qualities. It had always increased the risk that they could be betrayed. And suspecting one of the uncles she so loved had perpetuated that betrayal, and the murder of his own brother, was more than she could bear.

With the information her uncle had and the stacks of files and pictures Zack brought to her after setting her up in his office, she went to work trying to piece the puzzle together.

There was so much information. Years and years of information, threads so tightly woven with others that she knew she could spend years picking them apart. Even her father would have had a hard time with it after all this time.

Laying aside other pieces of information to follow later, Grace concentrated first on the weekly reports her father had filed in the two years before his death. He was thorough, concise, but still, pulling out what she needed while deciding what to ignore wasn't easy.

After creating another digital file, she began to log each piece of information and notate it back to others that tied in with it. It kept her busy, kept her from considering other suspicions, other lies, while Zack met with her uncle and cousins and the men watching the house.

Kin wasn't just a title given to some covert group. They were called Kin because family ties, loyalty, and a belief in the preservation of freedom bound them. Politics weren't an agenda with them. If the time ever came that America was betrayed by its own government, then the Kin would stand against it as well.

It was hidden in layers upon layers of secrecy, behind individuals, some supposedly not so patriotic, others with less-than-sterling characters. All tied to the family but with no obvious link to them.

Illegitimate children marrying into political families, while others laid out their own paths to place themselves in a position of strength, defined the Kin.

There had always been those who tried to betray them. What stopped them was that with the exception of the main family, no one knew what everyone else was doing or what they were really a part of. It was how they stayed safe.

But now, someone in that family was far too close to possessing information that would allow them to use it, to sell the secrets built upon over generations to weaken the defenses in place.

It came down to control. Someone believed they should have it, and hated Vince because he was strong enough to keep it.

The fact that the answers she'd needed to find hadn't been readily apparent during the earlier meeting bothered her. She could sense them, something she'd glimpsed in an expression that wasn't clear enough, kept teasing at her memory. A flash of guilt or knowledge. But so much had been going on, all of them talking at once in some cases, and all of them angry, that keeping up hadn't always been easy.

The information laid out around her kept her so deep in the past that when Zack came up to inform her it was time for supper, she looked up in surprise, realizing she was starving.

Grilled steaks and potatoes waited on the deck in the backyard, the succulent meat and fluffy potatoes grilled perfectly. A light breeze flowed off the water and made into the protected area, whispering through the mountains and easing around them.

"Come inside and talk to me for a bit." The request was more an order after they cleaned up.

Grace nodded hesitantly and followed him into the house, through the kitchen, and into the television room behind it.

A pool table stood at one end of the room, an old pinball machine not far from it. A large-screen television hung on the opposite wall with a large, overstuffed L-shaped couch and two recliners positioned for optimal viewing.

A well-stocked bar was placed close to the double doors, the mirrored shelf behind it filled with various bottles and glasses. He moved behind the bar, took down a short whiskey glass, and uncorked a bottle of whiskey before splashing some into the glass.

"Want some?" He held the bottle up in invitation.

Her brow arched. "I really don't think that's a good idea. You want me sober for this discussion, don't you?"

His lips quirked at the reminder that she didn't handle alcohol well at all.

"You really haven't gotten to have a lot of fun lately, have you?" he asked, the gentleness in his voice immediately capturing her attention.

Lifting the glass to his lips, he sipped the liquor, watching her closely, the thoughtful expression on his face causing her heart to pick up in speed and a sense of nervousness to rush through her.

He and Cord both had expected more from that meeting today, she thought. She had, as well. It was there, she just had to figure out everything she'd begun tying together.

"I expected Cord to call by now." She raked her

fingers through her hair, fidgeting as he rested his elbows on the bar and just watched her silently, sipping occasionally at the whiskey. "He's a little harder to read than most. Kind of like you," she told him. "But I can't stop feeling he didn't get something he wanted, something he expected. I thought he would have come up and talked to me about it before leaving."

"Hmm," Zack murmured, sipping at the amber liquid as she pushed her hands into the pockets of the soft, flowing skirt she'd changed into after arriving back at the house. "I like that skirt. It looks pretty on you."

The compliment threw her for a moment. She hadn't expected it. "Uh, thank you." She cleared her throat, her hands clenching in the hidden pockets of the pale cream and sapphire blue chiffon and silk.

When paired with the light, sleeveless summer knit top that buttoned just above the cleavage of her breasts, it gave her a soft, feminine look she liked.

"You always dress pretty," he murmured, shifting behind the bar as he continued to watch her with that thoughtful look. "I'd like to see you in cut-offs, a T-shirt, and sneakers, though. Just for the hell of it."

"I wear those to work in my flower garden." She shrugged, frowning. "We were talking about Cord, though."

He grimaced at the reminder. "I don't want to talk about Cord. He pisses me off enough whenever I'm forced to talk to him. I'd prefer not to talk about him."

He finished his drink, then fixed another, his movements unhurried, almost relaxed.

"That isn't what I've seen when the two of you are

together," she told him, ignoring the dark look he flashed her as he sipped at the drink.

"It's complicated," he admitted. "But still, not what I want to talk about tonight."

She stepped to the barstool at the farthest end of the bar from him and gripped the seat back as she watched him warily. "What do you want to talk about, then?" she asked, her fingers clenching on the wood of the barstool. "Besides my clothes, that is."

His lips quirked at that, his lashes shielding his gaze for a moment as he stared at her. "Your clothes are far more interesting, I have to admit." He grinned. "The lack of your clothes is even more interesting."

Grace could feel herself flushing. She wasn't certain how she could actually blush after the things they'd done together sexually. The heat moved from her neck over her face though at the same time her breasts swelled further, her nipples peaking harder beneath her bra.

Not that her body wasn't already primed for him—it was. She stayed primed for his touch. But at the mention of lack of clothes, it kicked into an accelerated rate of arousal. It was highly disconcerting.

He finished his drink, set the glass aside, and returned to his previous position, elbows resting on the bar as he leaned forward, catching his weight on them. His expression was still far too thoughtful, too watchful. He was looking for something without giving away so much as a hint of what he wanted or what he was thinking.

"Is that what we're discussing, then?" she asked, fighting to hide her nervousness. "The lack of my clothes?"

His lips twitched in amusement. "Only if you're taking them off."

"Take yours off first," she suggested, suddenly far too interested in this conversation. "Then we'll discuss whether or not I take off mine."

He laughed, surprised pleasure flashing across his expression as his teeth flashed in amusement. "You got me on that one," he admitted. "I'd personally prefer you take yours off first."

"Personal preference doesn't mean you'll get your way," she sighed teasingly, barely able to keep her heart from pounding out of her chest, it was racing so hard.

He wagged his finger back at her, the sensual intent on his face increasing as he watched her. "I owe you a spanking."

"So you said, on several occasions." She smiled, resting her arms on the back of the stool before laying her chin against them. "And I keep telling you I'm a good girl. Ask anyone."

"Hmm, but you wanna be bad, don't you, baby?" he drawled. "You like it when I make you be bad. Admit it."

Oh God . . .

She couldn't breathe. She could barely think.

He was far too dangerous, far too sexy.

"I'm still deciding." She gave a teasing little wrinkle of her nose and decided she liked him when he was playful like this.

Never admit to anything when it comes to the opposite sex, her Aunt Mary had laughingly advised her on more than one occasion. They don't need to know too much too soon.

A crooked grin tilted his lips before he scratched at

his cheek thoughtfully. "Think it will take you long to decide? I was considering other ways you could be bad. If you wanted to be, that is?"

"Now, Zack, I'm always open to suggestions," she assured him breathlessly, far too hot and creaming her panties like never before. "You'll just have to let me know what you have in mind. When the time's right, of course."

He eased closer until he was directly across from her before resuming his previous position, glanced behind her, then met her gaze with seductive intent. "Has a lover ever actually spanked you?" he questioned her softly. "Spanked that pretty ass as he fucked you from behind? Or at your sweet pussy until you were crazy to be fucked, only to spank it instead until you screaming for release?"

Her heart rate was going to strangle her any second. "No." Grace swallowed tightly. "No, can't say I have."

Anticipation filled the smile that tugged at his lips. "I could show you how bad you want to be, Grace," he offered, wicked, knowing hunger gleaming in his eyes. "If you wanted to stick around for a while."

If she wanted to stick around for a while?

Her heart stopped for precious seconds; she swore it did. She lost her breath, her ability to function or even think until it suddenly jumped back into action and slammed into her throat. "I could be convinced to stick around for a while," she finally answered, staring back at him, terrified she might be misunderstanding something.

Did he actually mean he wanted her to stay, even after all this was over?

"It could take a while." He nodded then. "Being bad isn't an overnight process, you know?"

She nodded at that. "I would imagine it isn't." Grace licked her dry lips nervously.

"And it would be understood there is to be no experimenting with anyone else." Something hard and possessive flashed in his eyes. "It would be just between us. Period."

Grace lifted her head from her arms and drew in a hard breath. "Zack, are you asking me to move in with you, after this is over?" She had to be certain. If she let herself believe it, then found out he'd meant something else, it would destroy her.

"I'm asking you to belong to me—just me, Grace. Beginning now," he amended, his eyes darkening with far more than simple lust.

"I already belong to you," she whispered.

He nodded at that. "No more running to the guest room because you're pissed. You sleep in my bed, we'll work out any problems that come up. We'll take things slow and easy, but we work at making it work. Agreed?"

Okay, that sounded easy enough. "Agreed." She finally nodded.

"Promise me," he urged, that sensual, dark hunger gleaming in the depths of his eyes. "Promise me, Grace. We work out any problems and make it work."

She felt dazed by her own arousal, and that look of wicked intent she could see on his face. "I promise," she agreed. "We work out any problems and make it work."

Just like any relationship, she thought. Not that she'd heard of Zack having many of those. Hell, she hadn't really had an intimate relationship herself. Having a lover wasn't the same thing. And Zack would never be like any other lover.

Straightening he stalked from behind the bar, Zack came around to her and as she turned to face him reached behind her to swing the barstool around. Strong, broad hands gripped her hips and lifted her to the seat, moving between her thighs, his hips pressing into the vee of her legs, the hard wedge of his cock cushioned against her sex.

"You know," he murmured, one hand lifting to cup the side of her head. "I've fantasized for years about corrupting all that innocence I see in your eyes." His head lowered, lips brushing against hers as he continued to stare down at her. "It might take me a long, long time to do that."

The all-too-brief kiss he gave her just left her hungrier for more.

"A long time," she whispered, her breath catching as the material of her skirt was pushed to the furthermost point of her thighs.

Grace held on to his arms, loving the feel of his biceps flexing beneath her fingers, the way the muscles of his shoulders rippled beneath his hard flesh.

She stared up at him, biting her lip to hold back everything she wanted to say, to confess as dazed anticipation rocked her senses.

"Sweet Grace." His lips brushed against hers again. "Love me, baby. Just love me."

Just love him?

"I always have." She fought to speak as she fought for

breath, excitement stealing her ability to process much beyond the sheer, overwhelming implications of the request. "Don't you know, Zack? I always have."

His head tilted, one hand cupping the back of her neck, the other bracing against the bar behind her as his lips came overs with such heated, hungry demand that it rocked her senses. He kissed her like he was dying for the touch, the taste of her. For all of her.

And she could only give him all of her, not that she'd held much back to begin with. All she'd tried to keep from him was that part of her heart that would keep her world from collapsing entirely if she lost him. But she'd lost even that part of her heart already, she admitted.

Holding on to him, her arms wrapped around his neck, her fingers burrowing through his hair to hold him to her, Grace reveled in him. The feel of him, the heat of his hard body, the sexual intensity that became so focused on her.

One hand moved to her thigh, lifting it along his, giving him better access to press the hard, denim-covered length of his cock into her sex. Heat spilled from her vagina, sensation tightened her clit and sent those spirals of pleasure rushing through her body and her senses. Drugged, drunk of the high his touch gave her, Grace reveled in every second of it.

So much so that the strident, irritating sound of Zack's cell phone didn't immediately register. Not until his lips pulled from hers, a frustrated curse slipping from his them, did she even acknowledge the distinctive, discordant ring.

"One of these days," he muttered, pulling back from

her slowly, regret and a flash of worry shadowing his gaze. "I have to answer this."

Jerking the phone from the clip at his side, he stepped farther away from her, rubbing at the back of his neck as he lifted the phone to his ear.

"What the fuck do you want?" he growled. Paused.

Tension snapped through his body like a live wire as Grace pushed her skirt down her thighs, watching him closely.

"What?" he snarled, his tone dark with fury now. "Like hell . . ." His voice lowered, but she still heard his side of the conversation. "It's too fucking soon . . ."

Turning back, his gaze locked with hers, and though he tried to hide it, though he was hiding it, she saw the tormented flash of grave, certain destruction in his eyes.

She should have paid more attention earlier, she thought. Whoever was on that phone, whatever was going on, was the reason he'd extracted that earlier promise from her.

"Fine," he snarled moments later. Paused. "I said fine, I'll fucking be there."

His hand jerked back and for a moment Grace thought he'd throw the phone. Instead, slowly, with deliberate care, he pushed it back into the clip at his belt instead.

Grace slid from the barstool, smoothed her skirt into place, and watched him silently until he turned to her, his expression savage with the fury filling it.

"Problems?" she asked mildly.

"So Lobo's convinced." His jaw bunched, that tormented flash of emotion she found so hard to define making an appearance once again as he propped his hands on his hips and stared back at her broodingly.

"Lobo's convinced it's a problem." She nodded, feeling a thread, a piece of information teasing at her mind. "Well, I guess you need to take care of it, then? It could be important."

"Grace." Dropping his hands, he stepped to her, then gripped her shoulders before stroking down her arm, seeming uncertain what to say for a moment. "I won't be long." He finally grimaced. "You're not alone either. Lobo, Calli, Dylan, and Eamon will be right outside if you need them. I'm not going far."

"Take me with you," she demanded, suddenly certain, knowing to the bottom of her soul that he needed to take her with him.

"Not yet." He dropped a hasty kiss to her lips and moved away before she could grab hold of him and strode from the television room.

Grace remained where she was until she heard the front door close before drawing in a slow, deep breath. Whatever Lobo found so important, Zack didn't believe it was dangerous to her or to him. He was furious, though. So furious that the sound of the Jeep's motor racing, tires screaming as they caught traction on the blacktop, could be heard even in the house before she watched the lights of the vehicle racing farther up the mountain rather than away from it.

There was a cabin located along that road, she knew. There were a few hunting cabins. . . .

She walked slowly to the window across the room and watched as the lights disappeared around the bend of the mountain, one hand lifting to the pane of glass as she stared at her own bleak reflection before stepping back and striding out of the television room.

Moving through the living room and entry, she glanced at the front door, the sight of Lobo leaning against the porch railing clear through the narrow side window next to the heavy wood door.

She didn't pause, but ran up the stairs to the guest room and quickly undressed.

Jeans, a dark T-shirt, thick socks, and her hiking boots. The cabins weren't far up the mountain, and she was certain she could slip from the house and get past Zack's friends without them seeing her. After all, they weren't expecting her to try to leave.

Slipping from the bedroom again, she moved quickly back down the stairs, grateful she'd turned out the lights before going up. There would be no chance of her being glimpsed as she made her way through the house, obviously dressed far differently than she had been earlier.

Lobo and the other two men, Eamon and Dylan, had been out front when she went to change, and Calli was probably with them, which meant the kitchen door would be her best bet. Besides, it was the most direct route to the road leading up the mountain.

"Slick." The feminine drawl was almost a whisper as Grace reached the back door.

She was almost in a crouch and reaching for the weapon she'd tucked into the inside of her boot before she stopped herself and turned slowly instead.

Calli sat on the counter in the darkest corner of the room. The other girl slid from her perch, settling silently on her feet as she crossed her arms over her breasts. "Sure you want to do that?" she asked when Grace didn't say anything. "Actually chase after him and see what he's hiding?"

There was a warning in her half sister's voice, one Grace clearly understood. There was no going back once she learned whatever Zack was hiding.

"I usually know what I'm doing whenever I begin a particular action," Grace assured her.

Calli breathed in hard and glanced away, her lips tightening for a moment as she obviously considered some problem.

"You'll get yourself killed out there by yourself," she sniffed disdainfully. "Like a fucking babe in the woods, no doubt."

Grace shrugged. "You know, I might take you a little more seriously if you didn't have such a fondness for four-letter words. Why don't you stay here where it's safe? I know where I'm going."

Calli's eyes widened in outrage. "You bitch!" she hissed. "Fuck you, Miss Prissy Pants. Me and my four-letter words get along just fine."

Grace stared at her sister silently, refusing to consider the pain she wouldn't let herself feel right now. Not now. Not until she found out why it had been so important to her that Zack take her with him.

"Your four-letter words show your immaturity and the depth of your lack of self-confidence," Grace informed her knowingly. "Now, stay, go, I really don't care. But make up your mind now."

"I could just call for Lobo," the other girl stated spitefully. "Then he'll call Zack, who'll come rushing back to soothe your ruffled little feathers. Or whatever." The suggestive tone and demeaning expression only drew a pitying glance from Grace.

"And a tattletale, too." She gripped the doorknob and

opened the door silently. "Do what you must, little sister, just as I'm doing."

She left the house, pausing outside the door long enough to catch the faint sound of the men still talking at the front of the house. Assured no one was watching, she sprinted from the porch, across the backyard, careful to stay away from the motion lights Zack had pointed out her first night there, and reach the tree line before pausing.

"Zack will kill me for this!" Calli snapped in a furious whisper from her side. "And it will be all your fault."

Casting a look heavenward, Grace wondered if God was laughing at her at the moment. She'd done the same thing to Sawyer and Deacon more than once when they'd tried to slip out of the house during her teenage years.

"I'll take the blame," she promised. "Now, let's go. Otherwise, he'll be back and in the bed asleep before we even get there."

Moving quickly, Grace made her way through the trees, Calli hot on her heels. She couldn't risk the penlight she'd brought with her, not until she was out of sight of the house.

"Put these on." Calli shoved something in her hands with a grunt of disgust. "You left and didn't bring a weapon, water, or anything. Dammit, you always carry a pack."

The gogglelike glasses Calli had shoved in her hands were actually night-vision goggles. Not the best, but easy to pack and wear.

"Before you leave, maybe you'll make me a list of what to pack," Grace suggested, moving faster now that she could see where she was going.

"Maybe Zack will learn to handcuff your ass to the bed," Calli sniffed instead. "I'm so going to get busted for this."

"Then go back." She was getting tired of hearing about it. "I won't tell anyone you saw me and you can just play dumb."

"Want to know how far that one will get me?" Calli drawled, her tone irate. "Or can you pretty much guess?"

They were all but running through the woods, a steady pace that wasn't straining, but didn't lend itself to conversation.

"Shut up," she ordered the girl.

"Can't run and talk at the same time?" Calli asked knowingly. "You should have stayed in bed."

Grace didn't answer, just kept her pace and concentrated on her landmarks. There were two cabins along this road; only one had electricity. She was counting on the cabin with electricity.

"You didn't get to train a lot when you were younger, did you?" Calli pointed out, easily keeping up with her and talking at the same time.

She hadn't gotten to train a lot. She'd learned what she needed to, but her heart hadn't been in it.

"Too busy playing with your Barbies and fixing your hair?" Calli snorted.

She'd never cared much for Barbie, and her hair wouldn't hold a curl, which made trying to style it pretty much a waste of time.

"I bet you were a freakin' cheerleader," Calli guessed in disgust. "Go team go, right?"

"Editor. School paper." Grace hadn't gone the cheerleading route either. "Class president. Valedictorian."

She was so glad she kept up with the jogging along the mountain trails on the Maddox property. If she hadn't, she would have dropped before the half-mile mark.

"What about you?" Grace asked. "I bet you made a pretty cheerleader. Short skirts and tight tops," she teased her sister.

It wasn't mean or snide, just enough, Grace hoped, to get the other girl talking.

"I really hate you," Calli injected with no small amount of surliness. "I really do."

"Uh-huh. Give me a cheer, then," she suggested, catching a glimpse of lights through the trees farther ahead.

"Reporter and editor, school paper four years running. Class president, valedictorian, and honor guard," Calli snapped. "Now, follow me or you'll get caught before we even get there. My ass is so kicked for this."

chapter twenty

Benjamin Maddox and Ureana Richards stood next to the fireplace, Ben's arm around his lover's small waist, his expression brooding and heavy in the low light of the living room lamp.

Like his twin, Ben was still tall and strong for his age, though his hair might not be so gray as Vinny's. Other than the slash of a scar over his left eye and one lower, along his jaw, he was still Vinny's twin.

Ureana, nearly fifteen years his junior, was still remarkably pretty. Tanned, fit, Ben often complained that he had to stay young just to keep up with her. At the moment, Ben looked every bit his age, though, and then some.

Sitting in the recliner facing the fireplace, Clyde Brigham actually had his feet propped up, boots off, his automatic rifle was leaning against the arm of the chair as he peeled and ate an orange, section by section, and watched Zack with knowing gray eyes.

Clyde's wife, Mena, was still bustling around the cabin, putting away clothes, making certain everything was ready for breakfast the next day while several of the hard-eyed men his uncle and Ben Maddox had saved and trained over the years stood ready in case of trouble.

"You're early!" Zack snapped, glaring at all of them as he paused at the entrance of the main room. "Dammit to hell, it's been less than twenty-four hours. You owe me three more days."

Clyde grunted at the protest and dropped his orange peels into the paper bowl resting on his lap. "Shoulda expected it," he mumbled around the orange. "He's an impatient bastard." He flicked his finger in Ben's direction.

Ben shot his lover's uncle a look of resigned disbelief. Ben wasn't the impatient one in the family, though his determination to return to Loudon had been making Zack's life very uncomfortable for the past year.

"I have three more days," Zack repeated through clenched teeth.

"Wrong. Time's up." Clyde tucked the last slice of orange between his lips and stared back at Zack blandly. A look that spelled mayhem if Zack didn't do something to rein his uncle in.

"And may I ask why my time is up?" Zack questioned him.

Get the facts, he warned himself. Before going ballistic, always get the facts.

"'Cause, word's already out that Grace is pokin' her nose into stuff." Clyde sat the bowl of orange peels on the table next to him and stared at Zack questioningly. "Unless you have something that piques my interest, then I'm of a mind to handle things my way, Zack." He gave his nephew a hard look. "So, you have anything?"

This was why Clyde couldn't get along with his older brother, Alexander Brigham. He didn't take orders worth shit, he ignored suggestions and pretty much did what he wanted to do when he wanted to do it. Screw protocol or anyone who stood in his way.

Zack turned to Ben. "You couldn't talk any sense into him?" He turned back to Clyde. "What the hell do you think you're going to do? Go in, guns blazing? This isn't Central America and it's damned sure not the Middle East. And we're not in the middle of a war zone here. And I won't have you turning it into one."

Why in the hell hadn't he brought Lobo with him? Talking sense into Clyde was like talking sense into his brother Alexander sometimes. Impossible.

"Someone's getting desperate, Zack," Ben stated, his voice calm though worry shadowed his eyes. "And whoever it is has enough ties into the agency that they've killed not one, but two prisoners being held for interrogation. If it doesn't stop now, then it could become more than just a Kin problem."

Zack could feel his molars threatening to crack as he ground his teeth in frustration. Clyde and Ben? His night had just gone from bad to worse.

"Three more days," he bit out. "Give me the time you promised me."

"That's three more days someone has to kill Grace!" Ben snapped, anger roughening his voice. "After that little meeting you took her to, whoever's behind this will be more determined than ever to kill her."

"I have her protected," he snarled, frustration claw-
ing at him now. Dealing with them was getting harder
by the year. "With Grace's safety at risk, Vince and
Alexander both will get to the bottom of this. Not to
mention Cord's determination to find out what's going
on. For God's sake, do you think they won't do it now
that Kenni's home? Her safety is paramount to them
now."

"And Grace could be killed before that ever happens,"
Ben protested. "Kenni's Vince's daughter, but Grace is
mine. And I'm tired of waiting to see my daughter. I
want it taken care of now."

"How?" Zack questioned all of them, disbelief causing him to stare at them in outrage as he rubbed at the
itch tingling along the back of his neck. "How, Ben? You
think you can just walk in from the dead, open your
arms, and she'll fly right to them and forgive you for
leaving her here? You can't do that to her."

"As you said, Kenni's home now," Ben pointed out,
a fist forming as his arm lay along the mantel over the
fireplace. "I can take my daughter with me."

What a fucking mess.

Zack shook his head before pacing across the room
while flicking his uncle a furious look. "This isn't the
way to do this." He faced them again, feeling everything
he'd begun to believe he could fix unraveling around
him. "It won't work."

"Says who?" Clyde asked, staring back at Zack curiously. "For you? You've always been sweet on her, Zack.
Think you can claim her and not tell her the truth?"

The sound of the front door opening had Clyde's

bodyguards moving smoothly to the doorway before relaxing and stepping back once again.

Frowning, Zack watched as Calli entered the room, her gaze going to her father, remorse clouding her eyes.

"Hey there, girl." Ben's expression softened as Calli walked slowly to him. "I thought you were at Zack's?"

"She was." Zack watched her suspiciously, seeing the way her lower lip trembled before she stopped in front of her father. "Why are you here, Calli?"

"I'm so sorry, Daddy," she said, staring up at him with genuine sorrow. So genuine, Zack felt the horror of what he knew was coming. "I'm so sorry. . . ."

"I'm so sorry, Daddy. I'm so sorry . . ." The words reverberated through Grace's head as she stood in the small entryway of the cabin, agony slicing through her heart, her stomach, nearly doubling her over with the grief and the pain.

"Calli-girl, why are you sorry?"

Calli-girl.

He'd once called Grace his girl, too. Once, long ago. So long ago.

She forced her legs to move, feeling reality narrow as she stepped into the living room and stared at her father for the first time in twenty years.

Calli stepped out of his arms and moved to his side, staring back at Grace, though what her expression showed, Grace didn't have a clue.

She felt as though she were walking in a dream, terrified she'd wake up, just as terrified it was real. Reality thinned and narrowed, the other occupants of the room barely noticed as she stared at the man she'd never believed would lie to her.

She never believed he would leave her.

But he was alive. . . .

Joy erupted inside her with such force, she nearly cried out with it.

He was alive. He wasn't dead. He was still breathing, he was still there.

Wasn't he?

"Daddy . . . ?" her voice trembled, hope and fear rushing side by side through her senses.

Next to him, Calli flinched, pain clenching her face as Ben Maddox took a step away from her.

"Hey there, girl," he said softly, staring at her with wary hope.

Calli's repeated flinch and fight to blink back her tears sliced through the agonizing joy, dropping her back into reality with such jarring abruptness, Grace felt dazed.

Her father was alive.

He was there with Zack's aunt Ureana, and their daughter, Calli. The lover and daughter he'd left her for. The daughter who liked to shoot guns, who liked to hunt and play with knives instead of reading books or cooking with her aunt. She hadn't been the daughter he wanted, but if he'd just told her how much it meant to him, then she would have tried harder. She would have eaten the fucking squirrel if he'd just explained.

"I would have learned how to shoot," she told him, her ragged voice barely recognizable as she clenched her fists and pressed them against her stomach, trying to still the gut-wrenching pain tearing through her. "I would have," she swore. "I would have learned how."

Confusion creased his face, and she knew he didn't believe her. Not that it mattered. He had the daughter who liked guns and hunting. One who wanted to learn how to spill blood instead of throwing up at the sight of it.

"I would have been good," she whispered, shaking her head, wishing this damned dream didn't seem so real. "I would have . . ."

Zack felt something in his heart twist with such wrenching agony, he couldn't bear it. Crossing the room, ignoring his uncle's warning look, he moved to her, watching her break apart, little by little, in front of his eyes was killing him.

"No." She stepped back, staring at him with such pain-filled eyes, he wanted to kill.

It wasn't a dream.

It wasn't a dream.

Grace stared around the room. There were too many people here whom she didn't know, their eyes filled with pity as they watched her. She couldn't break apart here. She couldn't. Not in front of them. When she left, they'd laugh at her, feel sorry for her.

Poor little Grace, even her father didn't love her. . . .

"You lied to me, Zack," she whispered. "You knew, all these years, you knew. Didn't you?"

She saw the answer on his face, in his eyes.

He felt sorry for her, too.

"Grace, you have to let me explain. . . ." Her father's

voice, firm and deep, drew her attention, his emerald green eyes darker, the scars on his face something she didn't remember.

"Let you explain?" It was incomprehensible. How could he ever explain something so horrific to her? "How?" she whispered, trying to make sense of it. "Why even bother now? What does it even matter now?"

"God, Grace . . . You don't understand," he tried again, taking another step toward her. "You have to let me tell you—"

"I do understand." She nodded quickly, unable to hear it from his lips. She couldn't bear to hear him say it. "I really do understand." She gave Calli a trembling smile, but her sister only turned away from her. "She's a good little soldier," she whispered. "She likes your guns and your war games, doesn't she? I'm sorry I didn't like them—"

"Grace . . . no . . ." Shock filled his voice as his eyes widened, staring between Calli and Grace. "God, girl, that's not why."

"Grace," Zack's voice so soft, so tender, whispered around her, his warmth eased against her. "Come on . . ."

He'd lied to her, too.

She jerked away from him, agony tearing through her brain, ripping at her heart.

"You're right. You're right. I should go." Desperate, agonizing, she could feel the screams wanting to loosen inside her, feel them shredding her soul as they had the night she begged her father not to be dead. Begged God not to take him away from her. Because she needed him.

The trembling of her lips was controllable now, the

tremors racing through her body threatening to tear her apart.

"You'll let me explain!" her father yelled at her, the sound ripping across her soul. "You will not walk out—"

"You lied to me! . . . You left me! . . ." The scream tore from her, so grating and serrated that Grace wasn't even certain it was her voice for a moment.

Pointing a shaking finger in her father's direction, she felt the fury that tore through her and wondered where it would go now that it was free.

"You left me," she repeated, a snarl pulling at her lips. "You didn't love me. I wasn't the daughter you wanted. And I should have known—"

"Grace, that's enough. . . ." Her father advanced on her.

Instinct had her moving back. He couldn't touch her. None of them could touch her. They would shatter her if they did. There would be nothing left of her.

"I begged God to bring you back. . . ." She laughed at the very thought of it. "I lay on your grave and I screamed and I begged God not to leave me so alone . . . to take me, too, so I wouldn't be alone with you gone—" A sob tore from her.

No.

She couldn't cry. She couldn't.

"At least you're alive." She shuddered, fighting to control herself, to push it back. "At least you're alive."

She turned to race from the cabin, made it as far as the rough, weathered porch before hard, familiar arms wrapped around her, dragging her to a stop.

"I'll take you back to the house," Zack promised,

holding her to him as he moved quickly to the Jeep. "Come on, baby. I'll take you back."

Take her back? To what?

"Make me wake up," she whispered as he lifted her into his arms and carried her to the Jeep. "Please, Zack, just make me wake up."

But she was already awake.

Staring through the windshield, she huddled against the door of the Jeep, the truth, all those little threads that had teased her for years, coming together. She hadn't acknowledged it before, hadn't put it together, because doing so meant admitting the truth. Her father hadn't been taken from her—he'd left her.

"Lucia suspected he was alive, didn't she?" Her voice sounded so rough, not at all like she remembered it. "How?"

"We don't know," he told her heavily. "We didn't even know anyone suspected until an attempted hack of Clyde's computers alerted him to a problem about two years ago. Ureana is a hell of a hacker herself. She tracked the intruder back to the Loudon property, but that was as far as she could go. Clyde was working on the identity Kenni was using, though I didn't know about that one until it was done and over with."

"She came into the office one day, talking about him," Grace remembered. "It felt off at the time, but . . ." She shook her head. "I should have known she had a reason. I told myself it was just another of those little games she played, trying to see if she could still hurt me."

She had. Grace had just learned not to let her mother see how much it hurt.

"And you knew all along," she whispered, refusing to look at him, terrified she'd lose her hold on the white-hot rage building inside her. "All along."

"He nearly died in the explosion that night, Grace," he stated, his voice sharp with anger. "It took two years to get him back on his feet, another six months before he could walk, his memories of the two years before it are still blurred—"

"And at any time, he could have had me brought to him!" she cried out, that lashing fury digging into her chest. "He didn't want to. He had his lover and the daughter who would enjoy everything he enjoyed," she sneered. "He has his little soldier. He didn't need me."

The Jeep rounded the turn into Zack's driveway, the house lit up, security lights blazing, and the three men he'd left to protect her standing on the porch, arms crossed and glaring at her through the window of the Jeep.

"You made me a promise tonight, Grace," he reminded her then, gripping her arm before she could leave the Jeep. "We'd talk if we had problems. I won't let you break that promise."

She turned her head and stared back at him, the betrayal so deep, so ragged, it hurt to breathe. "Why not?" she whispered, pulling at the grip he had on her arm. "You broke yours before you ever made it. All of you did."

"You'll see if you try to break it," he warned her, the promise hardening his gaze as he slowly let go of her arm. "I'll be a few minutes coming in."

He'd be a few minutes coming in? He could take all

year, for all she cared. She needed time . . . Oh God, was there enough time to ever stop hurting?

She shrugged at that. "That's okay, take all the time you want, Zack. I don't need you at all."

But she did need him.

She'd needed him to tell her the truth rather than letting Calli lead her into it. Her sister was so angry at her, disliked her so much, that she'd gladly taken Grace to that cabin. So angry . . . Calli hated her. Hatred was learned; it wasn't instinct. It was given life by resentments, by perceived hurts. If her sister hated her, then it was because her father had told the other girl what a disappointment Grace was as a child.

She was a disappointment now, too.

"Grace." Lobo was waiting as she stepped to the porch. "Calli didn't mean to hurt you."

"Of course she did." She stared up at him calmly, not surprised when he glanced away and breathed out heavily. "Let her grow up, Lobo. Just because she's a good soldier doesn't mean she's not still a child."

His head jerked back, his gaze meeting hers again as his eyes narrowed.

"The Maddox legacy isn't a nice one," she advised him bitterly, stepping away from him and entering the house. "It's actually a really really bad one."

She closed the door behind her, eyes dry and so tired she just stared at the stairs for long seconds before forcing herself to climb them. Once in the guest room, she stripped from her clothes and forced herself to put on a pair of loose pajamas before lying down to stare into the darkness.

* * *

Mad and Beau-Remi made their way from the cabin back to their camp within sight of Zack Richards's house. Neither spoke, what could they say? Even they hadn't known Ben Maddox was in the area, Beau-Remi thought. He hadn't told his sons he would be there. Something he hadn't told his daughter, but it was worse that he hadn't taken the tiny, delicate little girl who had loved him so much as a child.

"We should have taken her with us," Mad stated quietly as they slid beneath the overhang of the rock that protected them from sight. "We shouldn't have left her."

Joe's chains jangled from the water, the heavy splash a good sign that the caiman had found a midnight snack.

"She had Sierra then," he reminded Mad, not even bothering to irritate his brother with the Cajun lingo he normally used. "Then Vince lost Kenni. Or thought he did." Beau-Remi shrugged. "Hell, Mad, taking her woulda started a war, ya know?"

They could understand her feelings of betrayal, though. Beau-Remi had felt it himself when he was just a boy. Knowing who his father was, not being able to tell a fucking soul and having to be content with visits when the wife was gone. He'd fucking hated Lucia until he'd finally figured it out. It hadn't been Lucia's fault; it had been Ben's, no one else's.

"We gotta get this taken care of." Mad tapped one long finger against his bent knee, his gaze narrowed on the darkness as he spoke softly. "It's been a lot of years, Beau-Remi, and if it's not taken care of, then no one's safe, least of all Grace."

"Fuckin' bastard," Beau-Remi cursed again. "He

started all dis, Mad," the accent slipped. "Playin' doz games with de agency, makin' ever'one look over der shoulders all da time." He shook his head at the memory of how Ben had used the agency and the Kin against one another to find that bastard trying to take control. "An' you know dem brothers of his, they was always ass-kissin' dem agents. One of dem, dey know he's breathin' . . . dat's why dey go a'ter her."

"English, Beau-Remi," he murmured. "Come on, I know you can do it."

Beau-Remi snorted at the admonishment. "Wha' we do now?"

Mad continued to tap his finger against his knee, watching his brother thoughtfully. "Watch her back like we've been doing," Mad assured him. "We just keep her covered."

"Poor lil' Grace, poor lil' boo," Beau-Remi sighed heavily. "Men o' war got no business havin' such a sweet little tang." He shook his head sadly. "Our boo, she hurtin' now."

Mad glanced away from the anger in his brother's face. Yeah, Grace was hurting and he hated it just as much as his brother did. That was why they refused to be part of the Maddox family when they were younger. The continual games, the constant machinations, and the instinctive sense that someone in that family was willing to spill the blood of their own. Even as boys, they'd known with some instinct they couldn't explain that there was something corrupt there.

"I think it's time we go see Uncle Vince," Mad murmured as another heavy splash sounded from the edge of the river. "We need to get this done, Beau-Remi, and get home. We have our own things brewin', and I don't like the feel of things here. We take her with us if Zack can't ensure her safety. The rest of them can go to hell, for all I care."

There were too many secrets, too many lies that stretched too far. The lure of power had been known to corrupt many a good man, and the power Vince could wield, if he were a man to use it, was extensive. Someone wanted that power, and if they had to kill Grace to ensure they had the time to steal it, then they wouldn't bat an eyelash at doing so.

"Get some sleep," he warned his brother. "We'll go in tomorrow."

chapter twenty-one

*"Do you know how much I love you, Daddy?" The little
girl sat on the floor in front of the couch as her father
worked on his laptop behind her and she watched car-
toons.*

*"How much do you love me, girl?" The smile in his
voice caused her to giggle.*

*"I love you a bushel and a peck and a hug around
the neck." She sat still, waiting.*

"So where's my hug?"

*She jumped up from the floor to the couch and
wrapped her arms tight around his strong neck as that
deep chuckle she loved so much wrapped around her.*

*"You're my best girl, Gracie," he promised, holding
her securely to his chest.*

"I'm your only girl, Dad," she laughed.

*And he didn't say anything. He just hugged her tighter
before kissing her on the forehead and then asking her
about her day in school.*

She couldn't remember the expression on his face, she thought, frowning up at the ceiling. Somehow, over the years, she'd forgotten the smaller details. Like the scars on his face. She didn't remember the scars on his face. Had he gotten them during the explosion?

She didn't really care where he'd gotten them, she told herself, but she knew better. She cared. She didn't want to care, because doing so only underscored how much her father had meant to her when she'd meant so very little to him.

She had been replaceable, and he'd replaced her with a little girl who liked doing all the things he wanted to teach her. As though the sons he'd trained hadn't been enough. Most men didn't want to train their daughters to kill, but her father had been so disappointed when she cried over the squirrel he'd killed the night they went camping and refused to eat it.

Who was with them?

She remembered Cord, Sawyer and Deacon, Baer and Banyan, but there had been others there as well, boys whose faces she couldn't remember and whose names she couldn't recall.

But she remembered the disappointment in her father's eyes when she'd cried over the squirrel. Why did he have to kill the poor little squirrel? she asked him. What if it had baby squirrels that needed it?

Oh, Daddy, she'd sobbed, completely heartbroken that her father could do something like that, *how could you be so mean?*

And when he cooked it over the fire, she'd refused to eat, and she'd been so hungry. But her father hadn't packed snacks or chips or apples. He'd wanted to teach her how to eat off the land.

She refused to eat that poor little squirrel, though, or the wild creatures the other boys had killed, skinned, and cooked over their fires.

"Here, squirt." A bag of chips, a candy bar, and a ham and cheese sandwich dropped in front of her on the sleeping bag where she'd sat, trying not to cry after everyone ate all the animals they'd killed. "I went to the store down the road for my dinner. Good thing I figured you for an animal lover, too, huh? Critters don't taste near as good as ham and cheese with chips."

She looked up into bright, vivid violet eyes. They weren't green eyes like her father's and brothers' or cousins'. They were like jewels in a sun-darkened face nearly hidden by all the long, curly black hair surrounding it.

He plopped down on the sleeping bag next to her, followed by his twin. There were so many twins in the Maddox family, almost always boys.

Both of them unwrapped sandwiches and bit into them with gusto.

"Eat, and I'll show you som'din' cool." The twin winked teasingly.

"What is it?" She wiped her eyes, then lifted the sandwich and unwrapped it slowly.

"I have a caiman." He bent forward, those violet eyes sparkling in fun. "Your papa isn't happy wit' me either, 'cause I bring ole Joe with me."

If her daddy didn't like it, then she would make sure she did like it.

"I'm so mad at my daddy," she mumbled tearfully, her breath hitching. *"He didn't bring me nothin' to eat. And he killed that poor little squirrel."*

"Eh, sometimes he forgets little girls are supposed to be soft and sweet." He waved her father's supposed crimes away. *"That's what brothers are for, to make it all right when they forget."*

"My brothers don't like me," she confided, staring up at the young man somberly, not questioning why she'd trust him with that secret. But she remembered the outcast feeling that overcame her each time they were around. They would watch her, but they rarely talked to her. Never had they interacted with her as the two violet-eyed boys were doing.

"No. Not true." Disbelief filled his expression, though he kept his voice low so others wouldn't hear. *"An' you so sweet? Why would they not like you?"* There was the faintest hint of some accent Grace hadn't heard at the time. But she remembered thinking how pretty it sounded.

"Baer says I'm like Momma," she whispered, staring down at her sandwich, wishing her brothers liked her—because she knew, even as young as she was, that her momma didn't like her. *"But I'm really not."* She knew she wasn't. *"Him and Daddy were yellin' about it and didn't know I was there—"*

"Well, now, boo, sounds to me Baer needs to learn some manners, huh? I tell him you nothin' like that person, eh? Trust me, he listen to me right proper."

Who could not listen to the boys with such beautiful eyes, she remembered thinking.

She'd confided in the two boys that night as her father

and the other boys tracked through the trees and did their boy things. She hadn't wanted to go, because she was cold and hungry, and so sad for that little squirrel.

Her father had left her at the fire, promising all she had to do was call for him and he'd be there. But she'd been all alone until the twins showed up with their sandwiches, smiles, and gentle teasing.

She'd fallen asleep listening to that young man tell her stories about the caiman he'd promised to show her. She didn't know what a caiman was, but it sounded very fierce. And when she awoke the next morning, he and his brother were gone.

Her father never took her camping again, and Grace never forgot the disappointment in his eyes that night.

Calli probably killed and skinned her own wild game, then cooked it herself over the fire. Her younger sister likely didn't get frightened alone in the dark, and thought a campfire and sleeping bag was the place to be.

Her fists clenched as she rolled to her side, glaring into the dimly lit bedroom, hating the anger and resentment she couldn't seem to stop. Because it wasn't Calli's fault. It was her father's fault. He hadn't had to leave Grace behind to take his younger daughter camping. Even as a child, Grace would have understood.

She would have liked having a sister—

The bedroom door pushed open.

Eyes widening, Grace had little time to react before Zack was at the side of the bed.

"What are you doing?" she demanded, sitting up as he turned, stalked to the dresser, and gathered up an armload of her clothes.

"Did you hear me?" Grace jumped from the mattress,

hurrying to follow after him. "Zack, dammit, what are you doing?"

He moved quickly up the hall, then disappeared into the master bedroom.

Storming into the bedroom, she came to a hard stop at the bottom of his bed and glared at him, bemused by the sight of him shoving her clothes into one of his dresser drawers.

Her chin lifted defiantly when he turned back to her, arrogance tightening the features of his face as he met her glare without so much as a hint of wariness.

"I told you earlier, you sleep in this bedroom from now on," he reminded her. "You can move your clothes tomorrow, but tonight, you will sleep here."

"And what makes you think I'm in the mood for sex?" Her fists clenched at her side, anger churning with the loss and grief raging inside her. "Especially with someone who's been lying to me as long as you've obviously been doing." She wanted to scream, but if she did, she was terrified she'd end up sobbing instead. This was breaking her. She could feel herself shattering from the inside out and didn't know how to stop it.

"I didn't ask you for sex, I said you *will* sleep in this bed, with me, just as we agreed earlier." He stepped to her, gripping her upper arms and pulling her against him before she could avoid him. "And I hated every fucking day that I had to stare in your eyes and keep that truth from you. Every day that I knew by revealing it, I'd only be endangering you."

"You could have told me at any time in the past weeks." Shaking her head, she denied any reason he could have for not telling her. "At any time, Zack."

"Would you have believed me, Grace?" The sudden softness of his voice, the knowledge in his eyes pulled a sob from her chest as she fought to hold on to her emotions, hold on to the pain ravaging her. "Without seeing him for yourself, would you have believed me? Could you have accepted it?"

No.

No, she would never have accepted it.

"I'll never know, will I!" she forced herself to snap at him. "And I'll never know how much you'll keep from me in the future—"

"Don't you dare." His face was in hers so fast, she didn't even have time to gasp. "I'll be damned if I'll let you come up with an excuse to throw me out of your life like you do everyone else you think you might end up caring for or who might care for you. You made me a promise earlier, and by God, you will stick by it."

And he wasn't about to give her a chance to refuse.

Immediately his lips covered hers, stealing the protest she hadn't really considered giving and overwhelming the bleak, soul-deep pain with a pleasure she'd never known except for in his arms. In the rapidly growing storm that tore through the senses and seared them with rich, vibrant flames.

Wrapping her arms around his neck and holding on to him like a lifeline, an anchor to keep herself from falling into the pit of complete agony she could feel rising inside her, Grace took his kiss and returned it with her own. As she was rising to her tiptoes, a moan left her throat—and any thought of holding back or holding some part of herself from him didn't even exist. The only way to survive at this moment was in Zack's arms.

As she fought to push him as high as she knew he could push her, stroking against him, her tongue battling his, lips stroking, her fingers in his hair, holding him to her. The loose pajama top she wore was quickly unbuttoned, her breasts freed for his stroking hands, for his far-too-experienced fingers. Gripping one tight point, Zack exerted just enough pressure to send a flash of fire and ice surrounding nerve endings. The pressure eased, then returned, and the slight tug and grip sent the sensation tearing through her, arrowing straight to her clit before it tore to the depths of her pussy.

Her juices spilled from the aching depths, muscles clenching and desperate for penetration, for the pleasure-pain of each thrust filling her vagina.

She ached, she needed.

There were moments when she wondered how she'd managed to live without his touch, without knowing the powerful, rocking completion he gave her each time he took her. And she knew she'd never survive the emotional chaos building inside her if she gave in to it instead.

"Ah hell, Grace. I swear this is all I can think about anymore: how fucking good you feel.

How good he felt.

And he felt so good. Strong, broad, and warm.

Pulling her arms from around his neck, Zack pushed the material of her opened pajama top from her shoulders, his hands stroking down her back, his callused palms sensually rough, incredibly gentle as he tracked her flesh from shoulder to hip.

The feel of her the cotton pajama shorts she wore sliding over her hips and down her thighs, leaving her naked against him didn't seem completely fair to her. He should be just as naked against her.

She tugged at the elastic band of the gray knit pants that did nothing at all to hide the fierce erection beneath the material. Pulling the band back from the engorged crest, she slid the material down over his thighs, the backs of her fingers caressing the length of the shaft on a slow, downward glide.

Broad male fingers tightened on her hip, the other hand slid back to her breast, that incredible pinch and tug at the tip returning to sear her sensitive nipple with sensation.

Tearing her lips from his, Grace moaned at the pleasure, her lips running along his jaw, then his neck, to his hard chest. Licking at the tough flesh, nipping at it, she moved slowly downward, her fingers still stroking the pulsing length of his cock. She wanted to taste him again. She needed to taste him again. Needed the hard flesh filling her mouth, the taste of him making her drunk on the eroticism that built by the second.

"Dangerous, baby," he groaned as her lips slid over the muscles flexing just beneath his wide chest. "Control isn't my strong suit right now."

"Hmm. I have faith in you," she murmured, her rear meeting the mattress and placing her in the perfect position for what she wanted.

Her tongue slid over the engorged crest, licked over the wet bead that collected there, and relished the subtle salt and male taste of him.

"Grace, baby." Strangled and intense, the sandpapery sound of his voice sent a flush of feminine power rushing through her as his fingers slid into her hair, holding her head in place as he pushed forward between her lips.

Gripping the base with one hand, she stroked up the shaft until her fingers met her lips, then down to the base again. Slow, firm caresses, the pulse of blood beneath the ropy muscles pounding beneath her grip as Zack's thighs tightened with each downward stroke.

He enjoyed her tou.   uldn't fake that. Harsh, guttural groans rumbleu ... ms chest, subtle sounds of male pleasure that assured her he wanted more. That she was important to his pleasure.

As her mouth tightened around the crest, it pulsed warningly as another of those strangled groans sounded above her. Tension filled his body, the hands holding her head, the tight sac of his testicles in her other hand.

"Ah hell. Hell, Grace." Something wild filled his voice as his hips bucked just enough to drive the thick head into her mouth, retreat, and thrust again before he stilled.

The fierce, barely leashed control was evident in the sound of his harsh breaths, in the fingers kneading her scalp.

"Sweet Grace," he rasped. "Fuck, I love your mouth. Love it."

Sucking the hard flesh with firmer draws of her mouth, Grace swirled her tongue beneath the head, licked, lashed at the spot that never failed to make his thighs tighten, his breath catch with the pleasure of it.

She needed this. Needed to touch him, to pleasure him, to learn each caress, each stroke of her tongue that would induce the most pleasure for him.

"I'm losing it, Grace," he groaned, the tension in his body increasing by the second now.

The head of his cock clenched, the blood rushing through the veins pulsing harder.

"Enough. Ah God, enough." Before she could stop him, Zack pulled back, his fingers gripping the base of his cock as his expression tightened in borderline ecstasy, a grimace on his lips.

Leaning back as his gaze focused on her, Grace pushed herself along the bed, staring up at him from beneath her lashes as she came to her knees.

"Lie down," he ordered, watching her closely, intently. "Let me love you, Grace."

Her laugh, a teasing laugh, had his eyes narrowing on her. "Let you love me?" she murmured suggestively. "Are you asking for permission, Zack? How very unlike you."

Heat flared in his gaze, his expression tightening once more with the sensual, erotic awareness of a sexual challenge. Delivering the challenge heightened her own awareness as well. Grace's flesh was more sensitive, her need for him hotter, burning brighter through her body.

"Asking for permission?" he chuckled, the low, confident sound sending a rush of moisture easing from her body. "I was trying for more romance."

"Romance?" Her brows arched as she ran a hand slowly from between her breasts, watching as his gaze tracked the path her fingers took. "How . . . very . . ." She slicked her lips slowly as he forced his gaze back to hers. "Sweet . . ."

His lips twitched. "Sweet?"

"Definitely sweet," she assured him.

Her lashes dipped as her fingers slid between her thighs, easing into the thick, heated moisture coating the folds there. His eyes jerked down once more, his jaw tightening when she lifted her hand and brought her fingers to her lips, where she painted the lower curve with her slick essence.

He moved so fast, she couldn't have anticipated his next move. Before she could do more than gasp, he had her on her back, one hand immobilizing her head as he caught her lower lip between his teeth and licked the sheen of her juices from it.

"Sweetest pussy I've ever tasted," he breathed out, his voice rough as his lips moved from hers to the tight, hard peak of one breast. "Pretty, hard little nipples." He sucked one into his mouth, drawing on it with strong pulls of his mouth.

Flashes of sensation tore from her nipple to her womb with each hard, moist pull, each lash of his tongue. His fingers stroked the curve of her breast, creating a contrasting, softer touch that only increased the intensity of each.

Forcing her eyes open, needing to watch him, just for a moment, to see his lips on her flesh, to take in the intimacy of the act, Grace found her eyes locked with his instead. Held by the demand in his gaze, by the power of his need that she could see reflected in it.

Heavy-lidded, the gray shifting, first darker, then lighter and back again, like thunderclouds, like the storm raging through her senses. His expression was savage with pleasure as well. He wasn't just pleasuring her, he was finding pleasure in the act.

As she watched, he released her nipple only to move to the other, capturing the dark pink tip between his teeth as he watched her. The flare of instant, electric pleasure had her gasping. He kept drawing the hard point into the heat of his mouth and sucking it, the tip of his tongue stroking at it, and Grace couldn't help but moan.

With each draw of his mouth, her own need increased. Silky heat spilled from her inner depths, coating the swollen folds beyond and sensitizing her flesh further.

She needed him.

The desperation and overwhelming need to once again experience those moments when she was no longer a part of reality, existing only for the chaotic storm whipping through her was only growing. She needed to lose herself in him. Losing herself in the emotions and pleasure that whipped through her, that overtook her each time he touched her.

"That's it, Grace, just let it feel good," he crooned, his lips lifting from her breast, smoothing a trail of fire along her midriff to the center of her body. "Just let me have you, baby."

Her head fell back to the pillow, eyes closing. Fisting her fingers into the blankets at her side, Grace forced herself to wait, to relish every nuance of each sensation as Zack made his way lower.

As he pushed her thighs farther apart, his broad shoulders sliding between them, a brush of air wafted over the sensitive flesh between her thighs. A jolt of aching need slammed into her clit before echoing to her vagina and spilling more of the slick heat to the swollen folds.

"Are you ready for me, Grace?" the crooning temptation of his voice had her moaning brokenly.

She'd never been so ready in her life.

The feel of his tongue rasping through the sensitive folds brought her hips up in a jerk, the need to suddenly get closer, to have more, more instinct than just pleasure. Licking up, circling the straining bud of her clit, a rumbled growl of pleasure left his lips and tightened the tension straining at her senses.

One hand went to his head, threading through his hair to find an anchor, any anchor in the storm she could feel brewing through her. Each touch, each lick, each caress of his tongue to her swollen folds sent such pleasure surging through her that all she could do was cry out with the need for more. By time his lips surrounded the hard bud of her clit, she was crying out for him. Helpless pleas fell from her lips, the sounds ragged, the need whipping through her body like a vicious hunger she couldn't fight back.

She needed him. She needed this.

Forcing her eyes to open, Grace stared down at him, seeing the pleasure in his face as he devoured her, watching his tongue circle her clit, his lips pursing to deliver a hot, suckling kiss.

She couldn't breathe, couldn't keep her eyes open.

"Yes, oh please, Zack," she panted, the tension building, multiplying until she didn't know if she was being pleasured or being tortured.

"I'm right here, baby." Delivering one last erotic kiss, his head lifted and he was moving up her body, dropping heated kisses along his path until he reach her lips.

The broad, heated head of his cock pushed between

her thighs, parting the swollen flesh and lodging at the entrance of her sex.

She could feel it, pulsing with heat, ready to burn her with the most incredible pleasure. As his lips took hers in a deep, tongue-thrusting kiss, he pushed inside. Slow, aching inches parted the flesh of her vagina, pumping back and forth, taking her slow and easy as her cries built in her throat and he caught each one with his lips.

It was the most pleasure she'd ever know. She was flying in his arms, each stroke, each kiss, each hard lash of ecstasy throwing her deeper into chaos. And still, he held her with him. Clasping her close, he rode her through the storm, his big body arched over her, his hips moving fiercely between her thighs, his heavy and hot cock spearing into her and lashing her with sensations so wild, so strong, there was no way to fight them.

She didn't want to fight them.

Her nails bit into his shoulders, the distant realization that they were damp with perspiration, that both their bodies were slick with it quickly forgotten. Nothing mattered but this.

Zack.

Until chaos built, until lightning licked over her body, over her senses. Her back bowed, her legs lifting, knees holding tight to him, and when the explosion came, she swore she lost part of herself to him. Not just her heart.

It went far deeper than her heart.

She knew she'd given the very essence of herself to him. A part that could never be returned, but if she lost him, she knew she'd lose herself as well.

When it was over, when Zack managed to collapse against her and draw her into his arms, Grace felt sleep taking her, stealing her from the consequences of what she had done, what she had given to someone she feared might well walk away in the end.

If she'd expected that sleep to be calm and easy, she was wrong. It was plagued by nightmares, by dark dreams. The pictures she'd stared at for so long becoming collages, images moving from one frame to the next and making little sense, though she knew they should.

Through the darkness, into the nightmares, Zack was there, though. Holding her, taking the fear, and letting her focus on each picture that formed in her dreams, each bit of information and each hint of betrayal.

Until the truth, when her subconscious found it, was too much to take, too horrifying to contemplate, and she came away swallowing tears that no longer made sense and fighting a fear that when awake, she could find no reason for.

chapter twenty-two

Grace couldn't shake the hollow fear and sense of discord that overcame her when she awakened. Despite the fact that her father was alive, she had a sister, and Zack wanted her to stay with him. Still, she couldn't forget that sense of horror, or the images she was slowly remembering from her dreams.

Breakfast and most of the afternoon were spent in Zack's office. She ignored Zack when he came to check on her and ignored her uncle when he stood at the door, watching her. It wasn't until her father entered the room, dragged a chair next to her, and started going through the files that she focused on anything but the pieces of information she was gathering.

"I'm busy," she stated, pulling another file on the laptop and scanning each page. "I don't need any help."

Except, she probably did need some help and just didn't know what she needed.

"The two years before the explosion are so blurred, I

can barely remember any of it," he stated, rubbing his hands on his jeans before opening one of the files. "I've been over every file, every picture, and can't seem to remember why I even took them." His voice was quiet, almost a whisper.

"You were searching for the conspiracy," she told him, pulling bits of information from the file she was reading to the one she'd made herself. "You knew it was family, just like I do."

He stilled beside her. "Vince suggested that, but it doesn't make sense. Destroy the family, and you destroy the power we hold in this area."

"What if the one attempting to destroy it wants just that?" She shrugged. "The information is sellable, the location of the arms and gold would fund generations, or a lifetime of excessive spending. Or it could enable control of the Kin themselves, if enough of the Clan follows you."

"They wouldn't." He shook his head. "Take the family out, and this area is cut off from the Kin in general. No one but a member of the family knows enough to know how the hell to even use the power it would bring."

"A grudge . . ." She closed the file she was in and started going through others. It was there. She knew it was there.

"What grudge?" he asked.

Grace shook her head. "I don't know."

From the corner of her eye, she watched as he went through pictures, piling them much as she had the first time she saw them, but using a very different order, though he didn't seem to pay attention to what he was doing. Most of his attention was focused on her.

"You were three," he said a few moments later. "Brightest little thing that ever was." That couldn't be pride she heard in his voice. "We were at the park, and you told me one of your friends' mothers was spending a lot of time with another friend's father, and that maybe the father wanted to be the first friend's daddy." He chuckled at the memory. "Three years old. No one knew Mack Ronce and Delilah Day were having an affair, even me, and Mack was one of my men, until that day.

She paused. "It gives me a headache, having to watch everyone all the time, tracking their expressions and shifts, and noticing what's none of my damned business!" she snapped, leaning back in her chair, though refusing to look at him. "All my life, all I've ever heard is how regretful it was that I didn't do this like my father, that like my father." She trailed off, the pain she'd wanted to keep hidden returning. "I guess they weren't the only ones who wished I could be more like you."

It wasn't said with any sense of resentment, just of loss. God, how she wished she'd been good enough, just being Grace.

"You have it all wrong—"

"And I don't want to discuss it any longer." Pushing from the desk, she rose quickly and stepped around the other side of it. "You look at those damned files for a while. Maybe you'll remember something. Maybe then, you'll remember why I didn't matter."

"Dammit, Grace!" His tone was like the snap of a whip, and she ignored it as she raced from the office, only to run into Zack's chest.

Instantly, his arms were around her as she clenched her fingers in his shirt, searching for a way to remember that the past was past. Her father was alive. He was alive. And she loved him, no matter what.

"It's time to get out of this office for a while," Zack stated, his voice hard as she glanced up at him, though his eyes were trained on her father behind her. "You need a break."

"Yeah, that's what I need," she agreed, moving carefully around him. "Maybe some fresh air. I think I'll go out back for a while."

And Grace had to admit, nearly an hour later, that it was nice to be outside. The warmth of the late-summer air, the breeze from the river, and the sun beaming down on the yard were relaxing. Being alone had helped her to find her footing again, helped to force her emotions back under control. For now. They were weak, the hurt like a bleeding wound she couldn't close.

Well-established ornamental trees and flowing shrubs bordered comfortable seating arrangements on the covered patios.

Now, if Zack would just get the various friends and family, with the exception of his foster brothers and their mates, out of the house, then she might be able to enjoy sitting on the patio.

From inside the house, the drone of voices could be heard, despite the fact that the doors leading from the dining room and kitchen were securely closed. There were far too many people chatting, explaining, and generally catching up, not to be heard outside.

Zack's aunt, her Maddox lover, and their daughter, Calli; Zack's uncle Clyde and his wife, Mena, as well as their two sons, Gray and Lobo. Then there were four bodyguards she'd been introduced to, and the arrival of her uncle Vince and cousins Cord, Sawyer, and Deacon.

A houseful.

Far too many, as far as she was concerned. Too many eyes watching her, too many who knew her, pitying her. And the knowledge that if her uncle and Cord hadn't known for a fact that Ben Maddox was alive, then they'd at least suspected it. There was very little surprise when they were faced with the man the world believed they'd buried nearly twenty years ago.

"Oh, come on, Dad . . ." Calli's voice drifted through the small opening of the kitchen patio doors, irritated and filled with protest before lowering itself, the rest of her protest falling away.

Her father.

Her lips twisted in disgust at the title, but her heart twisted in pain. No one had meant as much to her as her daddy when she was a girl, and his death had destroyed her sense of security. A security she'd never managed to regain, she realized. And losing her aunt and cousin so quickly afterwards had only exacerbated the damage and reinforced the fear of loving anyone else.

She had friends, but not friendships the loss of which would scar her further. Losing more family—her uncle, her cousins—would be devastating, but if she lost Zack . . . She couldn't imagine what that would do to her. Zack had slipped into her heart over the years. She should have known that her intense fascination with him was far more than just arousal. Just as she should have known that her refusal to face Zack with their need for each other over the years was but one of the signs that she cared far too much for him. That he was too important to her.

"Hey, cuz." Sawyer's voice drew her attention as he stepped onto the patio, closing the door before sprawling lazily in the chair across from her. "You should come inside and be social for a while."

"Oh," she laughed a bit mockingly. "I think that's the last thing I need to do right now."

Sawyer's brows lifted at her protest. "Not every day a girl sees her father come back from the grave. It's a chance for answers, if nothing else, ya know?"

Her eyes narrowed on him. Sawyer was the negotiator of the family, the one who always tried to mend fences, see things differently.

"It's not every day a girl learns she wasn't good enough to go into hiding with her father either," she told him painfully. "That the daughter he had with another woman meant more—" She quickly shook her head. "I don't want to go over this again, Sawyer. Just let it go, okay?"

"Hmm," he murmured, then seemed to perk up. "I hear Magnus is ready to return to his momma," he said then. "That mean-assed little coot managed to get out of his crate and destroy half Ole Doc Branton's office. And I hear there's a little female Rottie there he was real sweet on." Sawyer was obviously fighting his laughter. "Maybe it's time to bring him home and get him a little girl Rottie, ya know? Some feminine companionship."

"You have a dirty mind," she muttered, crossing her arms over her breasts, refusing to listen to him. "If you're just going to sit here and be mean to me, then go back inside. You can practice your odd sense of humor on Zack's guests. I'd prefer to live in denial where Magnus is concerned. He's still a puppy. He doesn't need a female Rottie."

His expression stilled, the flash of anger quickly hidden behind an implacable mask. "Zack's guests," he grunted broodingly. "You're right, sweetheart, denial can be an excellent state sometimes."

She didn't comment; she couldn't. She'd never preferred denial over reality, but the last few hours had shown her the error of her ways.

"He was my favorite," Sawyer said long moments later, his voice almost too low to hear. "Damn, thought my guts were being ripped out when we were told he was in that truck."

A shudder worked up Grace's back. She still had nightmares about the night her aunt had awakened her, her face soaked with tears, and told her . . .

She'd screamed. For hours she'd sobbed, railed, and screamed for her daddy. Inconsolable, so steeped in grief that her uncle had threatened to call the doctor in and have her sedated. And he would have, had it not been for Cord, Sawyer, and Deacon.

Her throat tightened with that remembered pain.

"What can I say, Grace, to take that look of shattered pain out of your eyes?" he asked then. "It's the same look you had then."

Tears dampened her eyes and threatened to spill. "It's not the same," she finally whispered, swallowing tightly. "If he'd just left to stay alive, then he would have had me brought to him." She stared down at her hands, watching her fingers link together, then release. "How disappointed he must have been in me, Sawyer, to just forget me. To just start a new family, have another daughter . . ." Her lips trembled as she tried to smile, tried to push it back again, and failed.

It was ravaging her, shredding her insides, and she didn't know how to stop it.

"Hey, now, cuz." He moved to the cushioned patio sofa beside her, his arm going around her shoulders. "Remember, you were like five or six, and Ben brought you on that camping trip with us when he decided we were all going to eat off the land for a weekend?"

Oh, she definitely remembered that one.

"He was so disappointed in me," she whispered. "That poor little squirrel broke my five-year-old heart."

" 'How could you be so mean!' you cried, sobbing like your heart was broke," he recounted. " 'There could be baby squirrels that needs its Momma and Daddy.' "

She fought to hold back her tears. "I wasn't the daughter he wanted."

Sawyer laughed, genuinely amused. "Then we weren't the nephews he wanted either," he informed her with a snort. "There was a store not more than a mile down the mountain, we argued, when he told us he was going to make you eat that squirrel. 'Well, that store might not be there when you need it,' he went all gruff on us," Sawyer chuckled. "So now, old Beau-Remi, he just tilts his head and stares back at old Ben like he's done lost his mind and says, 'Well, use the one across the road from it. You kill all the little critters you hafta, but that wee cher,' as he called you, 'ain't gonna go hungry long as Beau-Remi has a dollar to buy a sandwich.' Sticks his hands in his pockets, feels around, then looks up at Ben all

serious-like and says, 'Hey, man, loan me a dollar.'"
Sawyer was laughing through the entire last half of the
tale. "Well, now, while he was rambling on, his brother
Maddox, he'd done started hiking down that hill, 'cause
he had the money to buy sandwiches, after making sure
his sweet little sister liked ham and cheese. But when
Beau-Remi asked for that dollar, I swear to you, every
damned one of us was handing him money to buy not
just your sandwich, but ours, too. 'Ham and cheese tastes
a hell of a lot better than critter any night of the week,'
Cord told him with such somber insistence, we were
laughing out our asses."

"That was Beau-Remi?" She stared up at him in surprise. "I hadn't even remembered that until the night
I walked in on . . . everyone the other night." She
shrugged. "I talked to them every week until Luce was
arrested, and they never mentioned it."

"Yeah," Sawyer sighed. "They finally stopped calling and demanding to talk to you about the third week
after Luce's funeral, but they sent Vince a message that
they were coming for you."

"Why?" she asked, confused. "Why would they
care?"

"Grace," he sighed gently, "they're your brothers.
They always cared. If it hadn't been for Dad's stubbornness and, as I hear it, Ben's refusal to allow it, then they
would have taken you to raise when you were five. We're
lucky they didn't do it anyway."

Unfolding her legs, Grace turned to him, frowning.
"I haven't seen them." But even if they hadn't come for
her, they hadn't forgotten about her.

"I hate how you're hurting, honey. It breaks my heart." He leaned forward, his expression filled with compassion. "But I can understand why he did it."

"So Calli would be safe," she whispered. That was all it could be, because Grace would never have refused to go with the father she'd loved.

"Or tipping off whoever's been waiting to use you to draw Ben out," he told her softly. "Vince knew, but we only learned recently that there was suspicion Ben was still alive since right after Mom was killed. You and Zack were both being watched, and we never knew for certain who was watching. We never suspected it was Luce, just as we never suspected the others."

Rising to her feet, Grace could only shake her head. "It doesn't matter, Sawyer—"

"No, it doesn't," he agreed. "But, Grace, too much has been hidden from all of us over the years, not just you. Cord just found all this out himself. Alexander Brigham was conducting his own internal investigation even as Dad was frantically trying to identify whoever's been orchestrating all this, and they had to walk a very fine line to ensure you weren't harmed while they jumped through hoops to keep anyone from suspecting it. We came here this morning to discuss all this with Zack, and came face-to-face with a man we weren't even certain was still alive."

"He was involved in all this from the day he was able to function after that coma, but he couldn't have me taken to him?" She swung around furiously, facing with him with years of grief, of anger. "Stop excusing him, Sawyer. Stop trying to explain the unexplainable. His other family mattered more."

"Or your disappearance would have alerted them to the fact that he was alive," Sawyer suggested instead. "The choices he faced weren't easy ones, Grace, and they're not choices he hasn't paid for, I don't believe. Because if there's one thing I know for a fact, Ben loved you. He loved you so much that he was going to take you with him the night of that explosion. If he had, he would have been in the truck when it went up in flames rather than waiting outside it for the helicopter coming for him and Zack's parents. Both of you would have died, and he knew it. He knew it, and he was terrified to risk you that far again."

He had to be lying to her. But she knew Sawyer, she even knew when he was lying, and he believed what he was saying.

"He what?" Confusion swamped her. "He wasn't taking me with him."

Sawyer's expression was heavy with somber truth. "Yeah, he was. You were sick, remember? He was supposed to just be going to Kingston for parts for that old tractor of his. He was going to take you with him, but when he went to the house to get you, Sierra had put you to bed, because your fever was so high. You were still getting over that flu you had that week."

The dream she'd had of him next to her bed, so sad, his eyes damp with tears as he spoke to her. It had happened.

She shook her head. "He was going to take me?"

A movement at the patio door had her turning, had her facing the father she'd believed hadn't wanted her. "I was waiting to tell Clyde I wasn't going until you were better, when that truck exploded and left me in a coma for weeks," her father's voice said from the entrance to the house, grief giving it a hollow, pain-filled sound. "Zack lost his parents, and for months, they weren't certain I'd live. But I would never have just left you, girl. You were my sunshine, just as Calli is, and my world hasn't been right without you."

Zack stepped onto the patio and moved to her, his arm going around her to hold her against him.

"You were my girl, Grace," Ben said, his voice hoarse now, his expression lined with pain. "I couldn't leave without you. I wouldn't have left without you."

"And later?" She was breaking apart. She could feel the ravaged, broken emotions tearing free inside her. "Why later? You left me here when you didn't have to. You left me." She held on to Zack, her fingers digging into his arm.

"I did what I felt I had to do to keep you safe," he whispered. "If I'd taken you, then whoever's been determined to destroy this family would have known I was alive. It wouldn't have been a suspicion, honey, they would have known. And I couldn't be certain I could protect you and Calli if that happened. Not just Calli, Grace, but you as well. You're my daughter, too, and not a day ever went by that I haven't grieved because you weren't with me."

"Half the time, he calls me Grace." Calli stepped beside him, her expression lacking any snideness, any sense of resentment. "I've been called Grace so often that I even answer to it sometimes." She shrugged a bit uneasily. "Sorry, Grace, I do confrontation better than I do tact, I guess, and you wouldn't argue with me." A flash of shame eased across her expression as she shifted uncomfortably.

"I don't expect you to forgive me, girl," Ben said then. "I never imagined you would forgive me. But I won't hide anymore either and let my enemies focus on you. Now they can face me."

"They can face all of us." Vince stepped from behind his brother, followed by Cord and Deacon, Clyde and his sons. "The commanders will follow us, and I know that damned Beau-Remi and Maddox are here close by. That was a gator that got Richard James, and it's the one that follows Beau-Remi around like some kind of demonic hound from hell. I bet my favorite gun on it."

"Caiman," Grace whispered as she felt Zack's arms tighten around her. "He calls it a caiman."

The boy with the violet eyes and odd accent, and his quiet twin who had given her a ham and cheese sandwich when she couldn't eat the squirrel her father had roasted over a fire.

"They'll wait. They're my ace in the hole," Ben sighed. "They won't show themselves until we least expect it. . . ."

"I'm sorry, Daddy, they scare me," Grace whispered as she watched the massive Rottweilers he'd taken her to see. "They're too big."

"That's okay, honey. I always have an ace in the hole to look after you if we need it, girl," her father promised when she was four and was too frightened of the guard dogs he trained and wanted her to choose for a pet. "I just don't care much for their choice of guard dog. . . ." Beau-Remi's caiman . . .

Grace shook her head. "They're your ace," she said softly, her gaze meeting her father's, things Beau-Remi and Mad had said over the years, small pieces of memories from her childhood coming together. "They're your sons."

He nodded at that, pride flashing in his eyes. "Beau-Remi and Mad, Baer and Banyan. They knew if anything happened, you were their only priority. Baer and Banyan here, then if anything went wrong, Beau-Remi and Maddox would hide you in the swamps until I could get to you."

"Except Beau-Remi and Maddox have fought me every step of the way on it," Vince injected acerbically. "Those two have been a pain in my ass, Ben."

Every time she spoke to Beau-Remi or Mad, they would ask her how the family was treating her. She'd never taken them seriously. Now, years of conversations, sometimes hours on the phone if they called after Vince left the office, came together. But that wasn't the only information she could feel tugging at her mind, her memories.

"They're good boys," Ben protested. "And they loved Grace from the moment of her birth, Vince. You know that."

"And they still refuse to acknowledge me unless they have no other choice." Calli rolled her eyes as she cocked a hip and propped one hand on it. "They told Dad they wouldn't acknowledge me until their baby sister knew the truth." She flashed Grace a wicked smile. "I torture them anyway. And I'm good at it."

Grace focused on Calli, because focusing on her father would have broken her. "I would have loved being your sister," she whispered, Zack's arms tightening around her as her voice broke. "I would have been a good sister."

She would have been. Unlike her brothers, unlike her cousins, her sister would have known she was there for her, and she would have known Grace loved her.

"I know that, Grace." Calli nodded. "None of us have agreed with Dad holding back, especially lately. But as much as I wanted an older sister, I didn't want my chance to get to know her taken away from me either." She sniffed, then shot Grace a wink. "You know now, though, and I can be the brat I never got to be with you. You can feel Beau-Remi and Mad's pain for yourself. Too bad I couldn't make the rest of the uncles' lives hell, too," she snickered. "From what I've see, they're such sticks in the mud . . ."

Her uncles . . .

That fucking whoremonger couldn't even keep it in his pants when he was half dead, in those swamps. . . .

I warned Luce what a womanizer he was before she ever married him. . . .

At least he didn't corrupt Grace. . . . She's nothing like him. . . .

Too bad you can't see things like your father could. He could put puzzles together so quickly. . . .

You're lucky you're nothing like Ben, Grace. . . .

All said lovingly, all within the proper context, but she'd felt that something . . . even then.

She refused to put puzzles together, claiming they gave her a headache. She politely answered questions about her lack of ability to see things as her father did, as though she weren't certain what they meant. She'd been a child when he died, she'd often say. He rarely discussed how he saw anything. After all, a person didn't tell five-year-old children their secrets.

But someone had known. Someone had known what no one else had suspected she was capable of, and they'd gotten scared. They'd gotten scared, and they'd moved to make certain she hadn't seen anything else. And Grace hadn't realized at the time what had happened . . . Because she trusted. Because she'd trusted in a lifetime of warmth. Because she was so determined not to hurt, not to lose anyone else that meant anything to her, she'd ignored all the clues, the pieces to the puzzle that would reveal a killer.

"It's okay, Grace," Zack whispered at her ear as she felt the tremors quaking through her. "I have you. I'll always have you."

Her breath hitched and ended on a strangled sob.

She felt the strength in her knees weaken, felt that dam break inside her as a low, keening cry sounded from her throat. And she couldn't stop it. She couldn't stop it.

The cries escaping her were years of pain and anger, of losses that went beyond her ability to accept, beyond any tears' ability to heal.

She felt Zack swing her into his arms before he sat down heavily, holding her to him, his head bent over hers as the gut-wrenching horror of her father's death, her aunts, of believing her cousin was lost forever, only to find her again. Years of betrayals and the revelation that those she loved so much could lie so easily to her. And the knowledge that she'd closed herself off from them, rather than them shutting her out.

And through the cries and bitterness, the gut-wrenching sobs, and the realizations the bitterness spilled from her in the aching sounds of sorrow she finally allowed free.

She'd shed tears over the years, silent, wordless tears. They'd spilled despite her attempts to hold them back. But the grief-stricken sobs and keening cries she'd always kept inside, holding them back because facing the agony had been more than she could bear.

Holding her to his chest, Zack hid his face against her, the pain spilling from her something he knew he'd never forget, never risk again. She held on to him like a lifeline, and he held on to her just as tightly, certain if he loosened his hold on her, then both of them might collapse.

He felt dampness on his own face, felt the release of the moisture he fought to hold back. But this was Grace. God help him, this was his heart and soul, and if anyone deserved his tears, then she did.

"Grace." Ben knelt next to them, his hand smoothing down her shoulder as the pain of his own loss spilled down his face. "You were always my girl. Always, Grace."

Her hold tightened around Zack's neck, the sobs jerking her body until he wondered how she could stand it. The violence and grief spilling from her broke his heart. He could only pray that by letting it free, a part of hers would be able to heal.

"I love you, Grace," he whispered at her ear, holding her securely to him, letting the storm rage through her. "I love you. . . ."

She shuddered again—so hard, her breath caught

before another sob was pulled from her. "Zack, I know," she cried then, her voice weak but echoing with horror. "Oh God, I know who . . ." She seemed to choke on the words for a moment. "I know who . . ."

Who?

Zack stilled, his eyes lifting slowly to meet the sudden comprehension in Ben's gaze.

"I know who it is, Zack," she cried, the words barely coherent. "I can't believe . . . Oh God, I can't believe they would do this. . . ."

chapter twenty-three

It was almost over.

Standing in her uncle's office the next morning, Grace watched the lazy flow of the river beyond the backyard, a lifetime of memories playing out in her head. She'd played on that riverbank as a child with Beau-Remi and Mad several times. Baer and Banyan had always been in the background, though, warily keeping an eye on the caiman, as Beau-Remi called it, while it sunned itself, always within sight of the two teenage boys.

She wasn't scared of the creature, though he was scary-looking and hissed if she came too close to him. He'd shake his big thick neck, the heavy chain collar he wore jangling fiercely. Beau-Remi would laugh and chastise it, earning a sullen stare from black, slitted eyes.

Her mother was never around when the two boys were there. They only visited whenever Luce was out of town on one of her trips. She took a lot of trips, Grace remembered.

Sometimes her sister, Grace's aunt Sierra, went with her, sometimes her other aunt, Mary, and Mary's husband, Thomas, would go. But more often, Luce went alone.

Grace had loved those times when her mother wasn't there. Her father was always freer to laugh and show his affection to the boys whenever they were around. But he could take Grace with him as well, whenever he visited his friends. Friends like the Richards.

She remembered things about Luce and Aunt Mary. The arguments they'd had, the anger, even after Ben's death, that shadowed them whenever they were together. Mary hadn't cared much for Luce at all. Yet, Luce visited her often. Lunch or dinner, sometimes overnight visits, as though they were the best of friends, when Grace knew they hadn't been.

Why hadn't she remembered that?

"Teague and Lana are here," Cord announced from the other side of the office, where he watched from the window looking out on the entrance from the main road. "Egan and Jane and Camden and Gina are behind them. Mary and Thomas are just coming around the mountain from town."

Grace inhaled slowly, turned, and lifted her head to stare up at Zack, where he stood next to her.

"I have you, Grace." He cupped her cheek with his palm, his gray eyes calm, the storm settled for the moment. "We'll get through this."

He'd been promising her that since they first came up with the plan. Of course, whether or not a confession was made wouldn't matter. It hadn't taken long, once they'd known where to look, for Vince, her father, and

Zack's uncle Clyde to track down all the evidence they'd needed. Hacked computers and credit card accounts as well as the locations of bank accounts that hadn't been listed. So much evidence. So many years, decades of deceit, lies and manipulations.

For what?

For vengeance and for greed.

Mostly greed, she suspected.

"We going to do this, baby? We can run now if you want to." He'd made that offer several times.

Her family had all the proof they needed; she didn't have to be there. But she'd been used to draw her father back to Loudon, to make certain he actually died this time, along with his daughter. Family members she'd loved, people she would have stood with, stood for, and they'd betrayed the family even before Grace's birth. With patience, always staying hidden, always careful that the blame fell elsewhere, they'd left nothing to chance. They would never have been suspected had they not gone after Grace. In going after her, they'd brought Ben out of hiding far sooner than he would have emerged, and had forced Grace to remember parts of the past and events otherwise forgotten, to create a picture none of them had suspected—until she supplied the missing pieces. Then it was a simple matter for two twins, Vince and Ben, whose talents so complemented each other, to know where to find the proof and how.

There was a reason the family businesses had become as streamlined and effective as it was before Ben's "death." Just as there was a reason why the network of militias had grown so well during that time. Ben had the ability, charisma, and charm to draw people to him and invite confidences; he was then able to take what he saw, what he heard, and often foresee problems before they flared up. Vince's logic and leadership abilities would then come up with ways and means of dealing with any problems.

Before the attempt on her father's life, he had begun to suspect that a series of so-called accidental deaths weren't the accidents they appeared. With his most trusted commander, he'd begun to investigate and began suspecting something much more sinister. Systematic thefts of weapons and resales to private individuals outside Tennessee. At one point, several military automatic rifles were sold to a gang in Columbus—weapons Ben had identified as part of the Kin arsenal just before a bomb was planted in his truck.

"Heads up, they're all chitchatting in the driveway and heading for the door," Cord announced moments later.

"Ready?" Zack asked, his arm going around her back as she moved to the protected corner of the room directly across from where her father would step out of the supply room on the other side.

"Ready." She nodded.

It was almost over.

The destruction of a family was almost complete.

The office door opened.

"Vince, I had to cancel a hairdresser's appointment for this foolishness. As if I care what position Zack Richards has in this family," Mary told him with an air of long-suffering patience before flashing Zack a wink. "Good looks are always a welcome addition in the Maddox Clan, especially when paired with intelligence."

She entered with her tall, blond-haired husband, Thomas Chance. Once an agent himself with the Brigham Agency that backed the Kin, he'd been required to resign after his marriage to the Maddox sister.

"Nice to see you, Zack." Thomas stepped over to shake Zack's hand, his dark brown eyes warm but quizzical before giving Grace a peck to her forehead. "I'm glad to see you back, sweetheart."

"Thank you, Uncle Thomas," she murmured.

"Grace, sweetie, this family sucks when it comes to its girls," Lana Magden Maddox, Teague's wife, gave her a quick hug, her hazel eyes solemn. "And don't think I didn't chew Teague's ass for how he acted the other day, honey. Maddox men are just big assholes, right?"

"They can be," she agreed, returning her aunt's hug.

"At least Egan had the good sense to leave," Jane Westbrook Maddox snorted as Lana moved aside. She, too, hugged Grace, winked, and moved back for her husband, Egan.

"Sorry 'bout the mess, Gracie," he sighed, hugging her as well. "I've missed ya, though."

Her heart clenched at the softly whispered words against her ear. "Thank you, Uncle Egan."

"Get out of the way, Egan." Camden nudged his brother aside, shook Zack's hand, and gave Grace a quick kiss to the top of her head. "He's too damned slow, all the time."

Teague was the only one of her uncles who didn't hug her. He didn't even meet her gaze.

"Let's sit down and talk a minute, then," Vince announced, moving from behind his desk and perching at the corner of it, facing his family as his sons stood protectively around him.

They took their seats slowly, watching as Vince stared at all of them for long, heavy moments.

"You know," he began. "I've known a lot of shame in my life, and no small amount of tragedy. And other than the death of my wife, Sierra, I count today, as one of the most tragic. But I also count it as my greatest shame."

Surprise filled their faces, as well as confusion. In one, guilt flashed but for a moment before confusion filled it as well.

"Vince?" Mary whispered, distressed. "What are you talking about?" She reached for her husband's hand, gripping it like a lifeline. "What's happened? Is Kenni okay?"

"My baby girl," Vince sighed, shaking his head as Grace saw the tears that glittered in his eyes for a moment. "Eight years. For eight years I thought she'd died with Sierra. My sweet little girl, murdered, along with her mother, and I couldn't find who had killed them. No matter how hard I looked."

Silence filled the room.

Looking to the back of the room, he nodded. One of the agents there stepped from where he'd stood unnoticed and opened the office door to allow Victor Brigham and half a dozen agents to enter the room.

"What's the meaning of this, Vinny?" Teague spoke up, his tone bordering on anger. "Why are they here?"

Vince turned his gaze to his brother, abject pain and

sorrow filling his expression. "Did you know Lana and Egan have been sleeping together since before the two of you married? That she, along with your brother and his wife, has been systematically destroying this family?"

Shock, disbelief. Teague stared from his wife to his brother Egan, then to Vince. "That's not true," he seemed to wheeze. "No—"

"Neither of them is protesting, I notice," Victor Brigham boomed as he stepped to the desk beside Vince. "Think that's because they know Vince wouldn't make a move without proof?"

"Lana?" Teague whispered, searching for a denial, all but begging for one.

She rolled her eyes. "It's not exactly a crime," she drawled, shrugging.

Egan and his wife sat still and silent, watching Vince without expression.

"Vince . . . ?" Mary whispered, her voice hesitant. "Why are you doing this?"

Vince lowered his head.

Immediately, two of the agents stepped to the supply closet and opened the door.

Ben, Ureana, and Calli stepped from inside.

Calli stared at the family, tipped her head to the side, and gave a slow, clearly audible "Tsk, tsk, tsk." As she wagged a finger at them.

It was Ben who held all their attention, though, as he moved to stand next to his twin, leaned against the desk, and crossed his arms over his white shirt.

"You're right, Lana," Ben stated. "Infidelity isn't a crime." He stared at his brother with icy fury. "Murder is, though. I believe these agents are here to take you, Egan, and Jane in for questioning. I hope you fare better than Lucia and the agent who was murdered this week." His smile was hard. "Or the four agents that have been helping you make certain your secrets were kept. They'll be joining you in the holding facility where you'll be questioned."

Egan shook his head, a sneer on his face. "Hell, and here I thought Luce was crazy when she said Ben was still alive," he laughed, rising to his feet only to have two agents grab him by the arms and secure them behind his back.

Two others were fastening nylon restraints on both Lana's and Jane's wrists as they stood, chins lifted mutinously, glaring at Ben and Vince.

"But why, Egan?" Mary whispered, standing now, holding on to her husband's arm as he watched the proceedings warily. "Why?"

"You should ask your husband that, Mary." Alexander stepped away from Vince, catching her as Thomas was pulled from her, restraining her arms as she cried out and reached for him. "It's okay, Mary," he whispered, his arms going around her gently. "It's okay."

"You bastard!" Thomas snarled, struggling against the agents now, his brown eyes filled with fury. "That's why. Did you think I didn't know what happened before we married? You lying bastard."

Mary's face was ashen and filled with pain as Alexander held her to his chest, her green eyes staring at her husband in horror.

"I would have brought everything you loved down

around your ears," Thomas sneered at Alexander and Vince both. "And I still will. Do you think you could possibly have taken down something I've worked twenty-five years to destroy?" he laughed.

"Shut up, Thomas!" Egan snarled furiously, his expression tight with contempt.

Thomas's head snapped around to the other man. "We're not innocent until proven guilty, you fucking moron. What does it matter? We'll never see daylight again anyway."

Egan turned to his brother, some hope, some certainty of salvation flickering in his eyes. "No." He shook his head. "Vince wouldn't do that. Not to his brother."

"You did," Alexander stated, his deep voice grating. "You planted the bomb, you intended to kill Ben and his daughter. Just as you conspired to kill your sister-in-law and your niece. Your brother's daughter, Egan. Not just his twin, but his wife, his daughter. Do you think you'll find leniency in Vince's heart now?"

Desperation and shock filled Egan's face as it paled to a sickly white. "I'm your brother, Vince," he protested.

"No, you're not." Teague stepped back, the horror and betrayal rushing through him and reflected in his face, in his eyes as his fists clenched at his sides, his gaze going between his wife and his brother. "You're no brother."

"Camden . . ." he cried out.

Camden also stared at him in horror, one arm holding his wife, Gina, behind him as he watched his brother in disbelief. "My God, Egan . . ." he wheezed. "Why? Why?"

"Your brother?" Gina whispered. "My God. Sierra?" Tears spilled down her face. "She was like a sister to all of us. To all of us—"

"I'm your brother," Egan cried out again, struggling against the agents as they dragged him to the door. "Vince. Vince, please . . ."

Vince stepped forward, his fingers burying in Egan's shirt, jerking him nearly off his feet. "My wife," he snarled into Egan's face. "My daughter. My twin. My fucking world, Egan!" He was almost nose to nose with his brother. "I'd kill you myself if I hadn't sworn to our parents I'd never allow my position to cause me to harm one of my own brothers or my children. I'd kill you myself."

Egan spat at him, the moisture spraying over Vince's cheek. "I would have killed you next, you son of a bitch—"

The agents jerked him back and away before Vince could retaliate, before the rage and bleak grief rising inside his eyes could cause him to break the promise he'd made to his parents.

"Dad." Cord caught his father's arm with one hand, the other gripping his father's shoulder. "It's over. It's over. Let it end here."

The pain, betrayal, and grief filling the room were overwhelming, a family broken, a past once revealed showing the shattered lines that had divided it all along.

Her uncle's expression was twisted with hollow pain, Ben's no less filled with the grief of betrayal as his daughter, Calli, wrapped her arms around his waist and he held on to his wife, watching as another brother was dragged away.

And Zack held her.

The loss and sheer aloneness she'd felt for so long were gone, leaving behind only regret and a sense of loss. It wasn't her father's fault; it wasn't her fault. He'd been taken from her, and he chose the path he'd felt was the right one to protect her as well as the woman he loved and the child they had together.

Her father was back now. The danger to all of them revealed. She could face her future safely, with the man she loved.

She wasn't alone anymore. Zack had her.

"Take me home," Grace whispered as Zack's arms tightened around her. "Just take me home, Zack."

"Grace." Alexander Brigham moved to them as they headed for the door, then stood before her, his gray eyes as warm and kind as she'd always known them to be. "I need to tell you something."

She stared up at him, wishing he'd just let them leave. "Tory expects to see you at that party this weekend. I hope you'll be there. And no matter what I let Zack find out about the orders for interrogation, you'd have never been questioned." He smiled gently. "Kept at the estate for a while, but I'm confident you and Tory would have found enough nail polish and girly stuff to keep you busy. If that weren't enough, I received two messages informing me how much gators liked human flesh when they got good and hungry." He grimaced at that. "Call those boys off, if you don't mind? I might start having nightmares."

"Beau-Remi?" she questioned, almost amused.

* * *

"Beauregard and Maddox Remington," he told her softly but looking up at Zack. "I'll tell you this once, son," he said. "I loved your mother like my own children. It was her decision to leave with Richard, her decision to hide you from us, because she'd guessed there were traitors in the agency and in the Kin. The stories you heard were planted by all of us." His eyes moistened for a second. "She was my baby sister, Zack. Only your father loved her more than her family did."

"You know," Grace said with a heavy sigh as the Brigham patriarch strode back to Vince and Ben. "Know-it-alls really bother me. They really do, Zack."

"Poor baby," he chuckled, leading her to the open door. "And here there's so many in your life. . . ."

They stepped through the door. Just as Grace felt sunlight touch her face, an explosion shattered the quiet as a primal bellow sounded from the main entrance and another explosion ricocheted through the house.

Screams echoed around Grace even as she felt the agony pierce her chest, felt her breath lodge in her lungs and her body bounce backwards into Zack.

Curses, Zack's roar of rage, and a crash to the floor happened in slow motion as she fought to breathe, fought to remain conscious.

It hurt.

Oh God . . .

"Grace . . . Grace," Zack's enraged voice sounded distant, hollow as his face blurred above her.

She couldn't breathe.

Couldn't breathe . . .

"It's okay, baby . . ." Hard hands were suddenly beneath her breasts, fiery pain resonating through her as she felt him pushing at her, felt his hands massaging her, raking talons of fire through her senses.

"Breathe, Grace . . . damn you, breathe . . ." he yelled.

The command was followed by more bellowing from outside, then an agonized, enraged scream of horror.

Air suddenly filled her lungs once again, bringing a low, pain-filled moan as knifing sensations shot through her chest once more.

"It's okay. Stay still, honey, I think that bullet might have broken a rib." Zack's voice was hoarse as other voices echoed in her head, that bellow sounding again.

"Dammit. Fuck. Beau-Remi, shut that fucking gator up before I shoot him!" Cord yelled as two figures slid in on the other side of her.

Fierce violet eyes glared down at her, curly black hair framing a far-too-handsome face, times two. There were two of them.

"Eh, an' here I tink you don' shame Beau-Remi." The Cajun accent was smooth, filled with relief. "You good, huh, girl?"

"Hell. Kevlar." A Texas drawl from the twin image as amusement flickered in violet eyes. "Hell, Gracie. I thought we were too late."

"Joe got da foot of dat boug." Beau-Remi grinned. "Dat boy gonna limp to da gallows, yah?"

Her eyes slid to Beau-Remi's mirror image in confusion.

Mad shook his head. "English, Beau-Remi, English . . ."

She fought to breathe, what little air she could draw in not nearly enough.

"It's okay, baby," Zack whispered again, smoothing back her hair, his expression white, fear darkening his eyes.

"Hurts . . ." she wheezed.

"Ambulance is almost here, Grace," he promised. "The vest stopped the bullet, but something might be broke. Just a minute . . ."

Just a minute?

It hurt.

"She gonna go . . ." Beau-Remi said, the words making little sense. "Like when she broke da arm, she gonna go . . ."

Go . . . Darkness whispered over her, the shock, the pain, and someone said, broke something?

She couldn't handle . . . broke something . . .

The lights went out. Slowly, dimming more and more until darkness settled over her.

"Boug, you dum-ting." Beau-Remi looked up at Zack and shook his head. "You don' say broke sometin' to her." He glared at Zack as another of those deep, primal bellows sounded outside. "Joe, I turn you to boots you don' shut up!" Beau-Remi bellowed back, violet eyes gleaming with humor as he turned back to Zack. "Gotta love dees mountains, eh?"

"Zack. God, Zack . . ." Ben knelt beside his daughter, staring down in shock at the Kevlar vest she wore, then to Zack. "He was going to kill her. . . ."

Thomas's cousin, Mark, the only one of those they'd suspected but been unable to find, because he'd been with Thomas when Mary had received the request that she and her husband were needed at Vince's to discuss who would take Ben's place.

"I'm the suspicious sort." Zack could still feel his heart racing, still feel the fear that had nearly strangled him, worried the bullet had struck her in an unprotected area.

He could have lost her.

Right there, in the Maddox foyer, to a threat he'd never imagined made it into the house, he could have lost her. And if he'd lost her . . .

He would have lost his soul.

"Paramedics are here." Ben's strangled voice was filled with relief. "Beau-Remi, get that fucking gator out of the drive or they won't be able to get in. Good God. How the hell do you tame something like that?"

"Tame?" Beau-Remi rose to his feet and headed for the door. "You don' tame da win', jus' sometime, da win' follow you, eh?"

With that, he was out the door, yelling at the gator about boots and belts as Mad sat back on his heels and shook his head in amusement as the paramedics rushed in.

"Zack, my friend," he drawled. "He'll make your life hell."

Zack ignored him.

Nothing mattered but Grace.

Just Grace. And making certain he revealed the secret he'd been keeping for far too long.

She was his life. His heart and soul.

He was finished lying to himself and to her.

He loved her. . . .

chapter twenty-four

Three Weeks Later

Painwise, Grace proclaimed, broken ribs and bruised ribs couldn't be a whole lot different. She knew for a fact her bruised ribs hurt bad enough to convince her they were broken. Bad enough that they'd stolen her breath when they weren't making breathing excruciating.

After that, all it had taken was the suggestion something was broken. Something broken was worse than something bleeding out, as far as Grace was concerned. She could handle losing a little blood as long as she didn't look at the blood. But something broken inside her was another story entirely.

Lying in the bed three days later as evening began to soften the fierce glare of the sun over the mountains, Grace stared up at the ceiling, hearing . . . no voices, raised or whispered. No conversation buzzing from downstairs or bursts of laughter.

No irritated bellows of a reptile easily longer than Zack was tall.

Just normal quiet.

Next to her, Zack laid on his stomach, fully dressed, boots still on, his head buried beneath the pillow, where it had been for the past five minutes. And he was holding that pillow over his head with a death grip. His fingers were actually pale with the strength of the hold he had on that pillow.

"Zack? Is everyone gone now?" She tried to keep the amusement out of her voice.

After three days of dealing with her family as well as his, Grace had been certain the house would never be quiet again. Every guest bedroom was filled, every couch taken, and if she wasn't mistaken, that had been Lobo and Calli she'd heard arguing the night before over who got which end of the couch in the front room.

They were arguing loud enough that Ben had actually stepped from the guest room next to the master and bellowed down at Lobo to park his ass in the van outside.

The 24-7 movement through the house had gotten the better of Zack the night before, though, when his uncle had knocked at the bedroom door and loudly informed him, "That damned Cajun's pet is trying to eat the Rottweiler."

Of course, it was Clyde's Rottweiler's, Magnus's sire. Zack had yelled back that it sounded like a helluva midnight snack.

Then the dog had started barking, Grace snickered, and Zack groaned like a man tortured.

"Zack?" She said his name again, noticing his fingers tightening around the pillow. "You okay?"

He mumbled something.

"I didn't quite make that out." She grinned. "Come on, don't make me laugh at you, it hurts."

The pillow was jerked off his head, the narrow-eyed look he gave her one of suspicion. "You keep threatening to laugh at me, Grace," he growled. "That's not nice at all."

She had to bite her lip to hold back a spurt of laughter.

"Laughing really hurts," she assured him, unable to control the tug of amusement at her lips.

He shook his head at her, though the tug of an answering smile at the corners of his lips assured her he at least saw the humor in the situation.

"I know, baby." He rolled to his side, his gray eyes watching her with the same quiet, steady look he'd been using since she awoke at the hospital after the Kevlar vest she'd worn under her shirt stopped the force of the bullet Thomas's cousin had fired at her.

"It still hurts," she assured him, but she couldn't hold back her smile either, which kind of spoiled the effect.

"I love you, Grace."

That whole punch-in-the-stomach, can't-breathe thing slammed into her heart. The twinge of sensation had nothing to do with pain, though.

She hadn't had any painkillers—Zack made certain no one had a chance to push any down her throat either—so she couldn't blame drugs for the fact that she was hearing things.

She blinked back at him, licking her lips nervously. "Could you repeat what you just said?" she asked, tucking her hair behind one ear, more to find something to do with her hands than because it was in her way. "I don't think I heard—."

"I love you, Grace Maddox. I think I've loved you for as long as I've known you," he stated. And he wasn't laughing. He didn't even look like he was joking.

She cleared her throat. "I was really young."

"So was I," he agreed somberly. "Grace, you've always been more important to me than you should have been at any given time," he breathed out roughly. "I've never been able to stay the hell away from you, haven't you noticed that? I love you. Heart and soul, Grace."

He'd always been there.

The night her appendix ruptured, and he'd come to the hospital days later, when she called him. When she broke her arm, when she'd needed someone to stand for her, to hold her, to show her that she hadn't really been alone in her life.

"Nothing to say?" he asked, brushing the hair from her cheek that escaped from behind her ear.

"I always loved you," she whispered. "I never imagined . . ."

"What? That I could love you?" he asked, shaking his head. "You were like a princess in an ivory tower," he sighed. "I was terrified to try to touch you, to do more than worship you from afar because to me, Grace, you were—you are—perfect. The rest of us are just mere mortals who wish we could be worthy of your attention."

He'd said that once before. Nobody was perfect but her. She'd thought he was being mocking.

She denied the description, fighting back her tears. "No, I'm not perfect, Zack. But I am yours. I've always been yours."

His head lowered, his lips brushing against hers, his

gaze holding hers. "When you're better, I'll show you exactly how much I love you."

"Well, be easy, I could handle a little now—" she began.

"Zack, dammit, where did you hide the propane?" Clyde barked from outside the closed door. "How am I supposed to grill steaks without gas for the grill?"

"Dammit, Dad, the garage!" Lobo yelled from downstairs. "Get down here and leave them alone. He wanted to take a nap. . . ."

Mena ordered her husband downstairs then, and Clyde stomped down like an irritated bull. All thumps.

"I thought they were gone?" Grace whispered, now understanding why Zack had held the pillow over his head for so long. "Can't they stay in the RV?"

"I tried that last time they were in town," he growled. "I had to buy a new RV."

Oh yeah, she remembered Jesse saying something about "friends" trashing his RV a few years back.

"Are they ever going to leave?" she whispered, suddenly terrified they wouldn't.

"I love you, Grace." There was an air of desperation in his voice amid the comedy. "I love you so much."

"You can't kill family, Zack." It wasn't the first time she'd told him that in the past three days.

"I love you, Grace. . . ."

"I love you, Zack," she promised. "But trust me, there're laws against it."

"Justifiable homicide," he muttered at the sound of Clyde bellowing up the stairs again about steaks and seasoning. "Really justifiable."

"Don't kill him, Zack," she giggled, then winced at the tug of pain in her ribs.

"Why shouldn't I?" he growled.

She smiled. "Be nice, and when I'm all better, I'll show you why you shouldn't."

He paused, interest flaring in his gaze. "Promise?"

"Absolutely." She nodded. "Many, many times, I'll make it worth your while."

"Many times?"

"Many . . ."

His lips covered hers, the promise held between them, tempting them, teasing them. . . .

"Dammit, boy, she's not well enough for that yet." Clyde stood in the doorway, glaring at Zack. "Get your tail down here and help me."

Grace caught at Zack's hair, holding him in place as pure retribution flashed in his gray eyes.

"Many, many times," she vowed without a hint of the laughter she could feel welling inside her. "In ways you could never imagine—"

"I love you, Grace," he whispered again desperately.

"Now, boy, I ain't getting any younger," Clyde informed him. "But I'm sure as hell getting hungrier."

The sound of Zack's uncle stomping down the stairs moments later brought a wince to Zack's face. "Don't forget your promise," he growled. "Ways I never imagined."

"Ways you never imagined," she promised again.

"I deserve sainthood," Zack muttered, but he dragged himself from the bed and stomped in Clyde fashion to the door, where he turned and winked wickedly. "Remember, ways I never imagined."

"I promise," she assured him, happiness building inside her like a wave that refused to be held back.

"I love you, Grace," he said again.

"And I love you, Zack." She smiled back at him, that joy escaping. "Go feed Clyde, so we can get some sleep tonight."

Zack loved her.

Closing her eyes, she let herself drift off to sleep again, rousing only when Zack slid in beside her, the warmth of his body settling as close as possible, his hand lying possessively at her hip.

"Night, baby," he whispered. "Love you."

"Love you," she whispered back, and let herself believe.

She was loved.